PRAISE FOR THE K FACTOR

"This is a knock-down, drag out, no holds barred, ribald tale of treachery and finesse laced with a magical combination of historical accuracy and military acumen the likes of which only L.J. can (and does, once again) deliver. Bravo, bravo, bravo!!"

—Ron Clausen

"I have edited and proofread a lot of military thrillers in my 37+ years career, but none with the abundance of the realistic, authenticating detail of *The K Factor*. You manage to paint a convincing portrait of the nuts-and-bolts of military life and combat — right down to the exact equipment and ordnance being used. This was a wild ride, and your characters were real-people convincing, also. Hats off to you on a great effort. Tension, drama, electrifying exploits, and unforgettable characters make this a *must read* for the action, adventure fan."

—Frank Kresen

"The Mike Reardon series is one filled with action, adventure, and a lot of off the cuff craziness that provides for an interesting and cannot-put-the-book-down read."

—Mary Gramlich

The K Factor
(The Repairman Series)

L.J. Martin

Print Edition

Wolfpack Publishing
6032 Wheat Penny Avenue
Las Vegas, NV 89122

ISBN: 978-1-62918-668-9

Invictus

BY WILLIAM ERNEST HENLEY

Out of the night that covers me,
Black as the pit from pole to pole,
I thank whatever gods may be
For my unconquerable soul.

In the fell clutch of circumstance
I have not winced nor cried aloud.
Under the bludgeonings of chance
My head is bloody, but unbowed.

Beyond this place of wrath and tears
Looms but the Horror of the shade,
And yet the menace of the years
Finds and shall find me unafraid.

It matters not how strait the gate,
How charged with punishments the scroll,
I am the master of my fate,
I am the captain of my soul.

Prologue

One Year Earlier

AS MUCH AS HE LOVED spy novels and international intrigue, he had no idea he would soon be immersed up to his ice-blue eyes.

Pieter De Vries graduated from the University of Twente in Enschede, Netherlands, in 1980 with a Bachelor of Science in nanotechnology, and then went on to graduate school to obtain his master's and then his doctorate, from Oxford in the UK. His area of expertise was highly valued by Royal Dutch Shell, headquartered in his home town of Hague, Netherlands, and he joined them in 1992, working in a secret program involving the use of an ultra-centrifuge for separating uranium 235 from 238—secret, because almost twenty years, before Shell had lost $250 million US on the same program, and they weren't eager for the financial world to know they were trying again.

He was happy with his work but interested in geo-politics, and he was lured away for less money working for NATO, which took him to Belgium, assessing data and its validity on the progress of nuclear development in other countries, mainly

Iran and North Korea. Again happy in his work, but underpaid, he could not turn down an opportunity to join South Africa in 1987 to assist with their nuclear weapons program.

By now he spoke Dutch, French, and English, and he was soon to master Afrikaans.

To his great dismay, South Africa acceded to the non-proliferation of nuclear weapons in 1991, and he was forced to turn his attention to non-military uses of nuclear power, primarily electric power generation. He was immediately employed in South Africa by Escom, the largest producer of electricity in Africa, to aid in their domestic nuclear ambitions.

In 2012 his beautiful wife, Marta, whom he'd met at Oxford, succumbed to breast cancer, and having no children, he was adrift emotionally. He'd always yearned for adventure; he thought of quitting and sailing the world but was yet satisfied with the amount of his savings, wondering if he might outlive them. He'd spent over half of all he'd put away traveling with his wife to both Switzerland and Germany, in order to try various treatments. All for naught. More money in the bank was necessary.

In 2014, after a long successful career with Escom South Africa, it was announced in the *Mail and Guardian* that he'd accepted a consulting position in Korea and would be leaving South Africa. He did not divulge that it was North Korea who'd lured him away with half again what he currently earned, plus perks.

He gave Escom South Africa two months' notice.

After a leisurely lunch at Johannesburg's Michelangelo Hotel, near his office, he exits to take a bench in Nelson Mandela Square and continues reading the old Wilber Smith novel he'd picked up at nearby Exclusive Books. It is twenty minutes before he is due back at his desk. He is deeply involved when a gentleman of color takes a seat next to him, unfolds a *Times*, and begins reading.

Then the well-dressed man turns to Pieter and comments, “We hear you’re leaving Joburg, Dr. De Vries?”

A little surprised, as he does not recognize the man, he lays his book aside, runs a hand through his sandy peppered-with-gray hair and asks, “Do we know each other? I’m sorry, you have the advantage....”

The man’s smile flashes in his dark face, and he laughs; nice wrinkle lines form at the edge of ebony eyes. “No, sir, we haven’t met.” He extends a hand, which Pieter takes, and shakes. “I’m Charles Eddington. An honor to meet you.”

Pieter judges his accent to be American but with a slight English overtone. So, he asks, “American, schooled at Oxford?”

“More than merely intuitive. You have an ear for accents, even the slightest echo of one. Actually, I did a couple of years at Cambridge but born and raised in Houston, Texas, USA. My mother is English, so I guess it wore off on me.”

“So, we don’t know each other from university?”

“No, Doctor, we haven’t met. I went to Cambridge, somewhat after your time at Oxford, and then to work for the American Embassy in London. I’m now stationed here in South Africa...Pretoria, to be exact.”

“And your duty?” Pieter asks.

“Cultural Attaché.”

“CIA...so you spent some time at Langley?”

He receives another flashing smile from the man who’s introduced himself as Charles Eddington. The man looks around, over his shoulders, as if to make sure no one is close enough to overhear; then he nods, but only slightly.

Eddington continues, “Let’s say I have a close association with those folks, and we’d...they’d...like to have a conversation with you. One that could be to your great financial advantage."

Pieter merely stares at him, wondering how much the CIA knows about his new job, but, obviously, they know more than he wants known. "What possible interest could the CIA have in me and my work?"

This time Eddington laughs aloud. Then, his voice low, he says, "You're on your way to a country in which we have a great interest. To involve yourself in a program in which we have a great interest. We know quite a lot about you, Doctor. You had an excellent reputation at Shell and NATO. We believe, even involved in the work that seems to have consumed you for so many years, that you are no zealot, no believer in nuclear proliferation. You have been active in some, shall we say, liberal causes, environmental causes in Holland and Belgium, anti-apartheid causes here in-country, and always with a good heart and with your fellow man in mind. But you also support freedom and have capitalist, not socialist or communist, sympathies. That said, we're all attracted by money." Then he smiles widely again. "We understand you have an interest in sailing?"

It was a question, and with his mind swirling, Pieter hesitates before asking. "All Dutch have an affinity…a love-hate relationship with the sea. Yes, I'd like to sail far more than I'm able."

"Have you been to Maputo of late?"

Pieter is a little surprised at the sudden change of subject. "Not for more than a year."

"There's a nice Boreal 52-footer moored there you might like to see. Roller furling, power winches, of course, one-twenty-five horse Volvo, full worldwide navigational capabilities, all the bells and whistles."

Now it's Pieter's turn to laugh. "As if I could afford a million-rand boat—"

"Seven hundred thousand US is what she's worth. Our Drug Enforcement Agency owns her and is thinking of selling her to you."

Pieter laughs again; then his smile fades as Eddington continues, "For one dollar."

Pieter is silent for a long moment; then he clears his throat, picks his novel back up, and mumbles, without looking over, "I don't want anyone to know we've been talking."

Eddington returns to behind his newspaper and speaks through it. "Understood. I'll meet you for breakfast at the VIP Grand in Maputo on Sunday morning. Your room is paid for, as you'll arrive late Saturday afternoon. Sign for anything you'd like in the bar or restaurant." Then he reached into his inside coat pocket, pulled out an airline ticket, and slipped it under his thigh so it would remain when he left. "Here's a flight. We'll go for a short sail, so bring some deck shoes."

Eddington then rises and leaves.

Bloody hell, Pieter thinks, *even with the quarter million a year US plus luxury housing in NK I've been promised, I'll be a long time in affording a Boreal 52, if ever. I wonder how she's equipped,* he thinks.

Present Day

FLAT ON MY BACK, gagging, choking, trying not to breathe, for to breathe is to drown. Bound to a hard-wooden bench riddled with splinters, a heavy rag over my face, six ugly bastards surrounding me, laughing, while hoping to put me under with gallons of water. SEALs are supposed to be on our side...or so I thought. To say I'm wondering what the fuck I'm doing here would be the understatement of my life...but I digress.

Only days before....

"REARDON, YOU UNDERSTAND what we're about to tell you is above top secret, and, should you disclose it to anyone, you're destined for the graybar mansion." My old Marine Recon Commander from Desert Freedom, Thomas Scroder, leans on his knuckles and focuses cold, gray eyes at me, laser eyes that seem as if they could melt steel.

It's not the first time I've been asked to lay my life, and the lives of my friends, on the line for something my country wants done but wants nothing to do with...or, better said, to be blamed for. And is willing to pay to see it get done.

"How much?" I ask, presuming what I'm about to hear will more than likely get me killed—and not if I talk about it. I'd face the same fate if I merely accept whatever is coming.

"What kind of attitude is that?" the unformed general to his left asks, with a voice as gravelly as one of those country roads back near Sheridan, Wyoming, where I was raised. I feel as if I'm a hundred thousand miles from there at the moment. Although I'm merely in LA, near LAX, the international airport, in an old Hughes plant helicopter hangar. One I presume is a CIA front, as the other five guys at the gray metal table are in suits but with holdover military haircuts. Hairstyles not complemented by furrowed faces that look as if they've seen way too much of this lousy world. Obviously, this is not an official government building, as cigar smoke wafts from metal ashtrays made of some machined chopper part.

"First," the commander replies, "you might want to listen to the problem."

"First," I ask, "I'd like to know who the players are. These gentlemen..." I nod at the five seated suits.

"Okay, but even the fact you're meeting with them is secret. Understand?"

"I've already forgotten their names, even before I know them."

"Good. Shake hands with Alex Peabody, Assistant Director of the Directorate of Analysis—"

"CIA?" I ask, leaning over the scarred metal conference table to shake hands.

"All of them other than General Holland," he replies.

I know Holland from NATO and from the fact he cost me lots of dough as I risked all to rescue his daughter from Estonia and ended up with me, and lots of my guys, with the part of the goldmine known as the shaft.

Maybe he's trying to make up for it with this gig…whatever this gig is. However, he's not the make-up-for-it kind of guy.

Scroder goes on to introduce me to the other four: Rutgar Paddington, who he describes merely as a field agent; Anthony Bartolo, from the Directorate of Support. Felix Von Reif from the Directorate of Analysis; William Nuthouer from the Directorate of Digital Analysis; and last but hardly least, Duane Roanoke from the Office of the Director. He is introduced as Executive Director. I know enough about the CIA to know his position is or very near number three in the organization.

His very presence—and the fact most of the sections of the organization are represented—means to me that this is something very big. Way bigger, I imagine, than anything this Wyoming cowboy has ever been near.

Had I half a brain, I'd thank them all for dropping by and haul ass out of here. But my curiosity has got the best of me.

What the hell do they need with a former Marine who was railroaded out of the Corps with a general discharge? Who's likely on the watch list of their organization, the NSA, the FBI, half the law-enforcement agencies in the USA and several in Europe...and certainly the FSB, formerly Russia's KGB.

I remain standing until Scroder suggests, "Reardon, you'd better take a seat. This is going to take a while."

So, I do, as stupid as a box of rocks am I.

As soon as I do, I turn to Scroder. "And how do you fit into this, Commander? Since you're no longer a commander—unless you've re-enlisted."

"You'll see how. My company has acquired a drilling company that's involved in offshore exploration and has a couple of rig-mounted ships, offshore drilling ships, working near the objective. Rigs that can be used as a base of operations."

I shrug. "Okay, makes sense."

However, the answer to "How much?" turns out to be ten million good ol' American greenbacks, tax free—not that it might matter, as there are no pockets in shrouds, and when did you ever see a Brinks truck following a hearse?

It's by far the most dangerous play we've ever undertaken.

Our op is labeled "The K Factor."

Chapter One

Present Day

"KIM HYUN-HEE, the North Korean ambassador to China," I tell my buddy Pax Weatherwax, who's the only human I'm authorized to tell, since he, too, is going to be scheduled to assist in the operation, at my insistence. And he's the only one I'm allowed to choose, as the rest of the team is being provided—much to my chagrin. I want to know I'm with buddies who have my back as I have theirs.

My buddy Paxton Weatherwax was a fellow Desert Storm Marine who saved my bacon more than once. The last time he did so, he lost an inch and a half out of his left thigh, thanks to an AK47. He lost the inch and a half, won a discharge, a purple heart to add to his chest full of medals, and a bucket of dough. Still, even with a platform shoe, I'd take him as a backup before ninety-nine-point-nine percent of the supposedly tough guys I've come across. And Pax is not only double tough but triple smart. He's turned his disability pay into a business as an Internet service provider, with offices in four cities. He's kept me out of the all-seeing-eye of the fed for several years, routed my dough and messages through a half dozen cities in as many countries, and rivaled the NSA in digging up information needed in my dubious endeavors and the subjects of my attentions.

And he's more than just a buddy. I'd get between him and a Cruise Missile, should it come to that. But I would never confess any of that to the pussy hound who's beaten me out of more than one good-looking blonde.

"So, why the hell is Kimmy Hee so damn valuable?" Pax asks.

I'm back in Vegas, and we're having supper at the Italian Club. The management here eighty-sixed us for a while, after we had a major shoot-out in their parking lot, but then, remembering all the gumba boys who've come and gone—some literally gone—in the past, we were forgiven and allowed back in the joint.

We're at a corner table, talking in low tones, and I have some gizmo in my pocket—thanks to my new friends at the CIA—that blocks electronic transmissions. So if some spy is across the room trying to listen in with a tiny parabolic mike, he's blocked. And no one's staring enough to be reading lips. Half the folks in the place are wondering why they're not getting four bars on their cell phones. It kind of tickles me that they have to actually talk to each other.

"So," I answer, "Kim is valuable as he's the North Korean ambassador to China and knows more about the Chinese-Korean relationship—and North Korea's nuclear program—than anyone other than the North Korean Cabinet. He wants to defect."

"So?" Pax asks.

"So, the North Koreans have this interesting way of keeping their foreign travelers faithful to the little worm who runs the country."

"And that is?"

I finally have his undivided attention, which is hard to do, as only two tables away, two blondes, a brunette, and a redhead are enjoying straight-up Manhattans and plates of antipasto…while giggling and glancing our way. One blonde would be a distraction for my gimpy buddy. Four luscious ladies are a hell of a hill for me to climb when it comes to keeping his attention.

"That is, they keep a close family member. In this case, three—his daughter and twin granddaughters."

"In North Korea?" he asks.

"No, at the Ritz Hotel in London—of course, in North Korea, you dumb fuck. Pay attention here. I presume all the blood has fled your brain to your crotch with those four wooly crested bed thrashers checking you out."

He ignores my sarcasm and responds, "So, our illustrious government wants to hire some suckers to go get the ladies so Kimmy can come over? Obviously some suckers who won't be tied directly to the government of the USA?"

"Yep."

He smirks. "You're not quite the right shade of canary to wander the streets of Pyongyang."

"I'm impressed," I say, and am.

"About what?"

"That you know the capital of North Korea. However, they aren't being held in the capital."

"And there's no son-in-law who needs a rescue?"

"There is, but he's a faithful Colonel in the Ministry of People's Security...the MPS the Gestapo of North Korea. He has a plethora of concubines and seldom sees his wife and daughters. Neither our people, nor, so I understand, the ambassador, give a rat's ass if son-in-law gets drawn and quartered. Which, I'm sure, is the reason he's not invited to the party."

"Are we doing this for love of country or...?"

"'And,' *and* an 'or.' Love of country plus...two point five million for you, two point five for me, and another five to split between our crew, all tax free...and you don't have to go in-country. You'll be offshore in the lap of luxury on a high-class drilling ship, eating fat steaks, directing us poor suckers."

"Bullshit...while you have all the fun downrange?"

"We need intel, and Sol is out of commission. Besides, you're the only one I trust to run the brain tank."

Sol is the number-two guy at Pax's Vegas office—as smart a guy as I've ever met and a computer and internet guru. But he got tied up with some very bad dudes in our last operation and is now in a mental-rehab joint in Reno.

Pax is pissed that he might not be downrange with me, and grumbles, "We'll talk about it some more."

"No, we won't. You're backup. If it makes you happy, you'll go through the training with the rest of us and be only twenty minutes from the battlefield—and we hope it's not a battlefield. You'll be covering our flank from onboard ship with a quick-response team in case we're hit by a shit-storm."

"Knowing you, a shit-storm is inevitable. We can't take the Viking. He'll stand out like a wart on Scarlett Johansson's nose." Our buddy, Skip, who's been with us on lots of gigs, is half-again our size and blonde. Not exactly the body type or coloring to do an undercover gig in an Asian country where ninety-five percent of the population is undernourished.

"Nope, we'll have an ethnic Chinese CIA operative who's an expert on North Korea and can pass for one; two ethnic Korean cats, both former SEALs; and a lady helicopter pilot who's former Navy. And, you'll be surprised to know, a fifty-seven-year-old former bosun's mate."

"Great. Everybody needs some old knot-head squid. And the lady pilot? Korean, I hope?"

"Yeah, and butt ugly, so don't start scheming."

"You've been known to lie, even to a best buddy."

"Scout's honor."

"Right. So, why does the United States government need a couple of broken-down jarheads? Why not Blackwater?"

"Blackwater is way-too-well known. I asked the same question. And it seems the Chinese, and likely the North Koreans, know every SEAL, Delta, and current Marine Recon cat in the current services, as, not too long ago, the Chinese, or so the CIA believes, hacked into Pentagon records. They got everything, including DNA. And Blackwater's personnel records were among them. Luckily those separated from the services were not compromised. Hell, they probably can call our current boys and their old girlfriends up on their cell phones with the intel they hacked...besides, the feds have a cover that makes a lot of sense. Not only that: the dudes I met with implied that our President wanted no military personnel tied to this operation. Plausible deniability...just some half-crazy Americanos. But he wants it done."

"Wait, wait, wait No military? We're both jarheads from time past. You said two former SEALs and a lady squid—"

"'Former' is the operative word here...thus the cover."

"So, what's the cover?"

"The *Pueblo*."

"A village?"

"No, dummy—the *Pueblo*. You remember: the former spy ship captured by North Korea."

"Yeah, I remember. So, how's that a cover?"

"While we're kicking around north of the 38th parallel, we're going to sink her."

"Sink the *Pueblo*?"

"Sink the *Pueblo*. You remember the old bosun's mate who's coming with us? He's actually Filipino. His daddy served aboard the *Pueblo* and spent a year in a North Korean prison. He's dead, but his dying words to his kid were 'Sink the *Pueblo*.' The old man had studied the situation since he was released in 1969. He knew more about the *Pueblo* and her current location than anyone alive, including the CIA. He wanted her sunk, and his kid has picked up the mantle. The old man and the kid, if you can call a fifty-seven-year-old a kid, even studied the Korean language so they could sneak back in and blow her all to hell. And the kid is half Korean, from his mama's side, and married to a Korean."

"So, the North Koreans are using the *Pueblo* as a spy ship?"

"Nope, as an attraction and, to the embarrassment of the United States, as an example of western imperialism and the military superiority of North Korea For a few wons, you can visit her and laugh at Imperial America. The dead old man was head of a Sink-The-*Pueblo* organization, and his kid is now its president…more than four thousand dues-paying members…most Navy or ex-Navy, I understand."

Pax has to smile. "So, as a distraction, we sink her and make America happy. I presume she's tied up somewhere?"

"Yep, but sinking her might be a bit of a problem, as she's on piers, permanently mounted next to a dock on the Potong River. She'll sink, though, after we blow her bottom and her supports."

"Oh, Ollie, what the fuck have you gotten us into this time?" He's shaking his head, but with a crooked grin. I merely shrug, so he continues. "How much did you say, again?"

"Ten million."

"Ain't enough," he says.

"What the fuck do you care? Odds are we'll never make it back, and Uncle Sam won't have to pay up. We'll be consoled to know we haven't added to the national debt—*not*."

"A comforting thought. Thanks."

"My pleasure."

"When?"

"We leave tomorrow for Marine Camp Kinser on the west coast of Okinawa to meet up with the other volunteer crazies and get some training in a joint CIA/military facility. It seems since the fat little prick, Ding Dong, or whatever his name is, started launching wannabe ICBMs and building the big bomb, we have a training facility that replicates a typical North Korean village...and that's where we're headed."

"Ah, so, grasshopper. Can't wait."

"Which only demonstrates your lack of even the most simple logic and reason."

"Learned all I know from you, Reardon."

"Which ain't much," I reply and hand him one of the North Korean CIA handbooks I've been given and a Conversational Korean-English dictionary. "So here's some more learnin' for you. Study up, and then pack light—*very* light, as we'll be provided local duds. Needless to say you'll get some new rags at Kinser. And I'll get the latest in North Korean pajama wear."

***

While Colonel Cho, North Korean State Security Department, watches his every move and examines every item of clothing and document he packs, Kim Hyun-hee silently seethes. He is angry, and for a very good reason. Even though he holds the honorable position of North Korean Ambassador to China, a position considered even more important than Ambassador to either Russia or the United States, he's been removed from his former position as director of nuclear development, a position he was trained for and one he considers of strategic importance to the very existence of North Korea. But far more important, he fears the fact Supreme Leader Marshal Kim Jong-un has appointed his brother-in-law, Moon Kyung, to his former position. He is as young as and maybe even more impetuous than Kim Jong-un. And he is known to be shockingly unqualified.

The tiny country of North Korea, even with the world's fourth-largest army, is centered between the world's superpowers—China, Russia, and the United States.

One false move, and that fourth-largest Army could be destroyed with the push of any of three red buttons.

And the most tenuous of those are on the desk of China's General Secretary of the Communist Party, Xi Jinping. Supposedly North Korea's staunchest ally, China is the country they most fear. Kim Hyun-hee knows that one slip on his part, even the slightest irritation of Xi Jinping, and he, his wife, and two daughters will end up in one of Dear Leader Kim Jong-un's re-education camps. In fact, as he packs to attend an international symposium in Belgium, his daughter, Sen Mi-ran, and granddaughters, Mi-na and Hye-ja, are packing to be the guests of Fang Chan-dong, the Director of K Camp 1, near Kaechon. Guests—prisoners—to guarantee his return from Belgium.

No high government official travels from North Korea without his immediate family being detained, in order to guarantee his return.

As Kim Hyun-hee seethes, he begins to relax. If all goes well, this is the last time he'll be packing a bag under the stern eye of a Colonel of North Korea's State Security Department, an organization like America's CIA, responsible for foreign activities.

The last time.

Chapter Two

IT'S A LITTLE MORE than sixteen hours from Camp Pendleton to Kadena Air Base on Okinawa in a C-5 Galaxy, and we are soon to discover that, although the onboard food is fine, the Marine Corps still provides no booze. They haven't gotten any more civilized since Pax mustered and I was thrown out. Not to be out-maneuvered, my forward-thinking amigo, Paxton Weatherwax, was clever enough to pack an oversized flask with twenty ounces of Jack Daniels. The jarheads are civilized enough to have ice and glasses, even if plastic.

We're being escorted by a uniformed Navy cop wearing a U.S. Navy Master-at-Arms shield and a serious attitude, who's so uptight you couldn't drive a sixteen-penny nail up his butt with a sledge. But other than furrowing his brow deep enough so that we could plant a medium-size bonsai, he says nothing when each of us tops ice with three fingers of Jack until the flask is drained and we sleep, more than merely semi-shitfaced, in the uncomfortable tilt-back seats. There are a half-dozen other personnel onboard, but they are forward, and a few tons of generators and other equipment is secured aft.

My first time in Japan.

Okinawa is lots of multistory concrete buildings, both apartments and commercial, lots of them only two to five stories or so, lots of electric and phone lines, and like some other island countries I've visited, above-ground burials of the dead in crypts, which tells me there's a very shallow water table.

We catch a ride in a battleship-gray Navy bus and are escorted to the rear, again with several vacant seats between us and a few squids in the front.

And like other countries with our military bases, it's only high fences, a gate, and guardhouse separating a Japanese city from an American one. Except for a dozen pickets near the gate and a Toyota police car with a bored officer eyeballing the pickets, nothing seems out of the ordinary.

As we cruise onto the base, with typical housing of four stories and looking a little more like a prison cell block than base housing, I feel a little trepidation. Kinser was named for a young sergeant who threw himself on a grenade to save his buddies during WWII and who was posthumously awarded a Medal of Honor. We may be throwing ourselves on a figurative grenade for our country—and ten million bucks, which makes the effort way, way, way less honorable.

And if we disappear, no one will know of our effort. Maybe they'll name an outhouse after us, but I doubt it. Caca happens.

The bus stops at the curb in front of a building that's windowless and at least forty feet tall. On the approach, I could see it was a few hundred feet deep, and I can see as we dismount with our small duffels—we were instructed to bring only the most personal gear—the building is twice as long as it is deep. There must be eighty acres under roof. The friggin' building is so big it probably makes its own weather.

The Master-at-Arms opens a pass-through door into a darkened space, and, to my surprise, the cop closes it behind us without entering.

Several guys in odd, but I imagine, local dress—but white, black, and brown guys, not Japanese—ignore us, and we move forward to a lighted door out of which comes a stubby, swarthy Italian- or Greek-looking guy half a head shorter than either Pax or me and also in Korean native dress, and gives me a tight smile and extended hand as we near.

Someone from nearby yells, “If it ain’t USMC, Uncle Sam’s Misguided Children.”

“Reardon?” he asks, and I nod and smile, but my smile fades as his turns to a smirk. “I’m Commander Guido Garino. I hear you think you’re some kind of bad ass?”

Now that surprises me even more than the cop not following. Garino takes my hand and pumps it a couple of times, and then jerks me forward; the shit hits the fan as the guys we’ve passed are on us from behind. I’m good in an alley fight, but I’m taken completely by surprise and am pummeled to the hard-concrete floor by knees, elbows, and fists; a hood is over my head and my elbows sucked together behind me before I can get in a decent blow.

What the fuck?

I can hear Pax behind me, calling these guys some names that are likely not endearing them to us; then his voice is muffled, as if someone has stuffed a sock in his chops. Not wanting someone’s dirty laundry in mine, I grit my teeth and stay quiet as they roll me on my back, hoist me, drop me on a hard surface up off the floor, and strap me down. They make the mistake of strapping my chest first, and I raise my knees all the way up against my gut, and instinctively drive both feet into a voice to my left and feel them both bury into some guy’s gut. He *oofs*, and, before I can take much pleasure, the blows rain down on me again, and three guys have my legs pinned and strapped; I feel a towel pulled tight across my face.

"Now, tough guy," a voice growls, "let's see if you're half as tough as you think you are."

It goes on for what seems an hour but is probably no more than fifteen minutes, as four or five times I feel as if I'm going to pass out and know I'm drowning. I can hear Pax in the distance, coughing and spitting. He's stopped cursing the boys, and I'm glad he has, as I don't think we're in any position to antagonize them more.

Finally, it stops, and the towel and hood are removed. I've been water boarded.

I'm gratified to see one of them, a black guy who's even bigger than Pax or me, sitting on a folding chair, eyes bulging, still holding his gut.

The stubby, swarthy guy is grinning at me.

"Untie me, and I'll put that stupid grin down your throat," I snap at him.

"You guys are okay, but I ain't untying you until you swear to be a good boy. Former jarhead Recon, so we hear?"

"You hear right, asshole."

He laughs. "That would be 'asshole, sir' to you, but since you're now a fat, lazy civilian, you're forgiven..." He laughs again and then adds, "We're about to go to chow. You can come with us, or you can stay here and wait for another bath. Your choice."

Not a lot to choose from. Stay strapped to a bench full of splinters or go to chow.

"Chow," I say, and hear Pax being given the same options. He wisely chooses as I do.

The straps are loosened, and my adrenalin level recedes.

Swarthy extends a hand. "Garino," he says, still grinning.

"Reardon. That's Weatherwax."

"We know. And that's the last time you'll hear it or use it. From now, on you're 'Cheech,' and he's 'Chong.' But we'll shorten you to 'Chee,' as it's more Korean."

"I've been called worse."

He laughs. "And your buddy called us lots worse. In case you don't get it, we're your backup. And it helps if we respect you and actually give a shit what happens to your dumb ass. We don't gotta like you, but if we lay it on the line for you, respect matters."

"Justifiably," I say.

We start moving away, Pax surrounded by a half-dozen guys, as am I.

Garino talks as we walk. "You guys are now cousins. Stay strong, and you'll be our brothers before you leave here in ten days for downrange. We'll be taking nothing but Korean from now on, Chee...except for some educational lectures."

I smile for the first time since opening the door to this artificial world, as we enter a village built inside the building. A village with dirt-and-brick-like streets and clapboard-and-paper houses. If I had any idea what a North Korean village looked like, I'd swear we were in one.

"Downrange," I say to Garino, "might be a cakewalk after hanging with you assholes."

He laughs. "That's the idea, Chee."

Chapter Three

LUNCH ISN'T RICE and fish-heads, as I suspected it would be, but it isn't much better. We are given a generous ten minutes to down a bowl of fried rice and that iconic Korean dish, *kimchi*—fermented vegetables. A rather rancid cabbage, in this instance, with maybe radish and some orange chips that could be carrots. It is all washed down with a weak version of the Korean national drink, *soju*.

Garino informs me in careful Korean and helps me with my translator until I figure out we'd likely have *soju* that was much stronger when in-country if we have a chance for a drink, as much as one hundred proof.

They walk us out of the village to a classroom, also in the huge building, and begin speaking English as soon as we enter.

Garino waves me over to the desk at the head of the classroom, where an Asian guy sticks out his hand and says, "I'm Bojing, your instructor for the next few days and then your team member. Friends call me 'Bo.' I know who you are, so you and Weatherwax take a seat, and we'll get started."

"See you at 1500," Garino says and heads for the door.

"What then?" I call after him.

"A leisurely stroll around the obstacle course."

"Whatever," I say.

He laughs. "This is your last easy day, cowboy."

"What-the-fuck, over," I say and find a seat at the head of the class, next to Pax.

Bo holds a laser pointer and turns it to one of five bulletin boards and two blackboards, all filled with maps and pictures.

"Gentlemen," he says, "you're about to get the first cram course in all things 'NK.'"

And he begins.

"North Korea, the Democratic People's Republic of Korea, which we'll call 'NK' to speed things up, is a country of forty-six thousand five hundred square miles...for comparison, that's one fourth the size of California. Pyongyang is the nation's capital and largest city. NK is bordered on the north by China and by Russia along the Amnok and Tumen rivers, and to the south by the Republic of Korea, separated by the heavily fortified Korean Demilitarized Zone. On her west is the Yellow Sea and on her east the Sea of Japan.

"She has a standing army of one point two million and an armed reserve of nine and a half million. The small country of twenty-eight million or so has the fourth-largest army in the world—"

Pax can't help himself and interrupts: "So, we send in five guys, and, not counting the reserve, they're out numbered two hundred thousand to one."

Bo gives him a tight smile. "This, as you well know, is a surgical operation to extract three women. With luck, and if you'll pay attention, there won't be a shot fired. Now, may I continue?"

"Be my guest," Pax says, returning the tight smile. Then he adds, "I'll interrupt only if I know my buddy here doesn't understand."

"Very amusing," I say, but Bo ignores us and continues.

"At the beginning of the twentieth century, Korea was annexed by the Empire of Japan. After the Japanese surrender at the end of World War II in 1945, Korea was divided into two zones along the 38th parallel by the United States and the Soviet Union..."

As he talks, he's using a laser pointer on a map.

"...with the north occupied by the Soviets and the south by the Americans. Reunification was attempted but failed, and in 1948, separate governments were formed. The north became the socialist Democratic People's Republic of Korea, and the south, the capitalist Republic of Korea. North Korea, wanting reunification, invaded the south, which led to the Korean War. The Korean Armistice Agreement brought about a ceasefire, but no peace treaty was signed. Technically, they're still at war.

"North Korea calls itself a self-reliant socialist state and formally holds elections. They, of course, are a joke. Critics regard the north as a totalitarian dictatorship. Various media outlets have called it Stalinist, noting the elaborate cult around Kim Il-sung, who died in 1994. He is the country's 'eternal president.' Kim Jong-il, known as 'eternal General Secretary,' father of the current jerk, died in 2011. You know, like in China, the family name is first—'Kim,' in this instance. And 'Kim' is as common in NK as 'Smith' and 'Jones' in the USA.

"The fact is the country is a totalitarian nightmare. The worst human rights record in the world. Too many violations in North Korea to count. The Workers Party of Korea, led, of course, by a member of the ruling family, yields almost absolute power in the state and leads the Democratic Front for the Reunification of the Fatherland, of which all political officers are required to be members.

"It's a caste system worse than India, where justice is a joke. If you are suspected of crimes against the state, not only you, but three generations of your family become guests of slave-labor camps. It's post-revolution Russia...even worse.

"*Juche* is an ideology of national self-reliance, a creative application of Marxism–Leninism.

"You all know of the Korean War, when Jong-un's granddaddy tried to re-unify the country. We interfered, and it cost us fifty-five thousand killed, and there are still eight thousand unaccounted for. There was no peace treaty and technically we and the South are still at war with the North. That's how many *we* lost…more than three million Koreans and Chinese were killed."

It's my turn to interrupt. "Bo, do we really need a history lesson? Can't we get to the day-to-day so we'll know a little about what's going on the country? I mean today—not a couple of hundred years or even a few decades ago."

He's looking a little frustrated, and then his tone lowers to a growl. "Reardon, I'm going in-country with you. I'd like to come back out. I could give you a semester on the bastards to the north, and you still wouldn't know enough. This is just the icing on a ten-layer cake, and I'm going to make damn sure you know it. If your buddy here has to sit on his ass and try to figure out what we're doing in-country, then he needs to have a basic understanding as well. We can dick around here until midnight, and you'll still have to hit the obstacle course the instant we're done. If I were you, I wouldn't piss Garino and his crew off. They can be a real pain in the ass...and anywhere else you have a nerve located."

I shrug but keep my mouth shut.

"So, you're fully aware, NK is the most secretive and isolated country in the world. It's known as the 'hermit kingdom.' They have their health problems, mostly caused by undernourishment. Blindness as a for-instance: ten times the rate of cataracts than other countries. A seven-year-old in the north averages eight inches shorter and twenty-two pounds lighter than one in the south.

"And General, or Marshal, Kim Jong-un, is a fine fellow. Since he took office, he's killed one hundred and forty of his senior leaders, his uncle, and his half-brother.

"You all know of the demilitarized zone between the north and south. Two point five miles wide, only one million land mines."

For five hours, he bangs away, without looking at a note.

We walk out with a smattering of every aspect of NK culture: art, music, literature, cuisine—if you can call it cuisine, as since the war. the average height of a North Korean adult is two inches shorter than a South Korean adult, thanks to a meager diet. They starved to death damn near a half million in the famine of the mid 1990s, and their policy of "military first," or *Songun* as they call it, didn't help with money and resources literally going to arms before food.

As usual with my knowledge of a foreign language before I visit a country, I can now request a bathroom or a restaurant but not cover or extra ammo. I'm not sure what I've learned is helpful, however....

By the time we finish, I am deeply impressed with Bo's knowledge and am very happy he's on our team—not to mention he's a former SEAL, is as big as I am, is younger by at least five years, and looks like a bad ass. He's one of those cut assholes whose muscles have muscles. Even so, I'm a little surprised when he suits up in tee shirt and shorts and heads to the obstacle course with us. But when he strips his shirt off, I can see he's really not a guy to mess with. He's past the point where blue veins bulge.

Rumor is, though, all SEALs—current or former—are tight lipped, Bo was on the most secretive of the teams, SEAL Team 6, and by the scars I note on his back as he changes, he tangled with lots of tangos in lots of places he won't, can't, talk about.

I'm surprised to see Rutgar Paddington, who I met in that hangar at Hughes Helicopter. I had no idea he was coming along. However, he's in sport coat and slacks and is obviously not coming to do anything but watch, probably hoping to get a laugh.

The same dozen assholes who water-boarded us—we're now cousins, and I'm wondering what it takes for two old farts, relatively, to become brothers—are awaiting our appearance, and I don't like the grins they're wearing.

Chapter Four

PIETER DE VRIES RECLINES in his seventh-floor apartment, which, at first glance, he'd been very happy to receive as his luxury housing. He has a wonderful view and wishes the apartments had decks, so that, when the weather was good, he could sip his evening Vieux, a Dutch brandy that he is surprised to have been supplied with. The bad news is that the elevators operate only sporadically, even though Pyongyang, the capital city of North Korea, is blessed with a far more consistent supply of electricity than the rest of the country.

When hired, he presumed he'd go directly to work in what he was told was NK's domestic nuclear electric production program, but, in fact, is teaching at Pyongyang University of Science and Technology, with three classes of bright young students a day and an attractive twenty-five-year-old interpreter, who, he presumes, is also paid to spy on him. Particularly after she afforded him the privilege of her body and, after two months of him being in-country, moved in with him. He is intrigued by Su-mi—"Sumi," he calls her—and her exotic looks, and he thinks that, under different circumstances, he might love her. But it seems to him a little like loving something beautiful, like a coral snake or sleek wolf. Beautiful, but deadly.

She always smells of jasmine, and tastes like butterscotch, with skin as smooth as melted butter and eyes a very unusual color for a Korean—a deep emerald green, deeper than the finest jade.

He is seldom out of her sight as she interprets in class and lives with him, but more than once he's set her up by leaving a small piece of paper or string in the hinge of his Apple laptop or clamped in a drawer of his desk, or in the door to the second bedroom that he uses as a study, when he knows she'd be alone in the apartment. He often takes his exercise climbing the building's stairs at a run, and she can't keep up, so she stays behind in the apartment.

She never lets him down, and all his personal spaces are searched each time he is away. But he cares little. She satisfies his sexual appetite and is an excellent cook.

His in-country contact is a cook at the university cafeteria. "Duri" is the only name he knows him by, a Korean who'd gone to culinary school in Santa Barbara, California, and who speaks excellent English and is, like Pieter, in the employ of the CIA.

He has three other classes each week. One, when military officers, who he presumes work in NK's nuclear weapons program, attend a class and fire questions at him…questions he knows pertain to the military applications of his knowledge. The second is as a student, where he studies the Korean language and, in addition, where the instructor indoctrinates him in Korean lore and—this amuses him—in the bullshit surrounding the ruling Kim family. And the third is also as a student. He is learning to cook, and the only University employee qualified to teach him and who can speak English is his CIA contact, Duri. As he can't risk having a SATphone or two-way-radio, messages must be passed mouth-to-ear or hand-to-hand if written…but that is seldom, as it's so risky.

Just the questions asked by the military give him, and the CIA, great insight into what is underway, and most of it pertains to miniaturizing a nuclear bomb.

In addition to his salary from the Koreans, he is banking ten grand a month tax free from the CIA and has an escrow account that will convey title to the Boreal 52 when he completes two years in service. And at that time, he will no longer be in the employ of NK or the CIA. And he is looking forward to that time.

If he lives that long.

He's only been in the presence of Kim Jong-un one time in the year he's been in-country, and that was at a banquet celebrating the Day of the Shining Star, Kim Jong-il's birthday, the current Dear Leader Marshal Kim's father.

Pieter is surprised to have found the man fairly charming, with excellent English, who acts as if Pieter is as welcome as a sunny Spring day. Of course, he is aware of Pieter's knowledge of nuclear fission and that he is helping with the country's effort to become not only the fourth-largest army in the world but a nuclear power.

He is surprised and concerned when Duri informs him that he is to be in his apartment, which overlooks the Potong and, coincidentally, the *Pueblo*, on a given few days. He is to be home, sick, with binoculars.

He is beginning to wonder if he'll ever man the wheel of the beautiful Boreal 52-footer.

***

AND I THOUGHT I WAS in shape.

I go to the gym three to four times a week when not on an op. I do reps of ten, three times, pressing 250 pounds and the same with 400 pounds with the legs. Plus, lots of curls and other muscle-teasing exercises.

However, at the moment, I'm feeling a bit like a real pussy, as one of the SEALs lets us watch while he runs the part of the course we can see. I'm feeling like I should have been doing more aerobics. Way, way, way more aerobics.

Glancing at Pax, I can see he's a little apprehensive as well. Saving my ass while I wandered a dirt track in Fallujah, in la la land because of a near rocket strike, Pax lost a little over an inch out of his leg and wears a lift in a shoe, thanks to an AK47. Don't get me wrong: there's no one I'd rather have at my back, but it is an impediment. He's already pissed at these guys, due to their little initiation with the water buckets, and I know he won't hesitate going for a throat if they rag him. He ain't your normal computer geek. I'll stick close to him, not so much as to embarrass him by outrunning him, but to keep him from starting a battle with six or sixteen hard-ass, battle-hardened kids ten years or more our juniors.

Garino strides over and gives us a nod. "You guys ever hear of BoneFrog?"

"Nope," we both say. Then I add, "I know Bull-Frog, one of you flipper assholes with the longest time in service."

"Not this one. Some out-of-service guys started a private company to host obstacle-course events and improved on our Coronado course...change of elevation, water and vegetation, and more. We've taken a page out of their book for this course. Don't get in too big a hurry—you've got the better part of five hours ahead."

"Your guy just took a few minutes—" I say, but he laughs me out.

"You ain't seen nothing yet, sunshine. You got a long row of stumps to root up."

"Bring it on," Pax says, and I can see his jaw knotting.

I risk letting Pax beg off. "Hey, man, you're going to be popping bon bons on board the home ship, so there's no reason—"

"Fuck you," he says and glares at me like a cobra at a mongoose, and I know it's fist city if I press it.

Bo, our classroom instructor, sidles up beside us. "You Vegas hotshots mind if I come along for the ride?"

"We'll hang back and make sure you're okay," Pax says, and I roll my eyes.

"Do that," Bo says and flashes a grin that says something like, "Don't hold your breath as you watch me disappear." But he doesn't say it; he merely chuckles.

"Let's get her done," I say to Garino.

"You going in those cargo pants and hikers?"

"Why not?" I say.

He digs in his pocket and pulls out a stopwatch. Before yelling "Go!" and punching it, he snaps at Bo: "You got your phone in case we need a rescue chopper?"

"Fuck, no. I'll just bury Chee and Chong out on the course like we did the last half -dozen jarheads."

Fifty yards away is a cargo net climb at least forty feet tall, and before we get to it, there's a six-foot-tall log wall, and behind it a twenty-five-foot spread of water with a half-dozen logs you can use to cross—six-inch diameter logs that won't be easy to navigate.

"Go!" Garino yells, and the other five SEALs who've come to chide us yell their encouragement, in the form of insults, as the three of us head for the log wall, low enough that we can reach the top and damn near vault it. I'm even with Bo as we land and both start across the water hazard on logs. I make it ten feet before I do a header into the three-foot-deep pool and hear Pax grunt behind me and his splash. By the time I'm out, Bo has a twenty-yard lead; he hits the cargo net and goes up like a chimpanzee. Glancing back, I see Pax clambering out of the pool, and, when I reach the net, I yell at him.

"A fifteen-foot fall can kill you. Fuck winning. Let's finish in one piece."

I'm six feet up the forty when he starts. Pax is a strong dude and can out-lift me in the gym—probably overcompensating up for the gimpy leg—and he has no trouble going up the cargo net. By the time I'm at the top and throw a leg over, he's even with me, but Bo is on the ground. I can see him glancing back and get the feeling he's not doing his best but, in fact, is looking out for the old guys.

We hit a series of three-foot diameter pipes, at least fifty feet of tunnel, with six inches of mud in the bottom—harder to navigate than it might sound due to the clinging mud.

As soon as we're out there are six rope bridges, at least fifty feet across a trench, with its bottom more than six feet below; a single rope is strung up to two hand ropes on the sides. It, too, is no easy crossing…particularly when you're gasping for breath.

There's a two-inch-thick rope that you have to hang like a sloth from and hand-and-feet work your way across more water. Then there is a series of ropes that you use to swing over more wide trenches, and the last one is too wide to swing across and you swing out as far as possible and drop into mud at least a foot or more deep.

It's amazing how much slogging through deep mud takes out of you.

And it goes on and on, with some repeat obstacles, some new ones, but each more and more a torture. As our part of the island is fairly flat, they've created forty-foot-high hillocks with a steep side either front or back. Thickets of clinging shrubs higher than our heads, with no discernible path, add interest and difficulty. We're more than an hour into the course with at least four-mile-or-more runs between sets of obstacles. When we reach the sea, it's nearly dark, and the floating platform three hundred yards past the low surf is lighted, so we have a target. Bo is perched on the edge of the float, his legs dangling in the water, looking like he's at the pool at the Ritz waiting for the waiter to bring him a drink with an umbrella.

There's a Polaris MRZR, a four-seater, off-road, UTV-type contraption parked nearby, with a 50 cal mounted on top, and four of the six SEALs who've been dogging us are leaning against it. Obviously, they've had it topped with a six-man rubber boat, an IBS, as its surf side. I guess they are there to rescue us if we don't make the swim.

As there's been lots of running, I must wait for Pax. The SEALs give me a condescending wave, and I salute them with the middle finger as I'm catching my breath.

Pax arrives, puffing as he laughs at me, a strained laugh but a laugh. "You resting, fat boy?"

"Yep. How's your breast stroke?" I ask.

"I'd rather be back at the Italian Club stroking the breast of that blonde."

"We ain't gonna finish unless we start." We're both puffing pretty good.

"A hundred mile…journey begins…with the first step," Pax gasps, and I turn and hit the surf.

As dry as my throat is, it's salt water, and a drink is out of the question, but washing out the mouth without swallowing helps…for a short while.

It's September, and the weather is mild, not overly hot or cold, but the Yellow Sea racks me, chilling to the bone. So I stroke with purpose, stopping only to glance over my shoulder a couple of times. My body's so hot from the run I feel like I should be steaming.

Pax is better in the water than on terra firma and damn near beats me to the raft. Neither of us are setting any records, swimming with light-but-cumbersome hiking boots and cargo pants. Thanks to the mild weather, we're wearing muscle-fuck tee shirts, mine a "Molan Labe" 2nd Amendment promotion and Pax's stenciled with "You make me wish I had more middle fingers"—a sentiment that's applicable at the moment.

The one advantage is the water wipes away the inch of mud that's built up on shirtfront, pants, and hikers…not to speak of face and hair.

Bo is still perched on the side, dangling his legs. "Outswam the sharks, did you," he says and laughs.

"So far," I offer.

"Fuck the sharks," Pax says, but he's puffing pretty good, his voice raspy.

"Let's take a blow," Bo suggests, and I know it's on our account, as he's been resting.

"Too friggin' cold," I say. "We're okay…right, Pax man?"

"I'd rather be beating the water than having my teeth rattle."

I turn to Bo. "In case we beat you back, which way?"

"Not likely, but we reverse the course and go back the way we came. It's equal fun both ways."

"Lead the way, leatherneck," I say to Pax, and he hits the water and strokes out.

The SEALs have turned on the lights of the MRZR so we have a beacon, as the sun's well down.

It seems a hell of a lot farther going back than it did coming, and it seemed a hell of a long way coming.

Garino is waiting in a lawn chair under a mercury lamp, a can of Coke in hand—I'm sure just to add insult to injury. Bo has stayed with us all the way back, and we finish side by side. The last mile run was more of a trot, but we made it.

Both of us now have our hands on our knees, and I don't know about Pax, but I'm nearly puking.

"Five hours. Not bad for civilians," Garino says. Then he adds, "Chow?"

"Fucking A," Pax says, but his tone is not as sassy as his words. "I can…eat the ass…out of a skunk."

All I can think about is the sack, but I'm not about to tell these guys that. And I learned a long time ago that, when you're under pressure, you need to hydrate and calorie up when possible.

That said, the rice, *kimchi*, and *soju* taste pretty damn good, but the sack, a rolled-out bamboo mat, leaves a lot to be desired. Every bone in my body aches; my muscles hurt so badly I can feel my heartbeat in my biceps and thighs, but…we made it. I can't imagine that the hard mats on the rough wood floors will offer much solace.

The last thing Bo says, after he shows us to the hooch we'll occupy, is, "This is the last easy day, boys. Weapons on the morrow, then another thrilling and entertaining lecture. Sleep tight. I'll roll you off your mats at 0430. At BUD/S, this is how we start every day…before the real work begins."

"Fuck," Pax says, and that's all I hear until Bo is kicking the door in the morning darkness. I slept like the proverbial babe.

Chapter Five

WE'RE BOTH FAMILIAR with the AK47, and the Type 64—a copy of the FN Browning M1900—and the Type 66—a copy of the Russian Makarov—both semi-auto pistols. But the Type 58, 68, and new 88 assault rifles are new to us. Garino is conducting the class and explains that there are more sophisticated arms in use but not by the Korean People's Army Ground Force or the reserve. These are the weapons we'll most likely encounter, but won't carry. We go to the range and familiarize ourselves.

Then it's front and center in the classroom again with Rutgar Paddington, formerly introduced only as a field agent. He looks like a spy, tall and thin, a bit of a ferret, with eyes always searching and quick head movements. His eyes are light blue and his hair on the blond side of brown. I can't help but ask.

"Are you going in-country with us?"

"Yes, but way in the rear with some tan cream, which I'm already using, a dye job, and soft, very-dark contacts. Don't sweat it. I was on the North Korean desk at State before I joined the company, and my Korean is better than Bo's or the other guys who've just arrived. They've got to sit in…" He walks to a doorway and yells out; soon the rest of the team enters. Five operatives, each of whom have been promised a million bucks. All former Special Forces of some kind, including our lady helicopter pilot.

"You fucking liar," Pax says as she enters, and I know immediately what he means.

"I said 'dog-butt ugly,' but I didn't mention how foxy some dog-butts are."

"Right, a-hole."

Rutgar turns the meeting back over to Bo.

"Lady and gentlemen," Bo begins. "This is Mike and Pax, after these lectures known as 'Chee' and 'Chong.' Chee has been on similar operations in Afghanistan, Uzbekistan, Estonia, Russia, Paraguay, and Albania…or so says the memorandum I've been provided. He's the team leader…which means he's the eye of the shit-storm."

It seems to me Bo has a little trouble spitting that one out…I'd guess he thinks the job should be his. But he continues….

"Chong, who was associated with all those operations, is a computer guy and your main, in fact only, contact with the outside world while you're in-country. Both former Recon Jarheads. You'll note we're not using any last names, as you've already been instructed. What you don't know you can't give up."

Then he waves Pax and me over and makes introductions.

"Ladies first," he says. "This, gentleman, is as fine and accomplished a helicopter pilot as you'll even meet. Ji Su—friends call her 'Su.' Did three tours in that hole, Afghani-shit-stan."

We shake with the lady, tall-for-a-Korean, pilot. Pax, of course, clings to her long-fingered hand a little too long. The lady has a bobbed haircut, raven-wing-black hair, of course, with ebony eyes that sweep the room like she's watching for incoming MIGs. Perfect teeth, a sincere smile, and absolutely perfect unblemished skin, with lips red enough that no paint is required. Hard to tell much about the bod except she's tall and thin, but I'd like to see lots more of that unblemished skin. I get the impression the top items of interest are bound down in military fashion, but the coveralls she wears don't reveal much.

When Pax finally drops her hand, he gives me a look that singes my eyelashes. I can't help but grin.

"And this," Bo continues, "is Gun Ho—believe it or not, one of the most popular male names in NK. Former SEAL, and he has often proven to be gung-ho. Gun Ho is a fair hand with demolition."

"'Gun' okay?" I ask as I shake.

"Better than 'Ho,'" he says, with a laugh, "and that's how I was known in the teams." He has a genuine smile and a grip like a concrete foundation re-bar guy who bends steel for a living. I'm glad I get my paw back un-mangled. He's two inches shorter than either Pax or me, probably an even six feet, and four inches wider. The guy has no neck, and his shoulders seem to flare from under his tight-to-skull ears. I'd hate to challenge him to pushups, pullups, or clean-and-jerks.

"And another Frog, Jin Soo, known as 'Jinny' to his friends, but you should get used to his given Korean handle. He was a com guy in the teams and will carry both SATphone and the latest in radios that will reach the mother ship, *Black Gold*, from anywhere in NK."

He, too, has a shake like coiled steel around your hand. No smile, but a nod and straight-in-the-eye contact. A solid guy, in every sense, as every SEAL seems to be.

And the final guy is about five feet, four inches, gray hair shaved to a quarter inch, tatts on both exposed arms and showing under the V-neck-tee he wears. He's Asian, and part

Korean I presume, but it'll be hard to deny his adopted country as his tatts will give him up.

"Butch, say howdy to Mike and Pax," Bo says and can't help but grin.

Butch, we're informed, is the son of the former bosun's mate on the *Pueblo*. He has watery eyes, a three-day stubble as gray as his buzz cut, and enough hair growing out of his ears and nose that it's pretty clear he's past picking up discerning women in the saloons. The eyebrows make up for the lack of hair on his head. Two fuzzy two-and-a-half-inch caterpillars that have grown together. He raises one as he eyes us and shakes, saying nothing.

"Butch is half Korean and knows the *Pueblo* prow to rudder, as his father served on her and drilled her into his head, and will stick with me. Our primary task is sinking the Banner-class environmental research ship, commonly called a spy-ship, upon which his daddy served."

Butch has a soft voice, but determined, and adds, "Proudly served, which got him a year in a shit-hole, thanks to those pig fuckers and the pissant who leads them…his father to be exact, but the shit flows downhill and from grandfather to father to fat fucking a-hole current Dear Leader…and I'm looking forward to putting my old man's old home on the bottom of the Potong."

I ask, with a smile, "What do you really think, Butch?"

He nods but doesn't laugh. He's dead serious.

But I can't help but ask, "Can you keep up, Butch?"

"You joking, you dipshit? You wanna go a couple of rounds right now?"

"No, sir. But I'll be responsible for getting everyone home, and I take my responsibilities very seriously…so I have to ask."

"Sonny, I'm in my sixth decade, fifty-seven next birthday. I've damn near ridden my eight seconds and don't much give a shit if I come back or not. Like Dr. Strangelove, I'll ride the old girl to bottom and smile and wave at y'all on the way down. You worry about saving your own butts and whatever else y'all are up to in that dung heap. I'll worry about old Butch and sinking the *Pueblo*."

I smile, shrug, and shake my head. 'Old Butch' sounds more like a Wyoming cowboy than a former Navy bosun's mate, but as we are instructed not to know too much about our team members, I don't ask.

What you don't know you can't tell.

We all take a seat, and the next lecture begins.

And we find out how close we might be to nuclear holocaust.

Chapter Six

THE FIRST THING BO DOES is excuse Butch.

"Butch, head over to the canteen, and grab a cup of mud and a piece of pie. This talk is NTK…need to know only. We'll come and get you if need be."

"Pie is good," he says and is gone in a flash. The old boy moves just fine for his age.

"Moves alright for an old man," Pax says.

"You reading my mind these days?" I ask.

"God, I hope not. In your mind would be a terrible place to be."

"Gentlemen," Bo snaps, and we pay attention. Rutgar is sitting nearby, and it looks to me like he's monitoring what Bo has to say. And Bo begins...

"The mission is to extricate Sen Mi-Ran, the ambassador's daughter, and twin granddaughters, Sen Mi-Na and Hye-Ja. They are being held at Re-education Camp One, Kaechon, about twenty-five clicks northwest of where the *Pueblo* is permanently moored on concrete pilings. Each of you will have a battle plan, which you will not open until you're deployed in operational groups—"

I interrupt, "Why?"

"What you don't know you can't divulge, and, believe me, the Ministry of People's Security, the MPS, and the Bowibu, or National Security Agency, have ways of extracting information you'd rather not know about."

"Makes sense."

"Mr. Weatherwax—pardon me, 'Chong'—Ji Su and her unmarked chopper will be deployed on the *Black Gold* in the Yellow Sea just west of the mainland of the Republic of Korea...South Korea...only five clicks south of the border with the North and eight clicks off the Republic coast. Because of the angle of the coast on the Yellow Sea or west side, the *Black Gold* is almost due south of your objective."

He points to a spot on the map with the laser pointer.

"Su and her chopper, and Pax, will remain onboard *Black Gold* in TOC, control center unless there's an absolute no-other-solution reason to have her extract either of the two teams...or both, which we don't anticipate. Mr. Weatherwax...Chong...will be assisted on board the drilling ship by a computer whiz kid from NSA, one from the CIA, and one from DOD, and a drone operator from the Air Force who'll be controlling a Grey Eagle, launched from here if its use is absolutely required. TOC, tactical operations command, the control center is a state-of-the art facility with access to military and NASA satellites and some hardware that's on a need-to-know basis.

"The teams will be the TOC: Mr. Weatherwax and Ji Su on the ship along with the government team; Extraction: Mr. Reardon, Gun and Jinny, who'll extricate the ladies; and *Pueblo*: myself and Butch, who will demo the *Pueblo* and put her on the bottom of the Potong River in the capital city of Pyongyang. A drop by Ji Su will deploy a surface vessel up the river from the Yellow Sea to a spot ten clicks or so southwest of the city. Then we'll be surface towing the submersible vehicle, which we'll deploy to the two click and then abandon our surface ride and proceed underwater, by Dräger…re-breathers for you civvie fuckheads. We have a dam near the mouth of the river to traverse, but, luckily, there's construction going on and helicopters in use there, and we hope, we hope like hell, Ji Su can place three loads just upriver from the dam from her bird, painted and marked to match the construction choppers—"

"Why three?" I ask.

"Trip one will transport the surface vehicle and trip two the underwater device so Butch and I can get the final ten clicks upriver to within a quarter-mile of the *Pueblo* underwater. Then, when we know we're good to go, trip three will deploy us and our weapons. Then we'll recover some American pride and sink the soiled lady. The mini-sub is an SDV, a SEAL or swimmer delivery vehicle, the modern version of what's essentially a tube with a propeller stuck on the back. It can be as compact as needed, sized to fit just one warrior or as many as six. It's a 'free-flooding' vessel, which means it's filled with water. The warriors inside or mounted horseback, depending on type, breathe through their own scuba tanks, Dräger, or from onboard oxygen reservoirs. The other two will carry the Zodiac…surface boat…and our team and weapons."

"I thought Gun was the demolition guy?" I ask.

"He is, and his talents will be utilized along with you and Jinny. The plan is in your dossier, which you'll open and study after you're separated into teams."

"Okay. But let's get back to basics for a moment. I'm still in the dark as to why me, why a bunch of ex-military rather than active guys up to speed with all this gear—"

"As you were told, our government has to have plausible deniability. We don't want to start a war; we want to prevent one, and Ambassador Kim Hyun-hee is integral to that ambition. Prior to being appointed to his post, he was the head of NK's nuclear program. He was displaced by the Dear Leader's second cousin, who's a numbskull and a minor-league administrator. Dear Leader did not want to retire Kim, so he promoted him so his cousin could take the prestigious job. Another reason Kim wants to defect. It seems his pride is wounded. And Butch is our cover. The North has been tracking him and his father, and the Sink-The-*Pueblo* organization for years. So he, and the sinking, is a cover for the defection."

"How's that to come down? The defection, I mean," Pax asks.

"Above our pay grade," Bo says, with a tight smile. Then he adds, "But we have a time constraint. Kim will be at an International Symposium meeting in Belgium in five days, and we must have the ladies in hand, safely in hand, at exactly that time, or he'll be escorted back to NK under armed guard, or worse, killed in Belgium by the NK State Security Department, agents of which escort every North Korean of any stature when out of the country. If we don't get the ladies and Kim out, it could be years, if ever, that we have a chance to get such a high-ranking NK official, and maybe never a look into their nuke program."

I'm suspicious, so I ask, "So, there's no secondary motive to this op? Give us the whole story."

"Okay, most of which you already know. As I'm sure you know, it'll only take between thirty and forty minutes for an ICBM to reach anywhere in the U.S. from North Korea. They exploded their first nuke in 2006 and have been going balls out since. We've tried everything diplomatically to get them to stand down, to no avail. China, the big brother to the west, has been no help. Why, we don't quite understand—unless NK has discovered some mineral deposits we know nothing about. We suspect lithium or plutonium. They provide hundreds of thousands of tons of iron ore and coal to China, but China can get iron ore or coal from lots of places, and I happen to know we've offered to underwrite the additional cost of ore from Australia or South America...which they've ignored. I'm going to let Rutgar Paddington take over from here for a while."

"Gentlemen," Rutgar says as he rises and walks to the head of the room and takes the laser pointer. He turns and eyes each one of us in turn, taking a full minute to scope the room. Then he continues, "The so-called 'Dear Leader' is a fucking madman who's killed members of his own family and believes in the reunification of the Korean people and peninsula even if it means the death of more than half of his people and all those in the south. He has an underground labyrinth in which he and his can hide—deeper, we believe, than our biggest bunker-buster can reach. Now, let me do a quick-and-dirty look at why he's so confident...so wrong...but so confident.

"And even if we wipe him off the face of the earth, it could mean many millions of American lives and an economic disaster that could turn us into a third-world country. If you recall, the bombing of the twin towers and the loss of more than three thousand lives cratered the American economy for a good while. What do you think an ICBM with a nuclear warhead on an American city would do? Not to mention the loss of a million lives or more."

It's silent for a long moment in the room, and then he continues.

"North Koreans put nuclear warheads on short-range missiles in 2013. Now they've advanced to ICBMs. But they have yet to perfect the reentry...the cones have to be perfect and have to burn off evenly, or it will disrupt the trajectory. We think they're both trying to develop that skill and trying to buy it on the international market. So, yes—there's a secondary motive, but you don't have to concern yourselves with it. Of course, even if they miss their target in the U.S. by five hundred miles, it's still a devastating hit. So we're more than a little concerned.

"So, step one is to extract the ladies, and the sinking of the *Pueblo* is step two, along with Ambassador Kim Hyun-hee stepping into the American embassy in Brussels. We've spent more than a month getting rid of markings and even serial numbers on anything going downrange. Now we have two more days to familiarize you all with all that specialized, sanitized, equipment you'll have the use of for the balance of this operation.... I won't be here to assist, as I have another assignment on the other side of the world.

"But first, let's recon the battlefield, and, for that, Commander Garino will do the honors. Now, here's your toy and downrange expert. Commander!"

With that, Garino strolls in and takes the podium.

Chapter Seven

"LADY AND GENTLEMEN," he begins after he grabs the laser pointer and hits a spot on the map of the north. "I'm going to hit only the high points, so each team will have a general idea of what the other team is tasked with. Some particular details for each op will be in your orders, to be opened only when you're separated and underway…security concerns."

I wish they'd quit insinuating that we'll be captured and tortured. Do they know something we don't?

He continues. "The *Pueblo* will be reached by surface up until we're from ten to as close as seven and a half clicks from her location. A situational determination. The river is too populated from there on to go surface. Now to the extraction. The Kim ladies, married name 'Sen,' given-name daughter, Mi-Ran, twin twelve-year-old granddaughters Mi-Na and Hye-Ja, are in the guest house of the gentleman who is the head man at Kaechon Re-education Camp just three clicks northeast of the city of Kaechon, and fifty clicks northeast of Pyongyang. A fine gentleman, name, believe it or not, Fang Chan-Dong. A colonel, probably responsible for twenty thousand or maybe more—far more—deaths of his countrymen. If you get him in the crosshairs, don't hesitate unless it compromises your mission.

"There's a river nearby, the Taedong, not navigable by us with conventional craft. National Highway 65 is a couple of clicks, but like all transportation facilities…highway, rail, and air…heavily guarded. You'll go in by motorized paraglider, a miniaturized version of a Blackhawk Airmax 220, powered by a very small battery-powered motor, that our people have worked over to both gear correctly and to run silent. It's as quiet as an office fan. You'll jump in the dark, on the coming moonless night, four days hence. The same aircraft that puts you over the target will drop a pallet of three personal watercraft that will transport two adults each, one slightly modified to carry an adult and the two twelve-year-old granddaughters, who weigh less than eighty pounds each."

I interrupt. "Didn't you just say the Taedong in non-navigable?"

"By conventional watercraft. These jet buggies, Ski Doos, are hardly conventional and rated in excess of one hundred MPH. They've been slightly modified…they normally carry two, but one's modified with an extended seat to accommodate both young ladies behind the driver, and all with a pair of M4s each on the bow with three hundred rounds each, and an M-32A1 40mm 6-shot, aft-mounted grenade launcher to discourage pursuit...calibrated at one hundred yards… loaded with alternating frag and phosphorous."

I again interrupt, "With both M4s firing at once, you can go through six hundred rounds in about thirty seconds—"

"You know your M4s."

"—and that's not much of a battle plan."

"There are another thousand rounds on each Ski Doo in built-in saddle bags, but it will be all but impossible to reload while underway. The 6-shot M-32s have another twelve rounds also in the bags, all frag, but again, you won't be reloading them while underway. All weapons are controlled by your thumb and/or trigger finger while underway."

"Better than nothing," I mumble, and he gives me a hard-ass look; then he tries to continue, pointing to a blowup of what I presume are satellite photos, but I interrupt aagain, "How the hell are we going to get an aircraft over North Korea? I understand they have a decent interceptor air force."

"Trust me—we've done two dry runs."

"You have no idea how much I hate it when someone says, 'Trust me.'"

He shrugs and continues. "The big boss's home and guest house, Fang's little paradise, is a bit more than a hundred yards from the front gates of the camp, between it and the city. We surmise the ladies are housed just outside the re-education camp as a not-so-subtle threat to the ambassador, in Commander Fang's guest house. You'll have a couple of clicks or more from your LZ to Fang's complex and four clicks to transverse from their quarters to the river, all of it cross-country. Your Ski Doos will await, if all goes as planned with our local contacts."

"And if not?" I ask.

"If not, you'll find some LZs downriver and Ji Su and her NK-painted-and-marked X3 will rendezvous with you there. A Korean construction company marked "chopper," for obvious reasons. Again, plausible deniability. Every piece of equipment you utilize will be scrubbed of any identifying marks. Most of them re-marked Russian."

Pax interrupts this time: "X3…never heard of it."

"New, built by Eurocopter. Cruises at 300 MPH published, but our boys have tweaked her even faster, with a ceiling of 13,000-plus feet. But we have high hopes she won't be necessary. She's the world's fastest chopper, but not faster than the NK's MIG 19s…so it's stealth, not speed, we'll be relying upon."

My turn. "So I presume we jet ski to the Yellow Sea…then what?"

"Then Juliet will be waiting…."

"With a cold beer, I hope."

"'Juliet' is our latest, a Ghost Stealth fast-attack watercraft, a real battlewagon for her thirty-eight-foot size. Her design is an inverted 'V,' a faceted design like a stealth aircraft. She'll be virtually invisible to radar. This one has some armaments stripped out to accommodate her pilot, co-pilot, and the five of you if you ride the river to the meet-up a click out into the Yellow Sea. So again, we rely upon speed and stealth."

"So," I add, "all we must do is avoid their ground forces, air force, and navy, and we're home free?"

"Close enough. We will have a diversion on the far side of NK that will draw the attention of every branch of their military…but that's above our pay grade at the moment."

"Do we get checked out on any of this?" I ask but know the answer. If these SEAL boys had their way, we'd be drilling and running the obstacle course for a month at least…but it seems we have two time constraints: the ambassador being in Brussels and a moonless night. Oh, boy: a moonless night and a parachute jump into rugged country filled with the world's fourth-largest military and citizens brainwashed, for all their lives and the lives of their fathers and grandfathers, to love and protect the Dear Leader…and although I have two dozen jumps, it's been more than ten years.

Like Pax said, "Ollie, what have you gotten us into this time?"

***

KIM HYUN-HEE and his suite mate, Colonel Cho, who is acting as the ambassador's *charge d'affairs*, are going into their third meeting of the morning. This meeting is an attempt to construct an international agreement to restrict carbon emissions. It is all the ambassador can do to stay awake, and if he hadn't been constantly on the edge of his chair, knowing his daughter and granddaughters would soon be, with any luck, extricated from North Korea, he would have dozed.

It is still far too early for the event to take place, and he'll know by his own abduction by the Americans…an abduction that is, in fact, a defection…that his remaining family is safe in the hands of the Americans.

North Korea wastes little money on frills, *Junche*, economic self-reliance, and *Songun*, or military first, is the mantra of the country—meaning the economic self-reliance of the government, not the people, and military first even if the populace starves. The people will be sacrificed to starvation long before the military will do without anything. So, five-star hotels are not booked for anyone other than the ruling elite. Even Ambassador Kim Hyun-hee is relegated to a four-star, but that's fine, as, with his busy schedule, he is seldom in his suite.

In two much smaller rooms across the hall from his suite, at the Mercure Brussels Airport hotel in Haren-Sud, Belgium—a suite shared with Colonel Cho—are six NK State Security Department agents. Plainclothes, the elite of North Korean security operatives. Each of them carries a Ruger P-Series semi-automatic pistol, and, among their luggage are three Sterling submachine guns, a UK manufactured firearm. It's a testimony to western efficiency and expertise that these elite troops carry weapons not manufactured in North Korea, and to Kim Jong-un's intelligence that he approves of their use. They are superior firearms.

Everywhere the ambassador goes—every business meeting, every social event—the MPS is near, at least four operatives at all times, in addition to the CIA.

Never far from the four operatives, the ambassador, and Colonel Chu are a dozen CIA agents. Like their SSD, NK State Security Department, counterparts, they, of course, carry as well, but .40 cal Glock 22s, capable of full automatic fire in addition to semi. Never carried but available in their portable armory are 100-round drum magazines.

Before the ambassador even utilizes the toilet, the room is checked carefully by one of the operatives. However, they are late to one visit.

The Glocks are in both shoulder holsters and mid-back holsters, depending upon the manner of dress of the agents. They are as well trained as the MPS agents and much better armed…and they have the heavily weighted advantage of knowing they are the aggressor at a forum that has never seen an abduction.

Besides the facility's own security force, each member nation has armed operatives in support of their mission, onsite, guarding their own contingency.

The North Atlantic Treaty Organization, NATO, headquarters in Haren-Sud, Belgium, a suburb of Brussels, is a series of interlocking buildings, each rounded, shaped like the top twenty percent of a circle poking up out of the ground, with one third of the end removed, chopped off as if a giant had taken a meat cleaver to the architecture. Eight of these shapes are interlocked, each ten stories tall at the crown. Hundreds of offices, meeting rooms, and several auditoriums make up the huge complex of more than a million square feet of space.

Twenty-nine countries are members of NATO; North Korea is not, but has been specifically invited to the symposium, as they, like China, are a major contributor to the earth's environmental problems, particularly for a physically small country.

Rutgar Paddington, CIA field agent, arrives at Brussel's International Airport as the symposium ends its third of ten days of meetings and travels straight to his hotel. As planned, he and a dozen of his team are housed throughout the Mercure, as the abduction, should it come down, will be much easier to effect without a hundred or more other armed agents from twenty-nine NATO countries reaching for their weapons—as would be the case if it took place on the NATO grounds.

The problem is that, wherever the ambassador is when word comes that the women are safe, he has to defect immediately. When his guards, commanded by Colonel Chu, are informed that the women have flown the coop, his life will not be worth what is splattered on the floor of a chicken coop.

The lucky number of thirteen CIA agents are on hand, but only ten, including Rutgar, will attended their planning meeting in Rutgar's suite on the third floor, four floors below the ambassador's. Three agents are shadowing the ambassador, the colonel, and the MPS agents assigned to protect, and contain, their charge, Kim Hyun-hee, North Korean Ambassador to China.

One of the CIA agents, dressed in a janitor's uniform, has managed to slip a cell phone into the ambassador's pocket as he enters a NATO restroom, between meetings. Before he leaves the toilet compartment, he wisely slips the phone into his underwear.

All tone functions have been disconnected, and only the vibrate function is operable...and it vibrates for only one half of one second, to announce a text.

Now, all he has to do is wait for his personals to be tickled.

Chapter Eight

FOR THE NEXT TWO DAYS, we drill with the equipment we'll utilize, including making one jump with the paraglider and small motor, batteries good for a half-hour, with its eighteen-inch prop. The paraglider itself follows the jumper out, with a crewman acting as a tender timing its follow…otherwise, you'll be dangling from its shrouds until it's launched. The motor and its small prop are in place on the jumper's back as he jumps. In case we get screwed up, we wear an emergency chute as a chest pack but have to shed the engine and paraglider in order to have a chance at survival. We jump from a low three thousand feet, which allows little time for any emergency…but I do fine with the practice run. I'm suspicious that the pilot was told to give us the go from four thousand, not three, but I have no way of proving it.

No matter, we gain lots of confidence.

The last half of day two, we transport to Incheon, Republic of Korea, on the Yellow Sea…the west coast of South Korea. Pax and Ji Su fly her now-construction-company-marked chopper out to the drilling ship, *Back Gold*, but not before he gives me the finger and yells, "Break a leg. I'll call on the SATphone as soon as we're on station."

Butch and Bo prepare for their mission by learning the tricks of a small, rubber—but highly powered—surface vessel and a two-man sub, a mini-version of the Mark 8 SEAL Delivery Vehicle, or SDV, while Jinny, Gun, and I study maps and aerial photos of Re-education Camp one.

And we meet our NK in-country contact, Sook, who we learn is not only a NK military man but an employee of the National Security Agency. I ask how he is able to meet us south of the border, and he merely gives me a crooked-tooth smile. He will be responsible for having the Ski Doos awaiting us at the Taedong. He's got a face as round as a dinner plate and is an easy two hundred pounds packed into about five feet six inches. He's no taller than the average North Korean but a lot more ample. I guess the military eat a lot better than the average lower-caste laborer.

Only after we bid Bo and Butch farewell do we open our mission orders, a large manila envelope with detailed plans of the camp commander's house, guesthouse, and general plan of the camp itself. I'm surprised to learn that Camp 1 is fifteen clicks in width and more than thirty-five clicks long and includes a lead mine, a talc mine, more than one factory, and several thousand acres of row crops, rice, and orchards. And all is operated by slave labor...several thousand Koreans who've fallen out of favor with the Dear Leader and his gang of thugs.

The three of us are given KPA, Korean People's Army, uniforms, but I'm happy to say we will carry our own M4A1, fitted with underslung M203 40mm grenade launcher and Heckler & Koch HK45CT auto-pistols with ten-shot clips in 45ACP caliber for work in tight situations. We'll have some real knock-down power if we get in a scrap. Holstered are Glock 17s with full-auto switch. Under loose-fitting KPA jackets, we have our standard slings with battle rattle: a half dozen ten-shot magazines and a half-dozen grenades for the launcher, binocs, and a flashlight the size of a medium cigar. Each of us has a ditty bag with six thirty-round mags for the M4s.

As if that's not enough, we carry mag lights, and Gun is loaded with ten pounds of plastic explosive and detonators. Jinny has a satellite phone and signal flares in case we must call in Su and her chopper. Unfortunately, she'll be busy for a good while dropping Bo and Butch and their gear.

Our helmets have AN/PVS-7 night-vison unoculars mounted so they can be folded down, but they have only a forty-degree field of view.

The good news is we're very well equipped; the bad news is we can be shot as spies if caught, and legitimately so. Of course, the NK scumbags will shoot us nonetheless if caught.

Other than our sidearms, most of this gear will follow us on its own pallet and chute, for which Gun is responsible; he will carry a controller that will operate the chute's controls. Controlling a paraglider is, actually, quite simple. The controls and shrouds that you normally hold in your hand connect to the trailing edge of the wing. Depending on how you pull the controls, the wing will change shape and therefore change behavior. Pulling on the controls makes the glider fly slower. Releasing pressure makes it fly faster. If you want to turn to the right, pull on the right control, and release pressure on the left. This makes the right side of the wing fly slower and the left faster. Before you know it, you'll be turning right. Of course, it's all a matter of finesse and practice. And in this instance, it's a pair of small, battery-operated servo motors that pull or release, depending upon Gun's finesse with a hand-held controller, much like gamers use. The equipment chute has no prop or motor, so it'll be a bit of a trick for Gun to stay close to it.

He assures me he's had plenty of practice jumping with the device and operating it before Pax and I arrived on the scene.

But just in case, our equipment pallet is fitted with a locator beacon. If absolutely necessary, the beacon on the pallet has a small but intense strobe light Gun can activate.

North Korea has nearly the same population as California in one-fourth California's size, so she's densely populated. Consequently, our LZ is carefully chosen. One disadvantage is also an advantage: North Korea has very limited power-generation capability, and she's almost totally dark at night, so not only do we have a moonless night, we have few lights to deal with on the surface.

Among our toys are the latest in handheld radios that will not only communicate but will provide us with not only our own location but also that of the pallet of gear.

We also have handheld electronic interpreters, into which you can either type or speak, and it will give you on-screen or speaker English-to-Korean or vice-versa. Thanks to Paddington and the CIA, we each carry a ballpoint pen that is also a mace and knock-out gas dispenser. I've used them before, and the knock-out is effective and almost instantaneous. The trick is to stay out of the spray yourself, or the bad guy might awaken before you do. *Oops.*

We're going tomorrow at midnight, even though we're told we might be facing winds as high as twenty MPH.

Damn the luck.

***

PIETER DE VRIES WAS TO SHOW up at five PM in the university's cafeteria kitchen for a lesson in preparing *Gochujang*, a sweet savory sauce. *Gochujang*'s primary ingredients are red chili powder, glutinous rice powder, sugar or corn syrup, powdered fermented soybeans, and salt. In addition, he would learn to prepare *bosintang*, a dish that revolted him but was a North Korean favorite. A soup of dog meat boiled with green onions, perilla leaves, and dandelion, with a handful of spices. At least that is his excuse for showing up. In fact, he is to deliver his last evaluation of the questions asked by the military engineers and chemists during his last class with them. Duri will pass the information along.

Pieter is to receive instructions for something he suspects is in the works, something that can influence his staying in North Korea—something, he senses, that is even more important than his current mission.

Duri is rotund for a Korean, but, of course, he's a chef and works in a kitchen that has almost as generous a supply of food as do the government pantries. Needless to say, no pantries are as nicely stocked as the kitchens of Kim Jong-un's several houses. He imports food and liquor from the world over, reportedly spending more than a million dollars on booze, cheese, and exotic underwear for the many virgins—referred to as his "pleasure squad" and medically insured to be hymen-intact, all supplied to the royal palace from schools countrywide. Some as young as thirteen. Dear leader has a thing for pantries and panties.

He's got to be Victoria's Secret's number-one customer.

But, strangely enough, dog soup is primarily for the much lower class. Even rice is considered a luxury to farm and factory folk.

Pieter leans against a metal table and crosses his arms, trying not to look at the dog hindquarter resting on a bamboo chopping board. Sumi, who's followed him in, refuses to look either, but reaches up and caresses Pieter's cheek; then she excuses herself with, "I will be in the cafeteria, having a cup of tea."

"I don't blame you…wish I could go," Pieter lies. But both he and Duri seem to enjoy her walking away.

No one is within earshot, so Duri speaks as he bones the hindquarter, and with his hands and expressions, one watching from across the room would presume he is merely teaching the fine art of turning a dog bone into a plebian dish.

"A group of private mercenaries will be both here and north of here sometime in the next three days. They will, among other things, be interested in a luncheon to be held on the deck of the *Pueblo*—"

"What? Why?" Pieter asks.

"Who knows? But that's the operation. It seems there's a chance a group of foreigners will be boarding the *Pueblo* for a luncheon. Your job is to watch the ship from your apartment—you are to send Sumi to the university to report you're ill. An hour or so before noon, each day for the next three, you'll need to be alone in your apartment…and when you see two or three limousines arrive, make a SATphone call to the preloaded number with the simple message, 'Lunch is served.'"

"That's it—'Lunch is served'?"

"That is it. Now, to the *Gochujang*."

"Wait. How do I get rid of her for three consecutive days?"

"An errand, or whatever. You just do so. Or don't, so long as you make the call when and if you see limos arrive for a luncheon."

Pieter shrugs but is uncomfortable, and he shakes his head worriedly as Duri places a large clay pot on the table, in which the *Gochujang* will be allowed to ferment after its preparation.

Maybe he can push her out the high-rise window?

But he likes her, even if she is a spy. Likes her far more than he's willing to admit, even to himself.

Chapter Nine

“GENTLEMEN,” GARINO INSTRUCTS us at 2100 hours on a moonless night, “you’ll be dropped from a Turkish-marked C-160, especially fitted with a rear ramp for ease of operation. We’ve performed this intrusion twice now and see no reason it won’t work again.”

“And their radar?” I ask, obviously concerned.

“Notorious power failures in NK, and one is timed to coincide with our intrusion. We figure we’ll have a thirty-minute window, as two of their facilities have had their backup generators compromised. It’s enough time—just enough, but enough.”

I can’t help but ask. “No one has said anything about rules of engagement.”

He chuckles. “You are envied by all of us, for there are no rules of engagement. You don’t have to be fired on to engage; you can rape and pillage, I guess.”

“Probably not much time for raping and pillaging, but since our military won’t be blamed, I guess I get it.”

“That said,” Garino follows, “I’d suggest you keep things as quiet as possible. If you rape, don’t get a screamer.”

"Very funny,” I say.

"We got a ready room at the bottom of the tower if you'd like to catch an hour before we mount up."

"*We*?" I ask.

"I'm going along for the ride and to make sure you get launched in good order."

"I wouldn't mind closing my eyes. Pax can sleep through a hurricane, but all I've ever been able to do is rest when a mission is on a short clock."

Both Jinny and Gun give him a shake of the head, so I'm going alone.

He points at a blue door in the bottom of a forty-foot square and one-hundred-forty-foot-high tower. I eye the C-160 as I head for the door. She's a fifty-year-old aircraft, and I'm a little surprised we don't have a newer ride, but then the Turks may not, and she's got Turkish markings...and the Turks are one of the few countries to fly commercially into NK.

As I suspected, I don't sleep but spend the time going over rudimentary Korean in my head until Garino opens the door and switches on the light.

"Time to rock and roll," he says, and, in moments, we're rolling down the runway with the scream of the C-160's turbo props precluding any talking.

I would have thought we'd set a course due north, as I know our intrusion is so located. However, as I glance at my watch, which contains a compass, we're headed west-north-west across the yellow sea. It won't take long to cross waters claimed by China if we keep on this course.

But as I suspected, after fifteen minutes and reaching what I imagine is cruising altitude, he banks to true north. I'm seated in a hard metal military seat but have a porthole, and, in the distance, I see the lights of another aircraft. We're running without any lights, and I'm wondering if the closing plane is an NK MIG set out to intercept us...or even a Chinese J-10.

Then I realize it's a passenger airliner, and I can see that our pilot is lining up directly aft of the airliner and closing the distance between.

In less than three or four minutes, I can see the wing lights of the airliner just ahead and above our position, and I begin to get it. We're tracking an airliner, probably originating in Beijing, China, and headed for NK's capital, Pyongyang.

We stick to this position for several minutes until the airliner begins his descent, and then Gun rises and waves Jinny and me up. "Five minutes to altitude. Hook up."

And he doesn't mean hook up to a line that will pull our chutes, but rather to our individual paragliders.

"Hang on," Gun says, and we grab onto handholds on the fuselage, and I see why, as the plane dives steeply and banks hard to the left, north, toward our objective. The aircraft levels off, and immediately Bo hits a toggle switch; the eight-foot-wide rear ramp drops away...and it's hand signals only, due to the roar of a 300-knot-plus turboprop aircraft trying to slow to nearly stall speed so we can launch.

My paraglider, I'm happy to say, is being tended by Commander Garino, and, although my heart's in my throat, I feel I couldn't be in better hands.

Gun is lined up in first position. I'm next, and Jinny is behind me, each of us with a SEAL to make sure our paraglider follows us immediately.

Gun's hand is in the air, and he's signaling with three fingers, then two, then one, and then, almost casually, he walks the ramp and disappears into space with the SEAL attending his paraglider close behind, but tethered to the plane with a nylon strap, shoving the paraglider package off behind.

I'm six feet behind and, taking a page from Gun's book, try to casually step into space. I'm slapped by cold wind and racked from boots to helmet by the jerk of lines. Gun has a tiny light about the size of a firefly, and, as soon as I have my directional lines in hand, I look for it and see him, already more than a hundred feet below, and use my lines to align myself toward him. I'm a little surprised by the prompt reaction of the paraglider to my tugs and "oversteer" two or three times before. Then I remember the servo motor and prop on my back, and I engage it with a toggle switch in my left sleeve that I pull down until it's tucked in that hand.

I glance to the west and see the C-160 in a dive until he's only feet over the low hills. The only reason I can see him at all is the faint glow of green lights disappearing as the ramp closes. Then he starts a steep climb.

The push of the prop gives me the impression I could fly to China should I wish, but it's good for only thirty minutes or so, which should be more than enough time to get us to our LZ.

Our handhelds are plugged into our helmets, and, as soon as I'm settled into my gentle descent, Gun's voice asks in a quiet and relaxed manner, "All good?"

Both Jinny and I answer at the same time: "Good to go."

We keep the chatter at a minimum, as one never knows who might be scanning channels, but Jinny adds, "I guess the pallet's behind me, but I'm having trouble locating. Strobe?"

Gun comes back, "Short as you can. Gentle circle to the left until you're in control of the load."

"Roger," Jinny says, and I keep my eyes on Gun. I don't want to lose sight of him, but even more so, I don't want to run over him and tangle us both up until we resemble a rock. It's still more than a thousand feet to terra firma.

"I got it," Jinny says. "And she's responding."

"Course 345, gentlemen. Try and get to my elevation, no more than 100 feet separating us. LZ is elevation 450 feet, and we've got about a quarter mile by a half to land safely, and remember: from this angle, it's about a ten-degree downslope, so compensate. The good news: no wind to speak of."

It's quiet for four or five minutes, other than the wind whipping from my own forward motion, as I continue to carefully gauge the distance between myself and the firefly that's Gun to my left, and glance right and see Jinny no more than sixty or seventy feet to my starboard.

Then Gun's voice again: "A hundred feet...eighty...sixty...fifty...ease it down, and wrap 'em up."

I think I'm only five feet—using my night vision, it's hard to judge—but am surprised when it's longer, maybe fifteen. My legs are hoisted, and then I hit, trying to keep my feet but pitch forward. I catch myself on rough weed-covered ground and am dragged for a couple of dozen feet before my paraglider folds and I get control.

I'm spitting a mouth full of North Korea and hear Gun again, only he's not talking to us.

"Sunshine?" he says.

"No rain," comes back, and I guess we've made contact with someone on the ground. It's a code I should have been advised of.

We're carrying our sidearms, but the M4s and other equipment are nestled on the pallet, wherever it landed. It's time I take the reins and do my thing, so I call Gun. "Pallet located?"

He comes back, but in a whisper. "Yeah, but not just by me. A local, uniformed. But be careful…it could be our contact, Sook."

Good thing we have suppressors on the sidearms and no rules of engagement.

Chapter Ten

PAX WEATHERWAX HAS RIDDEN through a short portion of a very dark night with a very competent Ji Su—she's asked to be called "Su"—at the cyclic. The bird is an X3 helicopter painted in the yellow-and-gold colors and design of a North Korean government contracting company. Identified by Korean characters, which he can't read.

They've flown over the brightly lit City of Incheon and across the Yellow Sea to a drilling ship, the *Black Gold*. The *Black Gold* is currently drilling in South Korean waters only thirteen clicks south of the North Korean mainland—dark in comparison with the South, as power is in great shortage—and one hundred twenty miles due south of Re-education Camp One. She's moored twenty-one clicks west of South Korea, just within her territorial waters, claimed at twenty-two clicks.

Needless to say, the location of the ship has been long challenged by North Korea, and repeated threats and close encounters with NK watercraft and aircraft are an almost-daily occurrence.

Pax doesn't know what to expect but, even so, is surprised to be hovering over the sixty-foot-square, brilliantly lit, landing pad of a seven-hundred-fifty-foot drillship with a beam of one-hundred-twenty-five feet, capable of drilling to forty thousand feet She's held in position by sophisticated bow thrusters responding to equally complicated GPS positioning units. Dead center on the deck rises an eighty-foot derrick crawling with roustabouts, roughnecks, and drilling hotshots just as if she were sitting in West Texas rather than on a ship in the Yellow Sea.

The landing pad rests atop a five-story structure Pax presumes is office-and-living accommodations for the crew, which can total as many as two hundred, with ninety-five percent being men. She's a small town.

Pax is surprised to be met, as he deplanes the chopper, by Mike Reardon's former commander, who's now a Vice President of Houston Offshore, the company which owns *Black Gold.* Thomas Scroder is dressed in coveralls and hard hat with a Houston Offshore logo embroidered on its pocket and stenciled on the rigid hat. He extends a hand as Pax walks out from under the rotor wash.

"Commander," Pax greets him.

"'Tom' will do," Scroder says with a smile. Then he turns serious. "Your people are set up in the lounge just off the helm and control cabin."

"Let's go. Our people should be on the ground in an hour."

"There's a coffee pot in the lounge—"

"You're reading my mind, Commander…er, Tom."

It's a short one story down the ladder to the helm, where he is introduced to the ship's captain, Fredrick Brinkerhoff, and first mate, Marty Skogen, and another executive from Houston Offshore, David Downie. Then he is quickly shown into the adjoining lounge, now a TOC, a tactical operation center, that now looks a little like a NASA control room reduced to a ten-by-twenty-foot gray metal room full of tables, chairs, and vending machines. Normally the tables are covered with boxes of donuts, pastries, and coffee cups, but now computers and monitors, all dwarfed by three fifty-four-inch monitors mounted side by side, almost fill the wall opposite the entryway.

One of the monitors is dedicated to a low-level NASA satellite, now tasked to the mission and passing its target every hour and twenty-five minutes. Another is dedicated to a map of the Re-education Camp One Area with real-time location, by different colored icons, of Mike Reardon, Gun, Jinny, and their North Korean contact Sook, via GPS locating devices each carry. The third is an overall map of North Korea with real-time evaluation of their military movements shown by a variety of icons, with particular attention given to MIGs and attack helicopters.

Three young people are manning—and womaning—the computers, and they stop, turn, and then stand when Pax and Tom enter.

Tom does the honors, turning first to a balding, pudgy kid who looks as if he might still be in high school, except for his balding pate. "Pax, this is Archie Turnston, from NSA," and they shake as Tom goes to a basketball-player-tall, equally young man. "And Terrence Walters, Department of Defense." Then he turns to a very attractive girl with blond hair down to the center of her back. "And Constance Nordstrom, CIA Directorate of Analysis. Her boss, whom you've met, Felix Von Reif, is down with some bug and is below in his bunk."

"'Connie,' if you would," she says and shakes with a surprisingly firm hand.

"Let's go to work," Pax says and can't help but glance down at a very attractive derrière as Connie goes back to her chair. Then he turns back to Scroder. "I presume this Mac is mine?"

"All yours, and room for your MacBook next to it."

"Reardon is in the air?" Pax asks.

"He is," the kid, named "Terrence," replies.

"Terry, right?" Pax asks.

"I prefer 'Terrence,'" the kid says as his fingers fly over his keyboard. "Check monitor two—you can see the speed he's moving at in real time. All three colored dots are merged together, as it's Reardon, Gun Ho, and Jin Son. Red for Reardon, blue is Gun, and yellow Jin. The other two dots are Bojing Hoy-Lee and Butch McNally, both onboard here and loading Ji Su's chopper with their underwater unit. They'll depart at 0300, about the same time Reardon and crew should be boarding their surface craft—"

"Ski Doos," Pax corrects. "It's okay to speak English."

"Ski Doos. By the way, it's orange for Bojing and white for McNally."

"Got it. Is the drone in the air?"

"The UAV was airborne an hour ago and is cruising two clicks south of the border on a conventional border-patrol course that NK is used to seeing."

"Okay. Now I guess all we can do is wait and watch."

"And the show begins," Connie says. "They are in the air, and it seems all paragliders have deployed properly."

We all have eyes glued to the big monitor showing each individual as they leave the plane, separated for the first time into red, blue, and yellow, and descend until each of them has come to a stop.

Each of the three geeks in the room is wearing a headset. Each is connected in real time to their home office.

Pax is provided with a headset ,and each of the young engineers has a switch so he or she can conference Pax in if their bosses wish. It looks to Pax like there might be far too many cooks in this kitchen.

"So it begins," Pax says, adjusting his headset and wishing he were with Mike. The simplicity of a battlefield, of downrange, is preferable to the politics of a control room.

Chapter Eleven

I CLOSE TO WHERE I can see Gun with my night vision, and, under the circumstances, I have my Glock in hand, screwing on my suppressor as I move. I used this firearm on the range and found it difficult to control on full auto, so I leave it on semi. Besides, we don't need the sound of even a suppressed automatic weapon.

As it happens, I'm the first to reach the pallet and the uniformed NK soldier who's busily trying to see what's wrapped tightly in shrink-wrap.

Moving as quietly as possible, I'm ten feet behind the guy. I know it's not Sook, our contact, as this guy won't go 120 pounds soaking wet. He's diligently trying to pull away the thick shrink-wrap and paying little attention. I get to within ten feet, slipping my Ka-bar from its thigh sheath, thinking I'll quietly cut his throat…when a voice, speaking Korean, rings out from behind me, and he jumps two feet in the air, turning at the same time.

I'm praying the voice is Gun and glance over my shoulder as he approaches at a brisk trot.

The nosy NK almost faints dead away when he sees me with gun in one hand, knife in the other, glaring at him.

Gun continues to yell as he trots up, and the snoop answers in a weak voice, hands wide, away from his own slung weapon. Gun, by far the best Korean linguist, wears an NK colonel's uniform, and both Jinny and I are dressed as lieutenants, so the snoop is obviously way outranked.

The guy is staring intermittently at our weapons, as they are likely something he's never seen. And, luckily, as dark as it is, he can't see how light-skinned I am.

He's nodding and shaking his head alternatively as Gun apparently reads him the riot act in Korean. I get about every twentieth word but keep as quiet as if I'm a mute, when Jinny arrives, Glock in hand, but he holsters it as he listens. So, I follow suit, removing the suppressor and sinking my sidearm into the thigh holster.

Gun waves the guy away, and he trots off, seemingly happy to be leaving. Then Gun turns to us, a sly smile on his face. He speaks in a low voice: "I'm sure he browned his skivvies when he saw he was talking to a full colonel. I told him this was a secret exercise to capture American and South Korean infiltrators we expect to arrive in a month or so."

"And he won't report this?"

"I advised him it would be a re-education camp if he said a word to anyone, even his wife. He's reserve and got a call because of some strange blip on a distant radar installation in the quadrant where he resides. Let's hope the C-160 got home okay. Exiting, even though he was right on the deck, but soon rising to altitude to deploy the Ski Doos, is bound to be a lot more dangerous than infiltrating in the shadow of that airliner. Let's get with it."

Jinny moves off and stands guard as we use our Ka-bars to slice away the heavy shrink-wrap and sort through our gear, most of which is packed in three backpacks weighing an easy seventy-five pounds each. As we do so, we get a triple click in our earphones, which means "Take cover."

Each with an M4 fresh from its wrapper, a couple of magazines, and a pouch of grenades, we ease back into the brush and barely get situated when we hear, "All clear, Sook and company."

We return to the pallet as Sook and another uniformed NK soldier saunter up. Without speaking, they begin cutting away the paraglider silk, and his associate drags it off into the brush.

"Watercraft?" Gun asks Sook, who's turned to helping us.

"Landed soft and safe. Unpacked and stowed in the brush a click due west, a couple hundred paces south of the suggested GPS."

"Ten four. Let's get half this load nearer to the camp and women, and then get it on and get the hell out of here."

"Not until we hide the rest of this," I say, and Gun nods. I have yet to assert my team-leader position, but it seems time. I don't want anyone questioning my decision if we get into a situation where time and decision-making are critical.

"My brother-in-law, Shin," Sook says as his companion returns from stowing the parachute. Gun nods, and I shake the man's hand. He's as small as the one Gun chased away but thin faced rather than a pie-plate, like Sook. Then Sook continues, "Shin will take the pallet and use it for firewood. He'll drag the wrapper away and dispose of it. And he has twenty-five pounds of rice coming for the help."

Among the goods on the pallet is a hundred pounds of rice in twenty-five four-pound sacks. I was surprised to learn that rice is only the food of the upper class in starvation-prone North Korea. We're going to hide it nearby, as it's great trading and bribe material should we need it. We haul it off into the brush and hide it in a pile of slash.

In only a couple of minutes, we have all three M4A1s unpacked as well as the three HK45CTs. We also have one AirTronic PSRL-1 anti-armor shoulder-mounted rocket launcher in case we get in real trouble with something heavy pursuing us. But it, four rockets, two of the M4s, and one HK will remain in a stash not far from our objective, as Bo and I, who plan to enter the house to recover the ladies, will have the short-barreled urban HK auto-pistols and our sidearms, and battle rattle with both shock and frag grenades on the belt, while Jinny will remain on the distant perimeter with the more accurate and longer-reaching M4 with its grenade launcher. Sook will be deployed a mile away to the camp's fence line, where he'll provide our battlefield diversion and blow a hell of a hole in the camp's electric fence. We hope that we will pull away guards from the camp as well as any stationed at the house.

We hope.

From our "our-eyes-only" orders, it's our understanding there is a major countrywide diversion to happen on the east side of the country, where a B1 and four F16s will make a slight incursion into NK airspace, hopefully attracting most of NK's air force many miles from our operation.

We hope.

As soon as our gear is arrayed, I double-click the radio, and Jinny rejoins us.

"Good to go?" he asks as he recovers the satchel charge that Sook will use. Sook will have a half-hour to cover the mile and a quarter to his assignment and a half-hour to get away into the hills before the timed charge will cause a hell of a boom. During that hour, we'll find a hiding spot for our spare ammo and weapons, and get in position a hundred yards from our objective.

I notice Jinny pull the SATphone from his belt; it goes to his ear, and then he walks over and hands it to me. Per the protocol we've established, Pax asks, "Supply ship *Jolly Roger*, you on schedule?"

"Ten four," I reply.

"Stay safe out there. We're watching. Back to work…" And he's off line.

I know he means he's at the ship, in front of the computers, and that NSA has re-tasked a satellite, and they have eyes on us…but it'll only be for a few minutes until it makes its one-hour-and-twenty-five minute, full-earth circumference and has eyes on us again. I'm told our bird is a low-altitude flyer only two hundred fifty miles in space and flies at seventeen thousand five hundred MPH, meaning she'll be overhead at that speed for a short time. All three of us have locator-beacon devices on our belts…how a two-inch-square device can communicate with a passing bird that far in space is above my pay grade, but I'm assured they'll know our location at least every eighty-five minutes or so. A hell of a lot can happen in an hour and twenty-five minutes, but it's way better than nothing.

Sook takes off to the north, carrying only his North Korean Type 66—a copy of the Russian Makarov—and the satchel charge. We head east to the camp superintendent's complex and the women. Bo and I each lug our M4s, an HK, and two spare rockets, while Jinny is encumbered with both weapons, one spare rocket, and the loaded rocket launcher.

It's easy going downhill but won't be so easy returning with three women in tow.

God willing and the creek don't rise, we'll return.

Chapter Twelve

THE BRUSH THICKENS as we move away from the long meadow, maybe a fallow field, and reminds me of a stint I did at Pendleton in California. The chaparral is not unlike that, and much of it shoulder high and even taller. Hard moving but good cover. I alternate between dropping my night vision and scanning the horizon—what little there is of it between the brush. If you've seen satellite pics of NK, then you know that, after sundown there are very few lights anywhere in the country, other than Pyongyang, where the elite have congregated.

Finally I see scattered lights in the distance and make out the gate to the camp, a twenty-foot-high opening sided and topped with what looks to be telephone poles, with hog-wire-filled gates and eight-foot-high strands of wire no more than a foot apart leading away on the flanks. I pull my binocs out of their case on my left side and see the wire has insulators—electrified. A hundred yards to the south is the commander, Fang's, complex of home and outbuildings. I smile to myself when I note he has solar lighting in the beds of the main house and around a swimming pool. A little ironic and frustrating as we were depending upon the black of night. The house itself is plain but spacious, as is the smaller guesthouse. where only the daughter knows we're coming. And she doesn't know the exact night. However, she's supposed to be ready every night for a fortnight.

Glancing at my watch, I see we have thirty minutes until Sook creates our diversion with the satchel charge.

Jinny, Gun, and I find a dark place in the brush and recon, agreeing to meet back here, where a twenty-foot tall evergreen rises up out of the heavy underbrush. It won't do to take the women to his sniper hidey-hole, as it will likely be on top of the bad guys' target list in short order.

I begin in a whisper, "Looks to me like the high spot in that outcropping of rocks about forty paces east, no more than one fifty from the complex, is your hidey-hole."

Jinny, who is carrying the M4, agrees. "I'd already zeroed in on that spot on the aerials and on Google Earth. Give me ten to get positioned."

"Good. Go," I whisper.

The three of us head quietly to the rock formation, and Gun and I relax as Jinny surveys the complex with his night vison. Then he settles in and positions his M4 and places in easy reach three extra thirty-round magazines and three grenades, two frag and one phosphorus. He spends a moment with a night-red pen light dialing in the night-vision scope on his rifle.

We wait in silence for the sound of Sook's satchel charge. The sound of our own breathing, the occasional hoot of an owl, the buzz and chirp of insects, and the screech of what's likely a night hawk, is all that there is to be heard, for several minutes.

I glance at my watch and whisper, "If he's on time, two minutes—" and don't get the rest of it out as the sky to the north is lit by a flash, and a heartbeat later, we hear the reverberating roar of the explosion.

Then sirens, which echo across the camp. Lights begin to come on in guard stations, including spots that begin to sweep across the many buildings and up and down the fence lines.

More muffled explosions—then dead silence and darkness. We'd been advised that the camp's generators would be compromised.

Gun and I saddle up, HK auto-pistols, night vision down, and begin to move downhill, and as expected, a flashlight appears in a back window of the guest house. which is now between us and the pool and the main house. The flashlight appears for a couple seconds only and is extinguished. As we near, we can see lanterns being lit inside the main house.

When within twenty-five yards of the guesthouse window, a vehicle roars away from the front of the main house in the direction of the camp main gate, where a half-dozen or more guards have gathered with lanterns and flashlights. At the same time, two uniformed NKs round the house and head directly for the guest house.

Gun is twenty yards to my left—we don't want to be taken out with one burst of automatic fire. I hear a click on my radio and a whisper, "Two tangos, my twelve."

Then I hear him yell in Korean, and the two uniformed guards, still at least a hundred feet from him, slide to a stop. He's yelling and striding forward in a military manner, straight at them. When he's within a dozen feet, they see his colonel's uniform and snap to attention.

All this while I'm in a crouch, headed for the window where the flash of light, the signal for the correct window, has originated.

Gun is rattling off orders in Korean and both guards spin on their heels and go back the way they came from, round the corner of the house, and are out of sight.

The window is being slid open as I near, and a nice-looking Korean woman waits, in a dark-blue kimono top and matching trousers, and waves me inside. She's not exactly dressed for my version of an extraction, but you take what you can get. Shiny silk must be a new version of camo. I sling the HK and vault through to land in what I presume is her bedroom.

"Daughters?" I ask in English and repeat the question in my limited, twenty-word Korean vocabulary.

She grabs up three small duffels and points to the door. I follow out into a short hallway. We cross to another door in absolute darkness, and she opens it. I follow her in, where two girls are sleeping on low pallets She snaps at them in Korean, and they are rubbing their eyes.

The plan, of course, was for the women to be dressed in dark pants and a dark, warm jacket, with hiking boots or at least tennis shoes, and to be ready to go.

Nothing ever goes as planned. Murphy's law.

I'm moving with my night vision folded down, and the woman has her flashlight in hand, now lit, so I have to fold up my unocular, as it blinds me. I can tell by the sound of the girls' voices and what I can see in the woman's sweeping flashlight that the girls are frightened to death, all wide eyes and blank stares. I surmise they have not been told of their imminent escape.

The woman—Mi-Ran, I assume, as she looks like the picture I've been provided—is doing all the right things. She throws a duffle to each of the girls and snaps at them in Korean. Then, showing some modesty, moves to me and physically turns me around so I can't watch them dress; then she snaps at the girls again. Having my back to three North Koreans was not in my plan, but I seem to be surviving. A five-foot-four-inches-tall woman and two five-foot, hundred-pound girls are not too scary.

I can hear them scrambling to dress.

"Okay," Mi-Ran says. "We go," and I turn to see the girls, dressed, but in sandals. And I wince, as one of them is dressed head to toe in neon blue. She'd stand out in Times Square. But there's no time to complain.

"Boots?" I question.

She shakes her head and mutters, "We go."

I lead, and, as I enter Mi-Ran's room again, followed closely by the ladies, I hear the rattle of Gun's suppressed HK and, far worse, the answering crack and chatter of weapons of the distinct sound of AK47s.

Then my ear bud crackles again, and Gun shouts, "It's CQB time."

I know enough about SEAL slang to know that's "close quarters battle."

Damn the luck.

Chapter Thirteen

MY RADIO, BUD IN ONE EAR, crackles. It's Gun again. "A dozen or more tangos from the camp gate and the main house—" and, as gunfire erupts, he goes silent. Not a good sign, but the women have to be my priority.

I go through the window first; then I sweep the area with my night vision. Seeing nothing, I turn and help one of the girls and then the other through the window, and, finally, Mi-Ran.

One hundred yards up the hill, through the brush, I hear the suppressed M4 crack. It's Jinny, now a sniper, firing at targets I can't see.

Then the pop and whoosh of a grenade being fired, then another and another, and the explosions, a count of three from the firing, are behind us and near the main house. The spray of phosphorous lights the night as a fountain of white-hot liquid fire arches behind us.

I lead the woman into the brush, with Mi-Ran locked with a hand clutching my battle rattle—and I presume each of the girls being led in turn—we make our way through the brush. I don't want to go directly to Jinny's position, as the flash of his weapons, even suppressed, will be a target and likely draw the fire of every house and camp guard on this end of the facility…and that may be a hundred or more.

As we move through the brush, I hear Jinny calling Gun. "Gun man, come back? Gun man, you down?"

Our mission is to get the women out at all costs, even beyond the mantra, *Leave No Man Behind*.

I find the tall evergreen and arrive at the same time as Jinny Glancing back, I smile. Fang's house is on fire from the phosphorous grenade. Too bad he's not frying, but he was likely in the first vehicle to head for the camp.

"Keep moving," Jin says. "I'll wait for Gun…but I think he's history."

"Then come with me—we'll need your firepower."

He's quiet for a second and then snaps, "Look, Reardon, I know this is supposed to be your op, but *Leave No Man Behind* is deep in my marrow."

"No time to argue. Catch up if you can. Give me the SATphone."

He does so without argument.

So I add, "I'll radio when we reach the watercraft and try and wait if you're on the way. Keep your GPS active so we can see your twenty."

"I can get out of country on foot if I have to. Go—get on with the mission."

So, I do, and the women follow as we continue to climb. In moments, I'm happy to crest the top of the hill and get out of sight of the camp and compound. Then Mi-Ran pulls me to a halt and starts talking in Korean. I shush her with a finger to my lips, and she points.

"Hye-Ja," she says, and I see that one of the twins has lost a sandal and that her foot is bleeding from a gash. "Damn," I mouth.

My first-aid kit is about two inches by two inches by six inches and in my small pack. I drop my battle rattle and hand it to Mi-Ran; then I drop my pack and rip the kit up and slap a wrap, doused in blood coagulator, on the foot. I hand my pack, now only a few pounds, to the other girl. Grabbing the bleeding girl, I hoist her onto my back, wrap her legs around my waist, and she latches on like a leech. With my HK at battle ready, we move on until I come to where we've hidden the other two M4s, Jinny's HK, and the rocket launcher. I dump the girl, load six more magazines into my pack, leave my HK, and grab my M4. I snatch the battle-rattle belt away from the woman and hand it to the girl to carry. I load Mi-Ran up with the rocket launcher and the belt with three spare rockets. She looks frightened even to handle it but takes it.

Loading the girl up again, I set out toward the river and, I hope, the watercraft.

Without speaking, we climb a half-mile through the heavy underbrush, having to use my night vision most the way, dragging the women on behind as they hang onto the girl on my back. It's tiring as hell, like pulling a sluggish train through the brush and over rough and sometimes soft earth.

Stopping, I drop the girl to the ground, hush them all with another finger to my lips, and listen. I hear no pursuers. I dig my GPS out of a pants side pocket and check our location. We're nearly a third of the way to the watercraft. As soon as my breathing returns to normal, I heft the girl, probably a hundred pounds, back up and trudge up a hill…one of about five, if my memory serves.

Reaching the top of it, the second girl is now crying, and I growl at her mother, who, to my surprise, slaps the hell out of her. It works. I'm rapidly running out of gas, winded and muscle tired, but we can't afford to wait, so it's down another hill and up a third.

When we crest it, I bite the bullet, and, even though I'm almost audibly gasping for breath, continue on. This hill, on the down side, is much steeper, and I use the M4 as a walking stick, holding onto the suppressor and using the butt to gain purchase—but it fails me as the ground gives way. I must retain the weapon; the girl screams as she hits the steep slope, and we both roll into the brush below. Both girls are whining in fear, and mom is snapping at them.

I get back to my feet and to the women and get them silenced.

This time I lead the limping girl to the top of the slope and gather us together to rest.

But not for long, as I know there are patrols out trying to track us down.

We're halfway up the fourth hill, weaving our way through the underbrush, when I hear the *Wop! Wop! Wop!* of a chopper, and we haven't called for one. I shove the women under some overhanging brush and check our six, when a chopper clears the hill behind us with what must be a ten-million-watt spotlight on its belly…and it's heading directly for us.

Chapter Fourteen

AS THE CHOPPER PASSES overhead, no more than a hundred feet above us, I can see the Korean equivalent of a .50 cal., probably a 12.7mm, poking its ugly snout from the open side hatch. Like the women, I'm tucked under some brush. I'm silently cussing Mi-Ran, whose daughter is dressed in neon blue and shows up like a Times Square sign. The light sweeps no more than fifty feet from us, and, had it been on target—even occluded by the brush—I'm sure an astute observer would see the girl.

I breathe as the chopper disappears over the hilltop, but I nevertheless take the precaution of trading Mi-Ran my M4 for the AirTronic rocket launcher. The last thing I want to do is call attention to our location, and firing a rocket at the chopper would pinpoint us not only to the chopper and its machine gun, should I miss, but to whomever might be tracking us.

If I'm forced to fire, I can't afford to miss.

I wave the women out of the brush, and we continue moving up the hill, still hearing the *Wop! Wop! Wop!* of the chopper in the distance. Because I'm the rocket launcher with four spare rockets now stuffed in the pack on my back, the daughter with the cut foot, Hye-Ja, is forced to walk on her own. Her mother and sister try to help her, but she cries out upon occasion, and, each time she does, I shush her, and her mother gives me a dirty look.

Glancing back as we get higher on the hillside, my mouth goes dry. At least four dozen handheld lights are stretched out on the second hill behind us. A line of tangos, pursuing soldiers that may number twice that many.

As the cut daughter is the one wearing neon blue, it's a double problem, as she doesn't move quickly when instructed to take cover.

I stop every thirty paces and check the hillside ahead with my night vision to make sure we're close to brush high enough to use as cover, but it's thinning as we near the crest of the hill.

I'm beginning to wish I could call for Ji Su and her chopper for an extraction, but it's a last resort. And risking an extraction by chopper is probably more risky and expected by the enemy rather than any initiative by water.

We're in the open as we hurry over the hilltop, but it's fairly flat, so, easily traversed. That's the good news. The bad news is that the chopper hunting us is less than a half-mile away, with navigation and high-powered spotlights on, and it's heading our way.

"Run!" I say in English, and I guess my meaning is clear as I start down the other side at a trot—as fast as the women can follow—and the chopper closes fast.

No question he'll reach our position before we reach the line of heavy brush fifty yards below. Damn the luck.

We're still twenty yards short when I'm washed with a light so bright that, when I spin and drop to my back, I'm blinded. I yell at the ladies, "Move, move, move" and have no idea if they obey as the chopper is only a hundred yards behind and maybe one hundred fifty feet high, and so loud I probably couldn't hear my own embedded earbud.

He's closing fast. Realizing he has his target, he pivots, slips to the side so his machine gun is facing our way, and hovers, but he's still sliding through the air my way from his prior forward momentum.

Luckily, the gunner is lousy, and, as flame flies from the barrels, the dirt fifty feet behind is exploding in showers from the heavy shells.

It's pure reaction, driven by fear, that allows me to discharge the AirTronic so quickly and so accurately…the rocket leaves true, and a trail of blue flame disappears into the chopper's side hatch and she erupts in showers of flame and metal fragments—the explosion so close it rocks me. Her tail rotor turns ninety degrees toward the stars, and she dives straight down. It seems less than a second when she folds, nose first, into the hillside and the fast-turning rotors explode, shattered into a dozen flying scimitars that would cut you in half. A secondary explosion from her fuel tanks lights up the night—and the brush.

I tuck, cover my head with my hands, make like a mole wiggling into the earth—and pray I'm not about to be decapitated by a hunk of rotor knifing through the air.

Things settle, and just as I'm about to roll to my belly and get my knees under me, another series of explosions and flying shards erupt as the chopper's remains burn. Obviously, it's the ammo storage. Then the ship's rockets begin to give us a July 4th fireworks show.

Some of the flying metal seems more accurate than the side gunner was, as shells and fragments fly so close I can feel the disturbance of the nearby air and see what look to be tracers.

Then all goes silent except for the crackle and roar of the fiery remains of the chopper, no more than a hundred feet away. And the brush is beginning to burn in a concentric circle around the shattered ship.

Dragging the rocket launcher, I crab in the direction the women have gone. As the explosions seem to be over, I get to my feet and run downhill to where I can see the three of them standing, nicely lit by the chopper's conflagration.

I motion to them to *Go! Go! Go!* and yell as I do; they turn and make for the brush and disappear just as the rattle of distant AK47 fire resonates and new eruptions of earth appear all around me. Thank God it's distant and inaccurate, and I follow the ladies, disappearing into the undergrowth.

With a platoon of tangos descending the hill behind us, some as close as three hundred yards if my night-distance estimation is correct, there's no way I'll be able to drag the women up the last hill and down the other side, locate the Ski Doos, and get us launched without coming under a hail of gunfire. The upper half of the hill is clear, and we'll be exposed to night vision or spotlight and in range for far too long a time.

So it's diversion time. We've been heading almost due west, to the location of the Ski Doos, but before we climb out of the brush, I find a game trail and turn south, moving the same way as the ridgeline of the hill and staying inside the brush. We're able to move much more quickly as we're running level.

The good news is that the dry brush on the hillside behind is roaring and growing with flames now shooting twenty feet high. No one is coming through that. I hope it spreads—but not fast enough to catch us.

We've moved a hundred yards when I feel the vibration of the SATphone in my thigh pocket. I slow to a brisk walk, which seems fine with the ladies, unplug the earbud from my radio, and plug it into the phone.

"Reardon," I answer.

"It's Chee, dumb fuck. What's happening?"

"Wish you were here. The more targets, the better," I say to Pax.

"I'm damn near there," he snaps.

"What?"

"At least help is. The unmanned aerial, the drone, with a Gatling gun, is ten minutes out. We saw the chopper go down via SAT, but the bird is out of visual in a mike or so…out of range. Good shooting—if that was you."

"Easy target. With thousand-yard guns on board, they pulled up in easy rocket ranges. Now the problem is a few dozen tangos are on our ass, maybe only a couple of hundred yards east. We've changed course to one eighty, but we've got to head back to two seventy very soon to find our rides. But I can't haul four friendlies and won't have time to bring mama-san up to speed on driving that hot rod."

"No sweat. It seems our contact wants a ride and has had some training."

"So…" I start to use Sook's name but think better of it.

"Yes. Seems his brother-in-law has been arrested, and he'll be tortured for info…not good news. We've been tracking Gun and Jinny, and they are somewhere in the camp…inside the damn camp…still, with their navigation devices. Looks like they're hiding in the snake's den. Any update on them?"

"*Nada*. Got to sign off and move. Keep your fire to the west-facing slope so we don't get friendly-fried."

"Ten four." I stuff the phone back in its pocket, move the pace up to a light trot, and am pleased that the ladies are keeping up.

After we've moved, I figure three hundred yards, I hear the faint whisper of the drone dropping to a thousand feet or so and then the sweet sound of a Grey Eagle, a fifty-six-foot wing span, lifting a nearly thirty-foot body capable of staying aloft for twenty-five hours, climbing to thirty thousand feet, and carrying a payload of a Vulcan cannon firing four thousand rounds a minute. She can keep up a constant rate of fire for many minutes unless she's also carrying her normal four Hellfire missiles, which limits her Vulcan ammo capacity.

As her mission is suppressing fire, the one-thousand-yard accuracy of the weapon is of little consequence, as, when she starts spitting lead and maybe firing a missile, lots of my pursuers will be hunting a hole….

And before we've travelled another ten yards, her muzzle flashes light the night, and the muzzle blast is a continuous roar. In return, a hundred or more weapons show muzzle flashes, now aiming up at the Vulcan, from halfway down the hill at our six.

I immediately switch course, and we head directly west, with the crest of the hill now no more than seventy-five yards above us. If we can make it before the drone expends all its ammo, it should be clear sailing down the far side.

And the brush fire roaring on the far side of the hill is our friend.

Then, to find our rides. I hope Sook is watching and waiting, and not hunting a hole himself due to the small war only a hill away.

I glance at my watch…three AM. Only three more hours of darkness, and light will likely be a death sentence.

Chapter Fifteen

BO, THE FORMER SEAL, and Butch, a former bosun's mate and son of the bosun's mate who spent a year in a North Korean re-education camp, are about to be placed thirty clicks above the dam on the Potong River and only seven and a half clicks downstream from the capital city of Pyongyang and where the *Pueblo* has been moored as an attraction for North Koreans…as an example of NK superiority and American imperialism. It was the third incursion into North Korea for Ji Su and her Chinese chopper that night, and now, three hours from dawn, her most dangerous.

The four-man IBS, a Zodiac, suspended below her chopper, is a standard SEAL boat but, like all other equipment on the op, has no American markings, not even a manufacturer's mark. In fact, all equipment has been carefully marked in Russian.

Butch and Bo, both in black wet suits, rappel only twenty feet into the Zodiac, and disengage the boat from the chopper. Ji Su pulls up and away to get her rotor wash out of play as they fire up the fifty-horsepower outboard and signal her with three blinks of their handheld night-red light.

Bo glances at his watch and notes the time: 0200. They have two hours to the final leg of the mission, which will put them only a quarter-mile from their target.

Underwater, dropped on a previous incursion, is a two-man submersible, which is brought to the surface by Bo with the help of a tank of compressed air. A Dräger, a re-breather, is for the last leg…two of which will be utilized on the final quarter-mile, or less, to the *Pueblo*.

The submersible, much slower than the Zodiac, will be towed to a spot three clicks from the Pueblo, where they'll sink the Zodiac, and then the submersible will be mounted by Butch and Bo. Underwater, they'll close the last two-and-three-quarter clicks where they'll make the final quarter-mile under their own power…and hopefully sink the *Pueblo*.

As the hundred-yards wide Potong flows at just over six knots, and as they'll likely be hunted, the trip back will be via the submersible and, all things being equal, at well over ten knots. Then she'll be scuttled a couple of clicks short of the dam, where they'll be extracted by Ji Su and her construction-company-marked chopper. Six choppers were at work ten hours a day on or near the dam, and the hope was the seventh wouldn't be noticed.

Bo is on the outboard and fires it up. Even towing the submersible, they are quickly making five knots.

He gives Butch a tight grin and suggests, "An hour-and-a-half to going underwater. Take a nap, old man."

"Hard to nap in the middle of a clusterfuck. All I want to do is watch the *Pueblo* take a deep six. Then I can meet my old man at heaven's gate and get an *Ooh Rah!*"

"You get one from me for having the guts to be in-country, particularly in this fucking POS of a country with its dirt-bag dick-head dictator."

"I ain't told no one, Bo, but I've been told I only got a couple of years, so if we get in a firefight, don't worry about me. You get away, and I'll do myself with my last cartridge."

Bo stares at him for a long moment and then snaps, "WTF, bosun! We don't leave ours behind."

"Yeah, but yours are usually young studs with lots to live for, or with a woman and brats at home who want to at least be handed a flag for their sacrifice and to hear "Taps" while theirs goes to rest. I ain't got none of those things. If it comes to the nut cuttin', you take care of Bo, and I'll take a few of those fuckers with me. I got a personal reason as my grandpa went down at Chosin Reservoir in nineteen hundred and fifty, before I ever got to meet him. These assholes rotted my old man in their shithole of a prison camp...and he was never the same again...."

Bo is forced to change the subject. "Heads up…or heads down. Surface vessel a quarter-mile ahead."

Intel had briefed them they might encounter patrol vessels on the Potong. Butch hunkers down but pulls his M4 close to his chest.

"I'm gonna beach us in the cattails, and maybe they'll pass on by."

He swings to the south shore and, luckily, pulls in under the overhanging branches of a thick-leafed tree. Bo kills the engine and digs his own M4 out from under the mid-seat dry storage.

Both of them, at almost the same instant, work the slides and chamber a shell. Then, it's wait.

The oncoming vessel is acting odd, swinging from one bank to the other as she progresses downstream. Bo is convinced it's a patrol boat, and if his swing from bank to bank puts the boat close to their hideout, he's sure they'll be spotted. And he'll have to go on the offense.

Bo rummages in the dry storage, pulls out helmets with night-vision unoculars, hands one to Butch, and fits his, folding down the lens.

"She's gonna come very close," he whispers, loud enough that he hopes Butch can hear.

For a full minute, he keeps the M4 at ready arms; then he relaxes and places it down.

"What?" Butch asks.

"Small fishing boat, dragging a net. Stay quiet."

The boat has running lights, but both are white, and Bo realizes they are some sort of oil lanterns. He smiles and waits. The vessel makes a turn back toward the far, or north, shore, and he can hear the *putt-putt* of a one-lung engine.

They lose only a few minutes, maybe fifteen, avoiding the fishing boat and are quickly turned back into the current. Then they're jerked to a standstill, as though they'd hit a rock.

"Damn," Butch says, almost going over the bow.

"The submersible got hung up on something. Come take the stick."

While Bo fits the re-breather, Butch moves to the tiller.

"Just keep her nosed into the current and a slight strain on the tow line."

"You got it," Butch says and gives the engine just enough to keep her under control.

Bo disappears over the side, is gone for only a handful of minutes, resurfaces, and humps back up into the Zodiac.

"What?" Butch asks.

"Hung up in some roots. Move, and give me the tiller."

He swings into the current and is pivoted by the fixed tow rope. When he's pointed downstream, he guns it. Her stern dips, and water pours in, but then the submersible pulls free, and the stern bobs up, pouring water aft. But the Zodiac is a self-bailer, and, almost as soon as Bo gets her pointed back upstream, she's dry.

And with them in wet suits, no real harm is done. Bo navigates back to the center of the wide Potong and picks up the pace. Hopefully, they'll make up the time. When he's back on course, he pulls his SATphone from the center storage, pokes in a single "1," and hits "Send."

Immediately Pax answers.

"Control," he says.

"We lost about fifteen minutes but otherwise good to go. Team one?" he inquires.

"In a firefight but nothing confirmed. Stay on track."

"Ten-four."

He repacks the SATphone, and then he sees another set of lights. This set is the conventional water-navigation display, or running lights, with red and green. The red is to the right, which means the vessel is headed for them.

"Dig out the AirTronic," Bo snaps at Butch, who moves off his forward bench seat, opens it, and shoulders the rocket launcher.

"Trouble?" Butch asks. Then he realizes it's a stupid question. "He's coming fast."

"I don't think I can make the bank," Bo says, and, before he finishes his sentence, a searchlight on the bow of the approaching vessel floods the water ahead of its bow…but is not on the Zodiac yet.

Bo pushes the tiller hard left, and the bow swings right toward the south bank, but, as he revs the engine, he yells at Butch, "Hand me the weapon."

He no more than gets it out than the floodlight washes over the Zodiac. Butch is trying to move aft and pitches on his face, as Bo swings the bow back directly at the vessel.

When they're within fifty yards, he cuts the engine, reaches down, and grabs the rocket launcher but is careful to keep it below and out of sight of the vessel.

A bullhorn blares a few words, obviously in Korean, and Bo waves, a big smile covering his face.

"What?" Butch asks.

"Shit hitting fan," Bo says and waves again. When they're at only forty yards or so, he snaps the launcher to his shoulder and fires.

The blue tail flame tracks directly at the patrol boat, and she reacts with the throttle shoved to the wall—but not quick enough.

The patrol boat erupts in a flash, and the explosion lifts the forty-foot vessel four feet out of the water, and she separates mid-hull and hits the water, now folding in the center as both ends fill with water.

She slips beneath the water with a sizzle and roar of steam as the flames extinguish.

"Damn," Bo says, as he passes the AirTronic back to Butch. "Hold on—we're gonna push it, balls out. Re-load. I'm sure that's not the only tango on the creek."

As they get no more than a quarter-mile upstream, towing the submersible as fast as they dare, a chopper passes no more than two hundred feet overhead, going balls out to the few still floating and flaming remnants of the patrol boat.

They can only hope they haven't been spotted.

Chapter Sixteen

IT'S QUIET FOR A FULL MINUTE after the last pass of the Grey Eagle. Handheld torches that had been extinguished begin to flash back on—distant fireflies on the hillside, at least a half-mile away. Not as many—by a good number—as there had been before the attack, but still too damn many. That's the bad news.

The good news is that we're topping the last hill and will be out of sight of our pursuers, at least until they top the hill. We'll offer them no targets.

And the better news is that, even with automatic gunfire still chattering in the distance, no gunfire is buzzing anywhere near us. It appears they believe we're topping the hill well north of where we actually are. We're safe, for the moment.

Just as we drop off the last ridge, with the river only a quarter-mile below, I realize how wrong one guy can be.

I hear the telltale dull thud of a mortar slamming into the firing pin at the bottom of the tube. Then another and another. At least three mortars are ranging our side of the hill. Luckily, the first, second, and third strikes are more than five hundred yards from where we're descending the hill. Our first hundred yards is rocky but brush-free terrain. The flashes of exploding mortars are distant but marching our way.

We're moving at a quick march, and the nearing explosions encourage our pace.

Both girls are sobbing, and mom is both chastising and encouraging, if tone means anything, as we begin to bust brush on the steep hillside.

I can now hear, but, due to the height and thickness of the brush, cannot see anything but the flash lighting the night sky. But the explosions are so near I can feel the shock. I yell at the ladies, "Down! Down! Down!" I set the example by hitting the ground and trying to make like a toad that's been flattened by an eighteen-wheeler.

They get it, and we all snuggle into the soft earth between stalks of brush with a dusty smell. Just as I think we've been bracketed by the mortars, the explosions begin to move away, marching back the way from which they came!

I'm certain within 30 seconds that the boys dropping the shells have misjudged our position. I yell at the ladies and lead the way at a trot, slamming through the brush, trying to be a blaze a rough trail.

After a very uncomfortable 200 yards of clinging brush and rocky terrain, I break out of the brush on a sandy grass flat and have to wait for the ladies, who also claw free of the brush. All three of them drop to hands and knees in the grass. No longer is there any crying—now they're gasping for air.

While we all collect ourselves and get ready for the last sprint to the river, where I pray Sook will be waiting with our rides, I grab my SATphone, and Pax picks up on the first half ring. "What's the turnaround time for the Grey Eagle?" I ask.

"No deal. Five clicks toward home and a pair of NK F-5As—MIG 17s to you—closed, and she's history. Get to your ass on the river."

"Jinny and Gun?" I ask.

"Hiding inside the camp. We tracked them via their GPS. There's a felt factory a click from the gate, and they're there hiding inside, probably in a pile of rags, the best we can figure. We have another operative creating a diversion, and, if possible, they'll haul ass your way...but not for at least thirty minutes."

"We can't wait three."

"They're big boys. Get the women the hell out of there."

"Ten-four. You got a location on Sook?"

"He's a half click south of you. I suggest you hit the water and float his way. Use the cattails for cover."

I get them on their feet and moving toward the tall cattails lining the Taedong—and, I hope, Sook and the Ski Doos.

We reach the inner edge of the thick cattails, and the water begins to deepen. The mother grabs me from the rear, and I turn to see her shaking her head, desperately.

"No, no, no," she says, and mimes swimming.

"No," I repeat and mime it back with strokes. "No swim?" I ask.

"No. No swim," she repeats.

"Damn," I say. Apparently, Fang's pool got little use. I probably should retreat, but the mortars have reversed and are marching our way. Then they suddenly stop, and I see why, as a row of torches top the hill behind us. And we're a half-mile from our ride.

I'm sorry to say the AirTronic and its rockets are too heavy to take, and we cast them aside. If these ladies can't swim, they sure as hell can't carry a load and do so, and I'm not going to turn loose of my slung M4 or my grenades.

***

Pieter De Vries was settling in nicely in his apartment, even though the elevator occasionally did not operate. Particularly when he arose before dawn, as was his habit. But, what the hell: he wanted exercise, and going down seven floors was not so bad. He ran, sometimes, when he had time, five miles. Two and a half along the river to a bridge where he crossed, two back to the bridge nearest his apartment building, and then across and a half-mile home. Normally, by the time he'd returned, the power had been restored.

The first time he arose while Sumi was still asleep, he was surprised to be intercepted by the MPS as he crossed the last bridge near his building. He was interrogated in the back seat of a police car, with cuffs on, for forty-five minutes. He suspected she'd called the police when she awoke and found him gone, but he didn't accuse her. She seemed amazed when he was late back to the apartment and told her.

"Oh, so sorry, Pieter. So sorry. Maybe you should wake me, and I will run with you?"

"As you wish," he said, with a smile. The next morning, he awoke her, and they ran off together. But soon he pulled far ahead of her, beating her home by twenty minutes. It was the last time she objected to his morning run.

***

GUN AND JINNY, realizing Gun might not be able to make the river, chose the hiding place least likely to be thought of by their pursuers…inside the camp.

Many of the factory buildings, at least a half-dozen, were lighted and buzzing with activity. They chose the only one that was dark—one with bales of rags stacked outside. Inside, there were bins of loose rags. They buried themselves in a bin.

Gun had been shot through the left side below the ribs. It was a through-and-through injury—in and out, clean. It hadn't clipped a gut, but he had a deep crease on his right thigh. They'd used both coagulating patches from their small kits. As tough as he was, Gun was moving slowly. As soon as they were settled in, Jinny got on the radio—taking a risk, as he was sure the enemy would be scanning all frequencies.

"Hey, Chee. Come in."

It wasn't but a few seconds when Reardon came back. "Status?"

"Safe for the moment. Our ride still there?"

"Half-click down from planned location. On our way there now."

"Looking for wheels. We'll play catch-up."

"Ten-four."

***

I HAVE A QUANDARY. Can't go back, can't proceed. Three wide-eyed, very frightened women at my rear, our ride a half-mile downstream.

God will provide.

As I'm contemplating trying to move downstream through the thick tangle of nearly impassable cattails, a twenty-five-foot log—its branches nearly all broken away and two-foot and longer stubs every three or four feet—is only twelve feet into the stream and floating our way.

I swim out and capture the leading end, the root ball, and with all my strength, I pull it my way. The top begins to swing out into the stream, but, holding onto the trunk, I reach back, grab mama-san by the wrist, and jerk her forward until she grapples for the trunk. The two daughters scream and reach to save mama, and I'm able to grab each of them and fling them into the stream, where all they can do is cling to the tree.

Then, with a mighty shove, I push it deeper into the stream with the shrill cries of the women piercing my ears as I'm yelling at them to shut up.

The passing thought, *Rescue them from a nice, warm house, drown them in the river*, passes through my mind as I cling to the trunk, which is beginning to swing around in the stream to lead the crown end downstream.

"Quiet!" I shout at the ladies, and mama-san calms and snaps at the girls; soon we're bobbing down the river in silence. And it's a good thing, as, looking back, there are torches sweeping the small clearing where we'd entered the water.

Now, if we can only figure out where to return to shore. I dig my GPS out of my thigh pocket and put a waypoint in, figuring it two hundred yards from our launch site. I move the cursor until I think it's a half-mile downstream, and I put in another waypoint.

Now all we have to do is float, hope the log doesn't roll and drown my non-swimmers, and then figure out how to get them from log to shore.

And then find Sook, who we can only hope is waiting, and take a leisurely cruise downriver.

Through a few clicks of tangos, if our luck is spent.

Chapter Seventeen

BO AND BUTCH HAD SUNK the IBS, the *Zodiac*, and are eight feet underwater mounted on the SDV, the swimmer delivery vehicle, closing the last two hundred yards to where a single bulb burns on the dock next to where the *Pueblo* is permanently moored as a display of American imperialism. Beneath the bulb, a guard leans against the light pole and seems to be asleep on his feet. When they reach a point where the water is no more than three meters deep, a hundred yards from the ship, they bottom the SDV and hoist their packs of C4 and detonators. Then replace the mouthpieces of the oxygen tanks, which are part of the SDV, with the rebreathers and, after turning on a low-red locator beacon, set out only three or four feet below the surface. But thanks to the re-breather, they have no trailing bubbles.

As they near the *Pueblo,* Bo can feel the insistent vibration of his SATphone. When alongside the ship, he surfaces close to the hull, retrieves the unit, plugs in his earbud, and calls TOC, tactical operations command. “Bad time,” he whispers into the unit the instant Pax answers.

“Detonators set yet?”

“No.”

"Return to your mother ship. A delegation of Iranian scientists are scheduled for a visit to the *Pueblo* at lunchtime. We want them. At least CIA wants them. DOD and NSA are still arguing."

"'Want them'?" Bo asks and then realizes what Pax means. He adds, "So we're to go to breakfast somewhere close and kill a little time chatting with the locals before we maybe turn some scientists into some Tehran version of yogurt?"

"Can you hang?"

"Oh, yeah, and go downstream in broad daylight."

"These guys are the top dogs of the Iranian nuke program."

"We'll hang. We'll have to cross the river, but there's a dock, a wide pier, low to the water but with enough room beneath, if I remember correctly. Advise when we're one hour short of show time."

"Ten-four," Pax says. "Break a leg."

"I hope that's all."

Butch is hanging onto an anchor chain, ten feet from where Bo is treading water up against the hull. He can barely see Butch in the darkness but sweeps his forefinger across his throat and points back in the direction from which they'd come. Butch is not happy—in fact, he looks disgusted—but he clamps onto the re-breather and drops beneath the surface.

Bo swims alongside him so they don't get separated and dead-reckons back to the SDV and the low glow of a red locator light.

They refloat the SDV to a couple of meters below the surface and head for a hideout under the dock across the river.

***

JUST AS I GET THE SATphone back in its pouch, the other thigh vibrates—the radio. I'm hoping it's Jinny, saying he and

Gun are on the way, but am equally happy to hear Sook's heavily accented English. "Are near?" he asks.

"Give us a red, aimed 270 degrees, in five minutes, and keep it until I signal back."

"Two seven zero?" Sook mumbles back and then asks, "West?"

"Ten-four." He has no idea we're coming on the surface of the river.

In a few minutes, I begin to stroke, aiming the remnants of the root ball toward the shoreline, and, luckily, I find footing on a muddy bottom. Just then I see a red light, and it's in someone's hand and coming down the bank to the water.

"Mi-ran," I yell at mama-san. "Shore." I have no way of knowing if she understands, but I reach out and pull her free of the log and aim her to shore. She realizes I'm standing and gets her footing as I reach for the daughter, Hye-Ja, with the cut foot, pull her free, and push her into the arms of her mother, who screams and grasps her mouth with a hand.

The log is again switching ends and is caught in the current with Mi-na, screaming to match her mother—and the log is beginning to roll, taking the girl under as it turns.

I dive deep, aiming downstream, hoping it's deep enough that I can get under the log and that I run into the girl as I do. I'm badly hindered by the M4 slung on my back, but it may just be our lifeline out of here.

But I don't run into the girl.

I surface on the other side, searching the surface with a hand over my eyes, the mother's screams still filling the air.

If our pursuers can't see us, they likely can hear us.

Again, I dive, following the log as it moves off downstream. I am kicked in the face by a bare foot, and I grab an ankle. I try to pull her away, but her clothes are caught in the stubs of the log. I work my way up her body as she kicks and hits at me, and grasp a handful of silk that's stretched taut by the tugging log.

I get a foot up, pry it against the trunk, and give a pull for all I'm worth. Suddenly, we're free, and I kick away, dragging her with me and quickly surfacing.

She's fighting me like a little wildcat, so I give her the flat of my palm, maybe a little harder than I should have, and she goes limp.

With my left arm hooked around her throat, her face above the water, I stroke for the shore, and her mother meets us. She's waded out to her armpits; she grabs her daughter but slips and goes under at the same time.

I grab her and, getting my feet under me, tug them both up onto the muddy bank, where we're met by Sook and the other girl, who pull the women up onto the dry bank.

Well, that was fun, I think. Of course, fun is relative. I've had dental work that was way more fun.

But we're ashore, and we're all breathing.

"Got go now," Sook says, as soon as we've shaken the water off. I had yet to notice, but the temperature is falling, somewhere in the forties Fahrenheit, I'd guess. The women, all dressed lightly, will soon begin to feel the chill—adding insult to injury.

And to add a double insult, I can hear the *Wop! Wop! Wop!* of another bird in the distance, and, a moment later, I see a spotlight searching the river surface a mile upriver, glimmering as it sweeps the surface.

Sook leads us twenty-five feet downriver, wading in knee-deep water, to a brown tarp hidden in the weeds, covering what I presume are our three Ski Doos.

He lifts an edge and waves us under, and, in seconds, we're in deep darkness, listening to the approaching hammering sound of a large bird, beating our way, a multi-million-lumen spotlight scouring the water and weeds for a target.

And we're a target, and a harmless one—*sans* rocket launcher.

Chapter Eighteen

JINNY SHAKES GUN AWAKE. "You can't get worse, man. If we're gonna make it, we gotta beat feet and get to the water. We got two hours to dawn, and I imagine this factory will light up not long after. Can you make it?"

"This is our last easy day," Gun says, with a tight smile as he throws rags aside. Jinny helps him to his feet, and he staggers out of the three-sided bin, supported by Jinny. Then Gun mutters, "My gut's swelling. Bleeding inside, I bet."

Jinny changes the subject. "You still got a bar of C4 and a detonator?"

"Is Kim Jong-un a fat dipshit?"

"We won't dust any civilians if we leave a little love behind. Maybe it'll get their attention while we breach the fence."

"Dig it out of my pack. Did you see those fuel tanks just outside the truck-size sliding doors?"

"Diesel?"

"Smelled like it to me. So long as it doesn't light up our location as we slip the fence."

"It's two hundred fifty yards to the fence. Have to be a hell of a fire to light us up that far away."

"Let's set it for twenty minutes."

"You can't sprint to the fence, ol' buddy."

"But I can make it in twenty. Besides, we're gonna purloin one of those wheelbarrows. If I slow down, we'll see how tough you are, and we can use it to hoist the bottom wire so we can slip under."

In less than ten minutes, they have a pound of C4 set in the warehouse for forty-five minutes and a pound outside, between two tanks of at least five thousand gallons each of diesel fuel, set for only twenty minutes. With luck, there will be a couple dozen guards or soldiers fighting the fire twenty-five minutes after the tanks explode. They'll get a surprise with the second blast.

They move out to the fence, Gun limping along with a hand on the edge of the wheelbarrow, pushed by Jinny. After a hundred yards, Gun trips and falls flat on his face.

Jinny kneels by him. "Taking a rest?" he asks.

"Fuck you, Farley."

"Taxi at your beck and call?" Jinny says. "Mount up, Custer."

Jinny helps him to his feet and lowers him into the wheelbarrow.

"Home, James," Gun says. Then he laughs and winces. "Fuck. Screw 'home.' Get me to the nearest scotch and soda."

Jinny moves out at a trot, pushing Gun in the wheelbarrow, the last hundred and fifty yards to the fence. He dumps him a few feet short, and, thanks to the fact it has wooden handles, shoves the wheelbarrow hard under the first two strands of electrified wire. Sparks explode, but the wire has nearly two feet of clearance below. Far down the line, a guard tower swings its spotlight toward the disturbance, but just as they do, the C4 and the diesel fuel light the night, and the shock careens Jinny nearly into the fence, but he recovers. He rolls under the fence, waves Gun over, grabs him by the wrists, and drags him under.

Jinny is able to free the wheelbarrow without touching its metal parts.

In minutes, Jinny helps Gun across a twenty-yard clearing and into the brush. Then he turns south.

"The Taedong is due west," Gun complains.

"Yeah, but there's a small compound of vehicles down a quarter-click from the gate on this side. All look like Yellow Cabs to me…and you ain't hiking four clicks over hill and dale to the river in your piss-poor shape. And I sure as hell ain't carrying your fat ass."

"Pussy. But fucking-A. A ride will work."

"You got a ride as long as your mule lasts. Get the fuck in…" Jinny again positions the wheelbarrow so Gun can collapse.

As they wind through the brush, heading toward trouble, the camp comes alive with vehicles, a fire truck flashing red leading a pair of military vehicles to the inferno that had been the fuel dump for the felt factory.

Then to their surprise, a distant explosion lights the night sky more than a mile distant.

"What the fuck?" Jinny says.

"A little help from some friends?" Gun asks, and Jinny shrugs.

"Let's find a ride," Jinny says, and begins pushing.

***

THERE'S SOMETHING OMINOUS about hiding under a wet canvas in a foot of water with a hard-breathing Korean in an enemy uniform and three shivering women, one now with half-a-leg of silk ripped away and the leg bared, while the beating rhythm of a bird likely armed with a 12.7mm machine gun, or two, and likely four or more air-to-ground missiles, bears down on you. And I've left my AirTronic behind.

But the bird passes, the downdraft pushing the canvas down around us, and the beating sound diminishes.

Sook and I peel the canvas away. He mounts one Ski Doo, and I help mama-san on behind. I take the rig with the extended seating and help the girls mount up. But I can't leave the last Ski Doo exposed, the rig planned for Jinny and Gun, so hanging onto her dock rope, I let ours drift out a little and carefully re-tarp the last rig.

Sook has fired his up and is idling facing upstream while I work. As soon as I'm finished, I jerk the radio from its thigh pocket and plug the earbud in as I'm asking, "Two souls out there?"

I wait for thirty seconds and am about to repack the radio when Jinny comes back. "About to have wheels. Can make the bridge in maybe ten mikes."

"We can't hang. We're mounted and about to make rooster tails. Your rig's covered with a Cleveland eleven-colored tarp and waiting." I use a code for "brown" because I don't want to give the color away, just in case.

I try to remember just where the bridge over the river is located, and then I advise, "Maybe a half or three quarters of a click against the tide." I'm trying to confuse whoever might be listening, knowing they'll have no idea what making a rooster tail is and hopefully not equating "against the tide" with "upriver."

"Ten-four. Safe journey."

"Roger that," and I return the radio to its pocket.

My Ski Doo fires at the first touch, but before I give it the pedal-to-the-metal, I quickly review my weapons. There's an arm switch and a fire trigger for each of the bow-mounted M4s, and the same for the grenade launcher.

Time to make like a dolphin and haul ass back to the sea.

Chapter Nineteen

BY THE TIME JINNY WHEELS Bo up to the wall surrounding the one-acre vehicle impound, he moves to help Bo out of the wheelbarrow and discovers him unconscious. Placing a finger on Bo's neck, he finds a weak but still throbbing pulse.

He considers trying to raise Reardon…Chee…on the radio and get him to call for a bird, but he knows they're in no position to be picked up. A full force is on the hills to the west; he's adjacent to a camp surrounded by guard towers, some, he's sure, with mounted 12.7mm machine guns and God knows what else.

Bending near Bo, he whispers, "I'm getting us a ride. Hang, pard." He moves along the wall to the far corner and peeks around to see the gates standing open, but there's a guard in position, nervously smoking a cigarette.

The guard is seventy-five feet from his corner position, standing in front of a human pass-through gate next to open truck gates. A single bulb is burning on a twenty-foot pole that serves as a hinge point for both the human and truck gates. Jinny doesn't want to fire, even a suppressed round, as a guard tower is located on the corner of the camp no more than one hundred yards from the vehicle yard.

He needs to distract the guard.

Bending, he finds a fist-size rock and heaves it over the wall. It makes little sound…must have hit in the soft earth. Scrounging around, he finds another and heaves it. This time, it clatters on a vehicle. The guard turns and moves to the human gate and stands staring for a moment but then returns to his position, leaning against the wall, smoking.

This time, Jinny bends and collects a handful of smaller rocks and heaves them over the wall, creating a clatter the guard can't ignore.

He drops his cigarette, grinds it out with a heel, unslings his long arm, and turns to move into the compound, slipping a flashlight from his belt as he does so.

Jinny moves quickly forward and takes up a position next to the gate, leaving his own M4 slung but palming his Ka-bar and slipping off his pack so he's as mobile as possible.

He's getting nervous, as the guard is taking his time. Then, just as he's about to take the chance of following the man into the compound, the dancing beam of the flashlight breaks the darkness. Jinny flattens himself against the gate as the guard kills the light as he steps through the opening. He never sees the blade coming as it's driven through his neck, severing the jugular on both sides. He manages to get his hands on his neck as he falls, and Jinny lets the blade slip out of the massive wound.

Kneeling next to the guard, Jinny wipes his blade clean on the man's trousers and re-sheaths it. He grabs the guard by the ankles and drags him inside, out of easy view. Then he fetches his pack.

He scrambles for the nearest vehicle, a personnel carrier that would be called a "deuce-and-a-half were it in a Camp

Pendleton Vehicle Impound. And, as is not uncommon in an active zone, the key is awaiting the driver. With his pack in the passenger seat, he works the gears and finds them familiar and easy.

In seconds, the truck is moving toward the gate and exits, only to come bumper to bumper with a smaller vehicle, this one occupied by four soldiers.

Jinny decides discretion is not the better part of valor and switches on his lights. Because the vehicle he's driving is taller, his lights are over the hood of the smaller one, and they blind the occupants.

He flashes his high beams repeatedly and blows the horn in a loud, continuous, blaring scream, and the other vehicle relents, slams it into reverse, and careens backward.

Jinny waves as if thanking the other vehicle for giving way and gets a wave and a *toot toot* of the horn in return. He swings right and is soon turning out of sight of the other vehicle, heading for the wheelbarrow and an unmoving Gun. He slides to a stop, jumps out, rounds the hood, strips Gun's pack away, and throws it and his M4 in the back of the carrier. With a super-human effort, he gets the bigger man up and into the passenger seat, slinging his own pack to the rear as he does.

He knows it will be only moments before the occupants of the smaller, Jeep-like vehicle discover the dead guard, so he hits it hard and soon is passing Colonel Fang Chan Dong's impressive house—now engulfed in flames—and guest house. Now it's only five or six clicks to the bridge.

By the time he's a kilometer down the paved two lanes, he glances in the rearview and sees two vehicles behind him. He pushes it to 100 KPH, and they are not falling back.

What he'd give for an AirTronic shoulder-fired rocket launcher. They've used all their C4—not that he'd have time to set a trap. At this speed, with his pursuers only a click behind, when he slides to a stop, he'll have only a mike, a minute, to set up a defense.

He's fucked, he decides. This may literally be his last easy day.

***

I DIG OUT MY RADIO—a little tough as the girl hanging onto my waist is about to cut off all circulation—and glance at the time. We have just more than an hour to daylight and twenty-five clicks or a little more to cover on a strange waterway with islands, flotsam and jetsam, and log jams, to reach the sea and Juliet, if the crew has the balls to hang as Jinny will be more than an hour past rendezvous time. And as fast and stealthy as Juliet is, she won't outrun a MIG and won't be able to hide from one in the daylight.

We have to average at least forty knots to reach the sea and our rescue boat in time for it to clear NK-claimed seas before light.

I ease in front of Sook and kick it up fifteen knots from the cautious twenty-five he's set as a pace. Mama-san is clinging to him like a remora on a shark, and both girls are tight behind me. Both Sook and I have on thick trousers with multiple pockets that thicken that area even more, long-sleeved shirts, vests, battle rattle, and mid-calf boots, and I'm feeling the cold with a fifty MPH wind. The ladies must be freezing.

We've both hit more than one floating log but skimmed over the tops easily. God willing, we won't hit one large enough to launch the ladies and us.

We settle into a steady pace, following the winding river, now sixty or seventy feet wide and who knows how deep. The reflection of the stars on the water gives us some pathway, but it's still so dark that, if we get a real impediment in our path, we'll likely be unable to stop in time. To try to turn would likely mean we'd take the bank.

Then to my pleasant surprise, the river widens and seems to slow—it's as if we're on a pond. I remember from my studying the route on Google Earth that there seemed to be more than one small lake, and I'm suddenly very apprehensive and slow. Then I cut back even more—and it's lucky I do. I'm almost at an idle, with Sook following suit at my rear, when I realize there's a line from bank to bank, maybe a hundred fifty feet wide. I get close enough to hear the roar of water and damn near get caught in the overflow of a weir.

A fucking weir.

Chapter Twenty

SWINGING QUICKLY, I avoid going over by no more than three feet. It looks as if the weir is only about six feet high, but I can't risk jumping it with the women aboard, and, so, I head for the bank, with Sook close behind. We nose up on a sandy stretch, and he comes alongside.

"Tell the ladies to make their way around and downstream, and we'll pick them up below."

He rattles off instructions in Korean, and the ladies set out to find their way around, but he's shaking his head, and his pie-shaped face has gone white.

"I let boat float over," Sook says, and for the first time he's wide-eyed.

"They'll wreck if we let them find their own way. We got to hit the weir at least fifty or sixty knots, on our feet, leaning back, so we hit the surface below at an advantageous angle and don't dig the nose in and flip."

"Cannot do," Sook complains.

I shrug, having to shout over the engine noise. "I'm sure your cousin will be happy to have you join him in the torture chamber?"

"Still, can no do," he's shaking his head as if I'd asked him if he wants a case of the clap.

So, I settle down and try and use my head. "You stay near the edge so you can watch me. You'll see how easy it is." I don't have time for me to screw around and try to pilot both boats, so I need him to get some *cajones*. I smile to myself, as I have no fucking idea if I can make this jump. It's a trick I've never performed before. I've made a jump on a five-foot lip on a snow-ski hill, jumped my Harley Sport maybe clearing twenty-five feet through the air, but a Ski Doo…never. But, hell's bells, you only die once.

Sook edges over to near the edge and keeps his bow pointed upstream and his rig gunned enough to stay in one place, as I run back upstream a hundred yards.

If there's a way to figure something better, there's a reason to wait and contemplate your next action. But if there's no advantage, the only thing you can do by cogitating is let your ass get more puckered. So I immediately wheel it, spin back, and give it all she'll take.

To my surprise I'm at 60 knots as I near the edge, so I level it off and get on my feet with a slight backward lean; suddenly, I'm airborne. I must be more than forty feet in the air and can't help but yell, "*Oorah!*" as I hit the surface and realize I'm alive and not deep-sixed. I spin the beautiful little boat and skim back to just below the six inches of water flowing over the more than one-hundred-fifty-foot-wide weir.

I'm laughing and waving at Sook to come on. He's looking at me like I'm crazier than his country's prime minister, but he shakes his head and disappears from my view as he heads upstream. I gun it toward the bank, where the ladies should be waiting, but I turn back as I get near the bank, just in time to see Sook's Ski Doo launch over the edge.

He's leaning back too far, the hull almost ninety degrees to the water; he hits hard and flips off the boat, somersaulting forward into the water, his body hitting hard, like a flounder hitting the fishmonger's floor. Luckily, he's used the dead-man tether-to-key, and the boat immediately powers down.

First, I've got to get the boat. I head for it and gather its dock line and immediately tow it back to the bank, where the three ladies await. Mama-san sees the problem, wades out, and takes the line as I spin it and go hunting for my compadre.

He's treading water, looking a little foolish, but not injured. I move up alongside and help him aboard. "Good job," I say. "The boat is fine."

"Fuck boat," Sook says, and I can't help but laugh.

In moments we've continued our downstream trip.

***

BO AND BUTCH ARE HUNKERED deep in the dark shadows of a fifty-foot-wide by three-hundred-feet dock along the shoreline, with only three feet of clearance. They're on the surface but as far under the dock as they can get, they have to be careful of bumping their heads when waves penetrate.

They're not surprised when a hundred-foot-long barge is pushed alongside the dock and they hear scuffling overhead as preparations are made to unload the cargo. They're unable to see what's mounded on the barge, but soon the smell of grain permeates the air. There's a loud clanking; an engine is fired up, the steady hum of what they presume is a conveyor belt begins, and voices ring out from the barge. Whatever grain it's carrying is being shoveled onto the conveyor belt.

Bo pulls Butch near. "You remember how deep it is where the barge is tied up?"

"Not very damn deep, but I think we can skirt the end and be okay."

"From your lips to God's ears. I asked Chong to give us an hour to get back to the ship. He says the nuke boys are coming aboard for lunch at noon. Maybe we'd better get a fifteen-minute head start?"

"I could give a shit, as long as I get to deep-six the boat."

"We're gonna be hung out like dirty laundry, and if I'm gonna go I want to make it worthwhile. Kicking the shit out of Iran's nuke program is worthwhile."

"So long as we sink the *Pueblo*. And if we kill some ragheads and fucking gooks—all the better."

Butch didn't give an inch when Bo quickly spun to face him. Rather, he asked, "Don't like the term 'gook,' eh?"

"Not my favorite," Bo growled.

"Then let me tell you the context in which it's used. Rear Admiral Dan Gallery, who wrote the definitive exposé of the capture of the *Pueblo* said it best: "A gook is an uncivilized Asiatic Communist. If that offends you, son, then you must not hate Commie cocksuckers like I do."

Bo found himself smiling. "Can't say I'm particularly civilized, but I sure as hell ain't no Commie cocksucker."

"Good, then let's kill us some ragheads and some gooks."

***

TACTICAL OPERATIONS COMMAND, TOC, or control, was busy. Archie Turnston was nose to screen on his computer and had been trading comments with his superiors at NSA. Terrence Walters was equally occupied with his at the Department of Defense. Connie Nordstrom had been the most cordial and helpful of the three, and after Pax had brought her a cup of tea, she kept his coffee topped off. Her immediate boss was aboard but had yet to show his face.

The red dot on the screen, Reardon, was moving steadily down the smaller river, and Pax had to presume Sook and the ladies were along for the ride.

It was the blue, Gun, and yellow, Jin, dots they are watching most closely. They'd obviously escaped the camp—they'd observed some of the mess they left behind—found transportation, and were moving at a high rate of speed toward the river, but the road would cross the river bridge a half click downriver from the location of their Ski Doo.

It was dead silent in the room, with all eyes on the monitor tracking the team, when light flooded the room. and a tall guy in a rust-colored sport coat and khaki slacks strode in. Pax couldn't help but notice his well-polished shoes that he wore with no socks—A. Testoni footwear, if Pax knew his shoes, about seven hundred a pair if his memory served. The guy wore a baby-blue silk shirt that, like the coat and pants, seemed perfectly tailored, and his hair was impeccable. Like the shoes, the doo must have set him back a couple of hundred.

He strode straight over, without closing the door behind him, to Pax, who was shading his eyes with a hand.

"Weatherwax, I presume?" he said, with extended hand while flashing perfect teeth.

"Yeah — close the fucking hatch. We're trying to concentrate on the screens, and you're blinding us."

The guy stopped short, and he dropped the hand as Pax spun back to the screen.

Pax heard the hatch slam and footsteps approaching from the rear, and a voice rang out over his shoulder. "I'm Felix Von Reif, Directorate of Analysis from the company, and this is my op."

Pax turned. "Heard you were in the sack with a bug."

"Shook it. Bring me up to speed."

"I thought this was a joint operation of DOD, NSA, and the company."

"It is, but I'm team leader."

"Maybe, but that red dot is my buddy, and he was told *he* was team leader."

"Not by me, and not by Langley. Now, bring me up to speed."

Pax turned to Connie, who'd buried her face in her monitor again. "Miss Nordstrom, isn't Mr. Von Reif your department?" He didn't wait for an answer. "Please zero him in, if you'd be so kind."

"Humph," Von Reif made a grunt, obviously upset that Pax had shined him on.

But Pax was occupied. He picked up the SATphone, hit the speed dial, and waited. It was a full forty seconds before Mike picked up.

"What? A little busy here, trying to stay between the banks."

"Radio Gun and Jinny, and see what's coming down with them."

"I'll have to slow down to hear."

"They're on the road, not the water."

"Ten-four. Will come back."

In a half-dozen minutes, the SATphone buzzed, and Pax grabbed it up.

Mike sounded more than a little stressed. "Can't raise them."

"The vehicle they're in has stopped at the bridge."

"Let me know what you know when you know it," Mike said, and rang off.

Chapter Twenty- One

IT WAS A HARD-RIGHT TURN onto the bridge. Jinny locked the brakes, slid into the turn, and leapt from the cab with both his M4 and Gun's in hand.

The tangos were only two hundred yards behind, having gained on the larger truck over the five clicks they'd come.

Jinny leaned around the back of the deuce-and-a-half and emptied a thirty-round clip at the leading vehicle, and, as he'd hoped it would, it slid to a stop, only a hundred yards behind.

He fit a phosphorous into the grenade launcher and let it fly. But it was high, flying over the Jeep-like vehicle — which he could see was carrying four soldiers — and between it and the following vehicle. The driver slammed it into reverse as Jinny reloaded with another phosphorous and was able to use exactly the same elevation as the Jeep was backing into, where the first shot exploded.

He timed the Jeep's retreat and fired again. "*Ooora!*" he yelled as he made a direct hit. Two of the occupants ran from the vehicle, on fire, and disappeared into the brush on the roadside. The vehicle trailing was a personnel carrier, much like the one they'd stolen, and soldiers were pouring out of the rear of it. All he had left was frag, unless he got to Gun, who was still unconscious in the front of the truck.

So, frag it was. He fired four as fast as he could — one into the brush on each side of their truck, one on target, and one behind.

Then he emptied another thirty-shot clip, spraying from roadside to roadside. He was out of C4 but not out of detonators. He set one for five minutes and dropped it in the fuel tank of his truck. Then, as the angry rip of gunfire filled the air around him, he hurried to the passenger side and dragged Gun out, down the bank to the river, and under the bridge.

They were out of sight for the moment.

For the moment.

When he reached the water, he dropped Gun, who went face first into two inches of river. Jinny grabbed for him to keep him from drowning, but, to his surprise, Gun suddenly lifted himself in a push-up position, coughing and spitting water. The bank beneath the bridge was slippery black mud. Jinny bent near Gun's ear.

"Shut the fuck up. I'm hiding you and going after the Ski Doo. Whatever you do, don't move. He dragged Gun up the bank, deep in the shadow of the bridge, and, as quickly as he could move, he smeared black mud all over him — face, hands, any place he could see that might show up. Then he scrambled to the edge of the bridge, where brush had built up when the water was higher, and dragged back a ten-foot-long evergreen, and covered Gun.

Before he headed out, he grabbed another small log, switched on his red mag light, jammed it between some branches on the log, and set it adrift.

Then he returned to Gun.

"If I ain't back by Christmas, catch a ride out of here."

"Go," was all Gun could get out. Jinny grabbed the grenades out of Gun's ruck and ran out from under the bridge, expecting to take lead any second. But he made fifty yards. Then he stopped, dropped his night vision, and scanned the bank behind. He turned back to searching for the Ski Doo. He'd slowed to a quick step.

He dropped flat when he was shocked by the rattle of more than one AK47; then he realized the sound was distant. This time, he didn't need his night vision as he looked back to see the muzzle flashes of at least four automatic rifles, standing atop the bridge, firing downriver, away from his position. His ploy with the mag light was working.

As he moved quickly away, upstream, the tangos were trying to deep-six a log with a mag light.

He couldn't help but smile as he chugged forward through the slippery mud and cat-tails.

Reardon said a "brown" tarp, but it was still dark as in a horny movie theater in the bowery, so he had to be careful. He dug out his GPS and entered a way point, not wanting to go too far past the half-mile distance Reardon had mentioned.

He didn't have much time to search, as when he checked the time, it was no more than an hour to sunup.

And they figured it would take an hour to get downriver to the Yellow Sea.

He kept moving, occasionally turning back and enjoying the fact that the NK soldiers were still chewing up ammunition firing at the retreating red light.

The last time he glanced, he could see them moving off the bridge and then another vehicle pull up, and all of them loading into the back. On the far side, from which they came, the road paralleled the river for a good way, and the vehicle sped off and down-river.

It was another ten minutes before he found the tarped Ski Doo, which fired up with the first touch of the starter. He left the running lights and headlight off and sped as quickly as he dared back to the bridge.

Gun was conscious but not making much sense. He dragged the bigger man down to the Ski Doo and got him in position. But he was wavering, barely able to keep upright. Jin removed his pants belt and tucked Gun's battle rattle in a saddlebag. He chose a canteen and five hand grenades to leave behind. Then he was able to belt both of Gun's thighs to the frame. He might fall backward but would still be aboard.

As Jin restarted the machine and was about to charge out from under the bridge, he stopped short. A light, a brilliant spotlight, that could be coming only from a helicopter, was visible, seemingly following the river upstream.

Toward them.

Damn, damn, damn, he thought. Then he caught himself and realized how fortunate it that he hadn't charged on downstream. Minutes passed as the bird neared, its powerful spotlight sweeping from bank to bank.

It roared overhead, blowing up ribbons of water from its rotor wash. Jinny let it get a couple of hundred yards beyond the bridge. Then the Ski Doo leapt from cover and created a wide wake as he pushed it to fifty MPH, as fast as he dared.

Now if only the soldiers who'd headed downriver had not set up to observe river traffic. With nothing but a few cattails along the banks, he and Gun would be sitting ducks.

Gun was leaning back, parallel with the water, his arms flopping, but there was little Jinny could do until he found some cover. Then he'd tie Gun's wrists together over his chest.

Chapter Twenty-Two

PAX SPOKE ALOUD, even though everyone in the TOC could see it for themselves. "Gun and Jinny are on the river."

A cheer went up in the room.

"Too late," Von Reif said. "They'll never make it to Juliet and the sea. We'll have to abort. Reardon and the women will be lucky to make it."

Pax slowly spun in his chair to face the dapper CIA executive. "I guess you company guys never heard of 'No man left behind.'"

"And I guess you never heard of plausible deniability? None of the equipment utilized in this op has US markings. In fact, we carefully used Russian markings. You guys were advised of the risk, and you've all signed releases should the worst happen. There's almost fifty million dollars invested in Juliet, her development, and only five of her classification afloat. We're not losing her for a couple of mercenaries."

Pax shrugged, looking nonchalant. Then he rose and took a couple of steps, until he was only inches from the equally tall Von Reif.

"Mr. Von Reif, you've got lots of very talented folks, and some very tough folks, working for you and the company. Right?"

"Damn right."

"But none of them are tough enough, and there's not enough of them, to keep me from shoving one of those seven-hundred-dollar shoes up your ass if any of our people get purposefully left behind. And that will be the most pleasurable thing I do to you. Got it?"

Von Reif blanched a little but then recovered. "I've got a job to do — "

"And you'd be smart to keep yourself in a condition to do it. And I promise you, if Reardon, or any of our people, go down because of a dollar or a fucking billion dollars you refuse to risk or spend, you'll taste that shoe, coming up from the wrong direction."

"This is my op — "

"Fine. Glad you think so. Stand back and watch it come down, and pray it works as planned, as I'm sure you were the head honcho doing the planning. Now I'm going back to work."

"And I'm going to find the head of security on this tub."

Pax ignored him and went back to his computer.

"Forty-five minutes to sunup," Connie reported as Pax retook his seat. Then she said under her breath, "And too many friggin' cooks in the kitchen."

"Thanks," he said and glanced at her as the hatch behind them slammed as Von Reif exited the room. Then he returned his eyes to the monitor and the red dot, Mike, moving downriver. Far behind, halfway back to the camp, merged yellow and blue dots were making good time. The merged orange and white dots on the Potong River, now in the middle of Pyongyang, the capital city, across the river from the

Pueblo, were still and unmoving, as expected. And they should be until 1100, when they'd begin moving across river to place nearly twenty pounds of C4 under a joint NK and Iranian lunch party — and under the *Pueblo*.

Connie winked a baby blue at him, and they shared smiles.

"ETA of Chee and the ladies," Pax asked, of anyone.

"A half-hour, plus or minus five," Terrance Walters answered. Then he added, "Juliet is our boat."

"But this is Von Reif's mission," Connie said.

"While we're arguing the fine points, we'll have everyone home."

Ji Su, who'd been leaning against the bulkhead, arms crossed, saying nothing, stood and stretched. "I'll go get any and all of them, should it get too hairy for the pretty little boat."

"Why did I never doubt that?" Pax said, still studying the monitors.

***

BUTCH AND BO WERE getting tired of bobbing, trying to keep from bumping their heads on the rough-cut planks of the pier above. They were trying to keep from sneezing while breathing the dust from the offloading grain. It wouldn't do to give away their position.

Bo stretched his arms to limber up. Then, bored with waiting, he turned to Butch. "Old man, what the hell possessed you to get involved with this op — the money, I guess?"

Butch chuckled quietly and answered, "Got no kids to leave it to. Ain't gonna be around to spend it…so it ain't the money. My old man loved that tub, and I loved my old man. Besides, I may be old fashioned, but I damn sure love the red, white, and blue, and if you insult her, you're on the fighting side of me."

"Sinking the tub isn't showing much love."

"I'm embarrassed for the Navy, and my country, so sinking her now that she's claimed by the North Koreans will give us all some satisfaction. How much do you know about the so-called *Pueblo* incident?"

"Just that she was a spy ship in North Korean waters and was captured."

"Then you don't know shit. We got some time, so here it is. Normally any Navy ship in the Pacific would be the responsibility of Commander, Seventh Fleet, but not the *Pueblo*. She fell under the command of Commander Naval Forces, Japan. They are, or were, basically a housekeeping command, taking care of bases and such. The only real ship they had under their command was the *USS Pueblo*. And since they didn't know their butt from a hot rock, command was nominal. She was really run by a bunch of fucking know-it-all young brats who were spies and had control — whiz kids who couldn't hit their asses with both hands. The Secretary of Defense is too often a civilian, and he has lots of these civilian whiz kids working for him. The command of the *Pueblo* was really in limbo. Even the captain of the ship wasn't allowed into the spy areas of his own command. Unheard of.

"So, when she was confronted by a hostile military force, the captain had to communicate with the whiz kids at Sec Def for orders, and that meant stumbling up the chain of command, with every gutless prick along the way wondering how it would affect his career. A hostile enemy ship with ten times her armament was commanding *Pueblo* to heave to, and the captain was waiting for orders from Washington, D.C.

"My father and the rest of the crew were in chains long before any orders came back. It was criminal, and leaving our people in North Korean prisons for a year was criminal. And all the buck passing afterward was typical, and criminal. So, are you sorry you asked?"

"A clusterfuck that doesn't surprise me," Bo said, glancing at his watch. "Sun's coming up soon, and we've still got a few hours. Why don't you take a snooze?"

"I'll sleep when the *Pueblo* sleeps in the mud on the bottom of the Potong...and my old man can rest easy."

Chapter Twenty-Three

I GLANCE AT MY GPS and see we're only two clicks from the mouth of the Taedong River, which is just four clicks north of our rendezvous with Juliet and our rapid exit to the good drilling ship *Black Gold*, only another fifteen clicks south across the Yellow Sea.

And safety.

It's a good thing, as the sky to the east is beginning to lighten.

Sook is doing well, we're cruising at forty knots, and the ladies are still managing to hang on — they must be frozen solid. The river is now very wide, having converged with several streams as we progressed. So wide I can't see the right bank in the starlight. I'm trying to stay in sight of the left. I presume I'll recognize the sea by its gentle undulations and the salt spray, but who knows? I'll keep checking the GPS.

There's a low fog beginning to thicken, which is good news and bad. Juliet has the latest in navigation and radar, so she'll find us easily, even in a thick fog.

I suddenly see running lights, a couple of hundred yards ahead, occluded by the fog but obviously bearing down on us…and, for an instant, I wonder if it's our welcoming stealth twin-hull; then I realize Juliet would not be running with lights.

It's got to be a bogie. I crank it hard right and cut across Sook's bow so he's aware, but he's already bearing right as well.

And it's none too soon, as a powerful floodlight suddenly streams our way, and the approaching boat swings to the port and follows our change in course. The light is doing them little good in the fog as it's panning back and forth. I slow and then come to a bobbing halt in the choppy water.

Sook idles up alongside; I sweep my throat with a finger, and he gets it, killing his engine.

One of the girls begins to cry to her mother; I snap at her to shut up, and her mother repeats the order in Korean. I can hear the thump of the diesel engine of what I presume is a patrol boat. I hope it's loud enough that they can't hear the girls' cries.

I pull Sook's boat alongside and whisper, "Let's see if she passes. If she turns more to intercept us, I'm making a run at her with the M4s and giving her my ass and the grenades. Idle away. As soon as I charge, if I have to, you haul ass for the sea with mama."

"It is suicide," Sook says.

"So is trying to run...."

"Okay," he says, restarts, and begins to move away. He's not more than forty feet from me when the spotlight passes him, stops suddenly, and pans back, landing on him and mama-san.

I have no choice, and I hit the starter and the throttle at the same time. When I figure I'm only seventy-five yards from what I now see is a Zhuk-class seventy-foot or slightly larger patrol boat, built in Russia, with 12.7 millimeter machine guns or larger on bow and stern, I hit both triggers of the twin M4s, and I'm spitting flame and lead.

As I'd hoped, the spotlight swings from Sook and mama-san to me and the girls, both of whom are screaming at the top of their lungs. But with the light now on me, I could care less how much noise they make.

The large patrol boat has at least eight feet of freeboard at the bow, and I fear my M4s are not elevated enough to get to whoever's manning the machine gun, which has just spit its first burst our way. It's easily seen, as every fifth round or so is a green tracer.

As it seems he's zeroing in on us, I break hard right, and when I figure I'm eighty yards, with the patrol craft behind us, I begin to hit the trigger of the aft-facing grenade launcher. I overfly the first shot, but looking back over my shoulder, I see it's a phosphorous and has exploded on the far side of the boat but in the water. Still it has arched and showered the deck with white hot globules of chemical.

I don't wait but fire all five from one launcher in half-second intervals and don't bother looking back to see…. Instead, I concentrate on getting as deep into the bank of fog as I can, as quickly as I can.

Now it's time to see what these Ski Doos can really do, for the sky at my six is beginning to lighten.

***

JI SU, A TEAM MEMBER and the bird pilot; Archie Thurston, NSA; Terrence Walters, DOD; and Constance Nordstrom, CIA, are gathered around Pax, and all are concentrating on the red dot representing Reardon and, hopefully, Sook and the three ladies. The dot is moving at a high rate of speed down the Taedong River and is less than a click from open sea, and five clicks from its scheduled rendezvous with Juliet, AKA Maine Systems Ghost. Four clicks behind, the merged blue and yellow dots representing Jin and Gun are moving — not as quickly as Reardon, but moving.

As they stare at the screen, the hatch flies open, and Pax glances back to see Von Reif, followed by Captain Brinkerhoff, first mate Skogen, and Mike's old force recon commander, Tomas Scroder.

"Not now," Pax snaps. "We're minutes away from picking up the women."

"I'm calling Juliet off," Von Reif says and moves to Constance Nordstorm's computer station. "Move, Connie," he commands.

"We're minutes away," Pax says.

"Tough shit. I've got a crew and an expensive vessel at risk, and this is it." He moves Connie aside and puts his hands on her keyboard.

Pax rises, and, in a swift movement, gathers up Terrence Walters' laptop and uses it as a sledge, kicking Von Reif aside, still in Constance's wheeled office chair. He rolls away and slams against the bulkhead. Pax pounds Walters' laptop into Constance's, smashing both.

"Get the fuck out of here," Pax yells at Von Reif, his eyes spitting fire, his tone fearless.

Von Reif rises but does not charge Pax, as Pax seems to expect. Rather, he turns to Captain Brinkerhoff. "Have your security remove him."

Brinkerhoff shrugs and turns to Scroder. "Who the hell's in charge here?" he asks.

"Reardon is team leader — "

"And I'm second," Pax says emphatically, returns to his laptop, and glances up at the main monitor. "Juliet is well inside NK water. She'll pick up the women in less than eight minutes."

"And," Von Reif is yelling, "if you'll look at the Korean forces monitor, you'll see a flight of MIGs leaving Pyongyang Air Base. They are less than fifteen minutes to target." He turns to Brinkerhoff. "Use your ship's radio to call Juliet off, Captain."

"Get the fuck out of here," Pax says. "We're a little busy."

As they watch in absolute silence, the icon representing Juliet is moving at more than fifty knots on a course that will converge with the red dot that represents Reardon and, hopefully, the women.

"Goddamn it," Von Reif shouts, but Pax glances back to see Scroder escorting the other three out. "Your ass is mine!" Von Reif shouts as the others move him along.

Ji Su moves and closes the hatch behind them.

"Sorry about your computers," Pax says over his shoulder to Constance and Terrence.

"Government property," Constance says with a laugh. "You'll probably get a bill."

They watch as the icon and the red dot merge, and both come to a standstill for less than a minute.

Then, drawing a gasp from all of them, the red dot moves at what must be nearly a hundred clicks per hour back toward the mouth of the river.

"What the fuck is he doing?" Pax mutters.

Chapter Twenty-Four

AS WE APPROACH THE unmarked U.S. Naval vessel Juliet, actually the product of Juliet Marine Systems and technically known as a Ghost, I get the feeling we might actually pull this off.

After the attack on the *USS Cole* in 2000, where some scruffy terrorists in a piece-of-shit boat managed to kill seventeen sailors on a billion-dollar destroyer, an inventor named Gregory Sancoff decided the Navy needed a vessel that could combat such a threat, and Juliet was born. A thirty-eight foot dual-pontoon, supercavitating stealth, radar-avoiding hull is powered by twin gas-turbine engines reaching a published speed of fifty knots…who knows what's classified. She can carry up to eighteen passengers or a weapons load that rivals an attack helicopter. The version to which I'm delivering the ladies has twin 20mm Gatling guns, Griffin rockets, and Spike fire-and-forget rockets. The Spikes are Israeli fourth-generation, man-portable anti-tank guided missiles and anti-personnel weapons with a tandem-charge HEAT warhead, developed and designed by the Israeli company Rafael Advanced Defense Systems. With this load, she will carry only eight passengers.

But armed as she is, she fears little.

As we disembark the ladies — none too soon, as I believe they would soon die of exposure — my radio vibrates.

"We gotta go," one of Juliet's three-man crew yells at me as I fish the radio out of a thigh pocket and hear Jin's voice.

"We got two patrol boats on our ass and another out front. But you must have done some good work on the big one, as she's on fire."

"Gun?" I ask.

"In and out of consciousness. I don't know…"

"Keep moving. I'm coming back for you."

"Nothing you can do — "

"Coming back. You copy?"

"Copy."

As I know Sook's weapons have yet to be fired, I change horses and yell at the crew member who's waving me over the pontoon and into a hatch. But I wave him off and yell, "Get the women to the ship." I put the throttle to the bottom, and the little Ski Doo damn near jumps out from under me.

The hatch slams behind me, and, from my peripheral vision, I see Juliet throw out a rooster tail from both hulls as she spins, rises out of the water, and is gone.

I turn back into the sun, which is now a fine silver line on the distant horizon.

I'm having to throttle back as I'm still in the sea, not the river, and the undulating rise and fall won't allow me to full throttle. Then the surface begins to flatten as I enter the wide mouth of the river. In less than five minutes, I can see the flaming seventy-foot patrol boat, now dead in the water. My phosphorous grenades, even though they had not made a direct hit, must have caught the wooden superstructure afire. She's almost totally engulfed, and crew members are leaping off the stern into the water.

As I swing to pass her on the bow side, I catch a glance of Jin and Gun passing on the stern end, and, rounding the patrol boat, I see two more smaller craft, now backlit by the sun, coming at full speed no more than a quarter-mile behind, throwing whitewater wakes on either side, muzzles of machine guns spitting fire.

I'd like to close and get my aft end their way, the end that bites with both phosphorous and frag grenades, but with two of them firing machine guns, I fear it would be suicide. So I spin and set a course that will bring me alongside Jin and Gun.

As I near, I can see a row of water spouts from machine guns as the pursuing patrol boats zero in on their small craft.

I want to yell at Jin to swerve, but it's fruitless as the engine noise precludes the sound carrying. But just as the water spouts swing over their target, Jin swings a hard-starboard turn. But it's too late, as I see Gun's side explode and fire shooting from the exhaust of the small craft. Had Jin not turned, the big shell would have gotten both of them. Then I realize their Ski Doo is faltering. Its bow dips, and I realize it's merely coasting, steaming from the engine compartment, which must have taken a hit.

The bottom falls out of my stomach, and my gut aches. I know myself and silently quell my anger and my ache for revenge.

Roaring up alongside, it's clear Gun has bought the farm as there's a gaping, fist-sized hole in the side of his chest, and his head is flopping from side to side. My stomach roils as I realize we've lost a man, my jaw clamps so hard I'm afraid I'll break teeth, and adrenaline floods my backbone. A dangerous proposition as anger causes one to get reckless…and reckless gets one a toe tag.

I reach for Jin but realize he's belted to Gun. Somehow their battle-rattle belts are attached, so Gun can't fall off the

Ski Doo. Tracers are cutting the air around us, and there's no time for anything but escape — if there's time for even that.

I'm expecting a shell the diameter of my thumb to eviscerate me any second.

With Jin on behind me and Gun dangling behind him, flopping like a fish out of water, I hit the throttle, and the game little craft leaps away. And it's a good thing, as both patrol boats are almost on us. They're both flanking us, both firing, and, rather than give it full throttle, I cut it, come to a rapid stop, and they shoot by, not a hundred yards between them, with us centered. How they miss us I don't know, but they do.

And, to my great surprise, one of them explodes. The dumb fucks have shot each other. My first laugh of the day. A sardonic one, but at least a laugh.

In the faint light of morning, I see a side channel, maybe a creek merging with the main channel, and gun the Ski Doo at the opening, only twenty or twenty-five feet wide. I'm hoping against all hope that the channel or creek is not deep enough to accommodate the patrol boat.

When I'm only fifty yards or so into the channel, I figure on firing some grenades. Then I realize that Gun's body is still trailing and is likely situated over the muzzles of the launcher. Had I fired, we'd surely have been blown all to hell with our own weapons.

We barrel in between five-foot-tall cattails marking the edges, and soon are two hundred yards into the winding creek and out of sight of the patrol boat.

Then I realize there's a bridge over the little creek, and I ground the Ski Doo in the darkness beneath.

I help Jin free himself from Gun's body, and we drag it deeper up the slope beneath the bridge, which is only one lane wide. We quickly camouflage him with mud and debris. My stomach is roiling and heat floods my backbone as we put a comrade in hiding. But neither are so bad as my heartsickness.

Both Jin and I still have our M4s slung over our backs with their grenade launchers. As quick as I can move, I go back to the Ski Doo and dig a half-dozen grenades from its saddlebags and a handful of clips for the M4s. Then I free it from the bank, turn it downstream, and gun it into the current back toward the patrol boat. I stuff my extra ammo in my rucksack. Crabbing, I follow Jin as he moves up the slope of the creek bank through the cattails…and realize the bridge is a single railroad crossing.

We reach the track, and I hear the chatter of the twin machine guns on the patrol boat, and, as there's no lead cutting the air overhead, I smile as I hope they're making Swiss cheese of the Ski Doo and will spend lots of time looking for the bodies.

I get my third smile of the morning as there's a train chugging along our way, its headlight still brilliant even in the morning light. It's an even more brilliant light than the patrol boat's flood.

"Ever hitch a train?" Jin asks.

Chapter Twenty-Five

"I HAVEN'T HITCHED A train in thirty years, but she's moving slow. The wrong fucking way — upstream — but slow. I guess they won't hunt for us going deeper in-country."

"Train's not a bad way to see the country," he says, and I scuttle along behind him through the cattails, staying low so we can't be seen by the engineer.

We let a half-dozen cars pass, and then we chug alongside and swing up between what appears to be empty coal cars.

Settling down between the cars, I see Jin reach for his GPS and put in a waypoint. He sees I'm curious and offers, "I ain't leaving Gun's body there. Sure as this is a shithole of a country, I'm coming back to get him."

"No man left behind," I agree, and we lean back to enjoy the ride but fear the gathering light of what appears to be a clear day.

We've got to find a place to dismount and hide out.

That may be more easily said than done, as with no lights shinning, we couldn't see how many houses filled the landscape, but, now, with the sun over the yardarm, it seems there's a farmhouse every hundred yards.

And plenty of folks moving around, welcoming another joyous day in North Korea.

It's a good thing that we're still dressed in KPA, Korean People's Army, uniforms and that Jin is fluent in the language.

Otherwise, we'd be in a little trouble.

Of course, if we're caught dressed in KPA uniforms, we'll be shot as spies. Which is a laugh, as we'd be shot, or worse, nonetheless.

Leaning out after we've traveled a half-mile, I see a group of clapboard buildings, one of them a barn large enough to hold a couple of semi-truck-and-trailer rigs. The train is picking up speed, and, if we wait, she'll be going too fast to risk a jump. I poke Jin. "Time to dismount," I yell, and he nods.

Jumping, I do a parachute-landing roll and end up on my feet. Then Jin crashes into me, and both of us fly into a field, ending up on our bellies among broad-leafed stalks more than two feet tall…and the odor almost makes me dizzy.

"Horseradish," Jin says and laughs.

I rise up enough to see farmhands entering the field a couple of hundred yards away; the area around them is devoid of stalks. They're carrying baskets and, I presume, harvesting the pungent crop, or the adjoining crop, which looks to be onions or garlic.

"Let's wander down the track like we're somebody," I suggest, and both of us rise. After a few strides I come upon a basket that's been cast aside, its bottom rotted out. I pick it up and carry it along. It likely looks odd with our uniforms, but, then again, what person carrying a basket full of garlic—even though there is none—would be suspected of doing any wrong?

We walk along the tracks until we're hidden by the barn, and then we dash inside. There are six-foot-by-ten-foot bins full of garlic in various stages of drying, and several of horseradish, lining both walls, with a twelve-foot aisle between.

Covering ourselves in pungent garlic stalks, in the rear of one of the bins, we hide out. Wishing it could have been potatoes, or carrots, or even radishes, as they would assuage our hunger, we bury ourselves. One can consume only damn little garlic and horseradish. Wish we'd found a barn full of fried chicken and French fries.

It's a good thing we've hidden ourselves well, as, at the end of the day, two dozen workers stumble in and empty three wagons full of baskets of harvested stalks and bulbs.

Then they vacate the place.

We decide it's time to move on, and, after a half hour of silence, we extricate ourselves. I'm pleased to discover a large chicken coop just outside the far end of the barn, and we recover a few eggs. Damn, looking like a couple of egg-sucking skunks, we took our fill…and I have to smile, as even they taste of garlic.

***

THE TOC ERUPTS IN a cheer when Juliet arrives back at *Black Gold* with the ladies aboard. With the exception of Pax, all descend several stories to the ocean-level deck to greet the women, who disembark the twin-hulled boat wrapped in blankets but still shivering.

And all are healthy, if cold.

As soon as they are safely in the wardroom of the drilling ship, sipping tea and warming the women up, Von Reif gets on his SATphone and calls his superiors in Langley. "Mission accomplished. It's a go for the ambassador." Then he rings off and turns to the rest of them. "Mission accomplished, ladies and gentlemen. Let's wrap it up."

Connie turns and surveys the room. Not seeing Pax Weatherwax among the group, she asks her boss, "We still have people in-country?"

Von Reif shrugs. "Independent contractors. They're on their own. I told them the op was over."

Ji Su looks incredulous and snaps at him. "Bullshit! You gave them assurances."

"You have the Company's agreement to pay on delivery. That's all. Those of you who survive have a check coming." Then he turns back to Connie, his employee. "Break down our equipment, and get ready to load up on the service boat." He glances at his watch. "She makes a run back in an hour."

"An hour," Connie says. "We still have people on or near the Taedong and the Potong."

Von Reif smiles as tightly as snake-lips and then asks, "What's this 'we'? You got a mouse in your pocket? Those are tough guys...they'll get home. The Company is packing up and going home, and, as far as I can remember, you work for me and the Company."

Thomas Scroder steps forward. "Mr. Von Reif, the service boat is, as of now, cancelled. The chopper was retained by Houston Offshore, and she's not going anywhere until our people are back."

"This is a CIA op — "

Scroder steps up until he's only a foot away, face to face with Von Reif. "Sir, the *Black Gold* is a Houston Offshore ship, and you just said your 'op' was over. So unless you want to be confined to your cabin until transportation is available — and it won't be until Reardon and his group are all accounted for — you'll stay below in the ward room or in your cabin."

"The hell I will," Von Reif snaps, pulls the SATphone off his belt, and starts to poke in a number.

Scroder snatches it out of his hand and slings it, in a high, arching path, overboard. Von Reif's chin drops to his chest with astonishment; then he recovers and turns to Connie.

"Give me your phone!" he commands.

"Don't have it," she lies. "Mr. Scroder took it from me."

Thomas Scroder gives her a wink, unseen by Von Reif.

Sputtering under his breath, his face growing beet red, Von Reif spins on his heel and heads for a ladder that will take him back to his cabin. After two steps up from the sea-level deck, he turns back. "Scroder, you'll pay for this…you and Houston Offshore."

"We'll see. Now, stay out of the way. *Black Gold* has a brig, Von Reif, and with all the friends you've made aboard her, I'm sure we can get lots of help letting you spend some time there. Suggest you go to your cabin and find a good book to read." He watches as Von Reif ascends the ladder. Then he turns back to the others. "Suggest you rejoin Mr. Weatherwax and see what we can do." Then he moves a step and places a hand on Ji Su's shoulder. "You still good to go?"

"You bet your sweet ass. Let's get it done."

"When we know what 'it' is, we'll give it hell."

***

THE RAVIOLI DE LANGOUSTINES *du Guilvinec*, brushed with truffle oil, were beyond compare, but what would one expect from *La Truffe Noir*, one of the finest restaurants in the world?

Half a world away from the *Black Gold*, Kim Hyun-hee is dabbing his mouth with a napkin, having just finished one of the finest meals in his lifetime, courtesy of the Chinese delegation. The ambassador feels a slight vibration on his inner thigh. He shares the table with five other Asians, including the

Chinese Ambassador and his beautiful female aide, and three from the Vietnamese delegation.

In various locations around the small restaurant, security forces stand aside and eye the participants and each other. Outside are a dozen cars filled with armed security and bodyguards who are smoking and doing their jobs, albeit somewhat at ease on a quiet night in Brussels.

Kim Hyun-hee had taped the small cell phone to the inside of his thigh…and the vibration can mean only one thing.

He glances at the Patek Philippe watch on his wrist, a gift from his Dear Leader, and sees that it's just minutes after eleven PM, meaning it's minutes after seven AM in North Korea.

The ambassador rises, excuses himself, and heads for the men's room. As he expected, Colonel Chu steps out from behind a huge bouquet of flowers in the entry and paces him.

"Alone, please," the ambassador says quietly, in Korean, to the large uniformed soldier who follows him.

"Why?" Colonel Chu asks.

"This is a Belgian restroom, fool," the ambassador snaps.

"So?"

"So, it's barely large enough for one, much less two. Wait outside."

"I will be near the door."

"As you wish."

The Ambassador enters the tiny restroom, a three-foot-by-four-foot toilet enclosure with a door that will barely clear a seated man's knees, a urinal on the wall next to it, and a lavatory with a man leaning on it whom the ambassador has only seen one time, and that at a distance across the room.

The man extends a hand, but the ambassador doesn't take it and rather puts a finger to his lips. "Chu, just outside."

"Fine, invite him in," CIA agent Rutgar Paddington says, in little more than a whisper.

"You are sure?"

"Sure."

The door swings inward, and Paddington steps behind it.

Kim Hyun-hee opens it and speaks in Korean, "Chu, please," and waves the man in.

He barely clears the doorway when Paddington shoves a stun gun against his neck, and he goes down like a sack of rocks. Then the CIA agent reaches into his pocket, recovers a small plastic syringe, removes the needle cover, and gives Chu a quick injection on the side of his neck.

"You have killed him?" the ambassador asks. "I did not want — "

"I've killed his will to fight…at least for a few hours."

"Aw," the ambassador says, relieved. Then he asks, "My daughter and grand-daughters?"

"Safe — out of country."

And the ambassador looks even more relieved.

Paddington reaches into a waist-high trash receptacle and hands the Ambassador a *thawb dishdasha*, an Arab robe, and a *ghutra*, a headdress that would basically hide the face of the wearer should he wish it to do so. Then Paddington digs deeper into the trash, removes another set, and quickly puts them on. Then he removes a Glock 22 from the coat that he'd cast aside and shoves it inside his robe.

"You ready?" he asks, and two men dressed in full Arab regalia exit. Rather than turning into the dining room, they turn through the reception area and out the door; in a few steps, they are on the pavers of Boulevard de la Cambre.

A black limousine, one of more than a dozen limos and town cars parked nearby, cruises up to the curb. As they reach it, Paddington opens the passenger door and bows his head deferentially as the ambassador enters. As they pull away from the curb, a four-door black Mercedes, with darkly tinted windows, pulls away from the curb across the boulevard, flips a U-turn, and follows. In addition to the two agents in the limo, another four are stationed in the Mercedes.

They turn onto the adjacent four-lane road, which sports a wide median, and accelerate away.

Paddington lets out a long, nervous breath, gives the ambassador a tight grin, and says, “In twenty-eight hours, you’ll be with your family in a five-star hotel in Washington, D.C.”

The ambassador merely nods but closes his eyes and leans his head back. It has been a long week awaiting that vibration on his inner thigh.

Rutgar Paddington is not so comfortable.

It has been too easy.

Chapter Twenty-Six

BO IS STIFF AND SORE from bending in the narrow space beneath the pier, across the Potong from the *Pueblo*. As he's almost a foot taller than Butch, the wait is much harder on him.

He glances at his watch and announces to Butch, "It's eleven hundred. Time to rock and roll."

"Let's get 'er done."

Bo operates the controls to submerge the SDV, and both of them adjust their rebreathers. In less than a minute, they near the bottom of the Potong and pass under the grain barge into the sunlit water.

Bo has to keep the bow turned upstream to offset the current. It takes nearly fifteen minutes to slowly make the crossing, but then they are in the shadow of the *Pueblo*. Both of them have their individual mission. Butch is to place a charge, two five-pound bricks of C4, directly beneath the keel, but it alone will not sink the ship, only flood her — but, hopefully, will kill everyone on deck above. She's held in place by eight steel pipes each twenty inches in diameter, welded to the hull below the water line, pile-driven deep into the Potong's muddy bottom. Each of those will have to be blown, and each receive a one-pound magnetically attached charge of

C4. Bo is responsible for five of them and Butch for three, plus the hull.

They meet back at the SDV and give each other a thumbs up and underwater high-five.

The charges will be radio activated, as opposed to timers, as it is imperative the secondary targets, the Iranian visitors, are aboard for their luncheon and fatal dessert.

Neither Bo nor Butch are aware of how the control room, TOC, will know the arrival of the visiting delegation of Iranians. All they know is that they are to receive a SATphone call when the time is right. The radio-signal activation is supposedly good for up to a mile, but, just to be sure, Bo maneuvers the SDV only one half-mile downstream, until he finds a warehouse with another pier they can hide under, and does so. The fact is that he's studied every foot of the banks of the Potong for miles, thanks to SAT photos, Google Earth, and in-country agents.

"Now we wait," Bo says and notes Butch's Cheshire cat grin.

Butch can't contain his enthusiasm. He guffaws and says, "I hope my ol' daddy is perched on a cloud, watching."

Bo nods and adds, "And I hope we get most of NK's nuke scientists and a good part of Iran's."

As he speaks, he picks up the SATphone and dials the single number that connects him to *Black Gold*.

"Chong," Pax answers. "Tell me you're on schedule."

"Good to go. Awaiting your order to execute."

"Relax. Stand by."

"Ten-four," Bo says and rings off.

He turns to Butch. "Relax, the man said."

"Fucking easy for him to say," Butch says but leans back and closes his eyes.

***

WITH OUR BELLIES FULL of raw eggs, we keep moving east, back in-country, the opposite way, we presume, that any pursuers would go.

We've walked only a mile or so when a paved highway joins the alignment of the railroad, on the opposite side of the tracks from our position. As I feared, after a dozen cars and a half-dozen trucks have passed, a military deuce-and-a-half comes along.

"Shall we hide?" I ask Jin as the truck approaches. It will pass only a hundred feet or so from us.

"No," he says, emphatically.

As I feared, they slow as they near, rolling to a stop opposite us.

The driver salutes and yells something in Korean, and Jin returns the salute, waves, smiles, and then answers.

They wave back and move on.

"What?" I ask.

"They offered us a ride. I said we were inspecting the track, and they bought it. Gave me an odd look, but bought it. We need to get the hell away from this track. They're going to begin to wonder why an officer is walking track."

The track has picked up a parallel spur, one that, I presume, is used for one train to pass another. For a hundred yards, we walk between the two.

There are two-dozen farmhouses and barns within sight, and I can't help but wonder where the hell we'll be able to hide, when my hopes are answered. Another train approaches.

In fact, when I look behind, there is a second train coming, now one from each direction.

We move down the rip-rap embankment to a stand of small trees and wait.

Luckily the train moving west, with a dozen or so boxcars, pulls off onto the side spur. We hide while the eastbound train passes. As the westbound begins to move, we run up the embankment and swing aboard between the cars. It's not the best spot, as we can be seen, but at least we are now traveling toward the Sea of Japan.

Back the way we've come.

I fire up the SATphone and dial.

"Chong," Pax answers.

"Chee here. Traveling with the sun. If this keeps up, we'll be looking for a lift in an hour or so."

"Shank's mare," he asks, again using lingo any NK listener will likely not understand.

"Negative, Johnny Cash and the *City of New Orleans*." Again, something an NK listener will not understand, but any music fan — and Pax is one — will know that's a train.

"Roger that. Standing by for coordinates."

With lots and lots of luck, we'll be squeezing a lime in a Corona in the *Black Gold* wardroom in a couple of hours.

With lots and lots and lots of luck.

***

BO AND BUTCH ARE wondering if they'd ever see the *Pueblo* go up in flames and steam as she sinks, when Bo's cell phone vibrates.

"Tell me we're a go," he says, not bothering with "Hello."

"The party will be on in ten to fifteen mikes. You clear of any shock wave?"

"Affirmative. We're on the clock."

"Wait for my confirm."

"Roger that." He rings off and turns to Butch. "Hang for fifteen; then the dance begins."

Again, Butch leans back and closes his eyes.

"You okay?" Bo asks, seeing Butch grimace.

"Never better. In fifteen, I'll be able to die a happy man."

"Let me buy you a fifty-dollar-an-ounce Kobe beefsteak back in Japan before you give up the ghost, old man. You'll get to palaver with your pa soon enough."

"I got a niece," Butch says, turning serious. "My only relative. I told Reardon about her, but you should know as well. My dough goes to her. Jennifer McAdams, in Manhattan Beach. Got it?"

"You'll hand her a copy of your will after I buy you that massaged chunk of Wagyu."

"Yeah, right. But if I don't, make sure Reardon follows through."

"Read you loud and clear."

The phone vibrates, and Bo slams it to his ear. "Tell me it's button time."

Chapter Twenty-Seven

PIETER DE VRIES HAS butterflies in his stomach. He's called in sick again and knows Sumi is suspicious of his illness, as he's been moving from bed to small kitchen to the windows, as nervous as a cat in a dog pound. The binoculars he's been given by his cook contact, Duri, are easily explained away. After all, their apartment is on the seventh floor, with a wonderful view of Pyongyang and the river and canals.

The SATphone he carries is another problem altogether. Duri had managed to slip it to him; he's managed to get it into the apartment…but it is hard to hide with an eight-inch antenna. Hard to keep out of the inquisitive, searching eyes of Sumi.

But, for the next hour at least, he's managed to get rid of her. Complaining of diarrhea, he'd sent her to a pharmacy for medicine. Much to her displeasure, but not so much as her displeasure of looking aghast at doing the laundry.

From his window, he has a clear view, only a half-mile away, of the parking area of the *Pueblo,* and he's both excited and nervous. His instructions are to report the arrival of limousines, and they are arriving. He waits until three line up as close as vehicles can get to the gangplank leading aboard and then makes his call. He says clearly, "Lunch time," the code word he was given. Then he kills the call and quickly hides the SATphone in a plastic bag in the toilet tank. Then he returns to the windows and his binoculars and stays glued to the ship—he knows something is happening but doesn't know exactly what to expect.

And what effect it will have on him. He hopes his reporting is merely informational, but deep in his fluttering stomach, he's sure it's operational.

He'll know soon.

***

BO TURNS TO BUTCH, who looks eager. "I wish we were close enough to see something other than smoke, but here goes."

Pushing the button on the controller, both of them smile as the report reverberates up and down the Potong. They're close enough to the edge of the warehouse wharf they're positioned under to see upriver and the billowing smoke and even solid pieces of the *Pueblo* that rise above the buildings that are in the way of their view.

Bo turns, and he and Butch high-five. Then Bo says, "Let's deep-six this baby and get in the current. Every gook in this shithole will be looking for someone to filet."

Butch laughs at the ex-SEAL of Chinese heritage using the term "gook." He guesses he's convinced him of the true definition of the word.

"Take 'er down, squid," Butch says, and in seconds, to the piercing sound of air-raid sirens echoing across the land, they are near the bottom of the thirty-foot-deep Potong and in the current, heading west at more than ten knots.

***

Peter De Vries is both elated and fearful as he watches the Pueblo shatter, and then his view of her is occluded by smoke and flame. The three long, black limousines parked near the gangplank are rocked and their windows blown out.

When the smoke begins to clear, he sees that she's shattered, but not sinking. Then what's left of her slowly begins to list to the river side, and she seems to shudder and then slips under the surface.

He's mesmerized by the sight, even if he feels like running for the elevator and trying to find his way to the border and out of the country.

Under the circumstances, he decides he does not want to be found with the SATphone, in fact, under any circumstance. So, he retrieves it, hurries out of the apartment, and decides to go up to the roof rather than down to the lobby. Not trusting the elevator, he takes the stairs. In minutes, he's on the roof, four stories above, and finds a four-inch pipe, a vent, probably a plumbing vent, that's large enough and drops the SATphone. He stands quietly and listens to it rattle its way deep into the bowels of the high-rise apartment building. Then he hurries back down to his apartment.

He's surprised to see that Sumi has already returned.

Before he can comment, she says, "You must be feeling better?"

"Not really, but I had to go to the roof to see better what the explosion was."

"You didn't take the binoculars," she says, accusingly.

"I forgot," he replies. "Excited, I guess."

"Captain Soon of the MPS just called and asked for you. I had to tell him I had no idea where you were."

"MPS?" Pieter asks innocently but knows and fears the Ministry of Peoples Security.

"The police. I would expect them to arrive here shortly."

"Why?" Pieter asks and shrugs as if he has no idea what is taking place.

"Because you are a foreigner, and someone has destroyed a national monument?"

"That boat?"

"The *Pueblo.* The captured American ship proudly on display in our capital."

"I'm Dutch—"

"And a foreigner. Expect to be one of many questioned."

Again, Pieter shrugs. But butterflies swarm his stomach, and he is so glad he's dumped the SATphone.

It is only minutes when a heavy knock announces someone at the apartment door.

***

JIN AND I CONTINUED TO worry, as we were exposed between the boxcars, and two men with strange weapons, battle-rattle belts, and KPA officer's uniforms look a little odd catching a ride on a freight train.

So, we decide to see if we can get inside a boxcar and climb the ladder, located on each end of the cars, to the roof. "Yippee," Jin says, with uncharacteristic zeal, "there's a hatch." He swings it open, and, in a heartbeat, we are inside and perched on crates, which, luckily fill the boxcar only halfway up.

"Good to be out of the wind," Jin says, and I agree with a nod of the head, which I realize he can't see in the darkness.

"With luck," I reply, "these crates are full of canned goods. You got a light?"

"Got my lighter," he says, and, in moments, after digging in his pockets, I hear the igniter spin on his Bic. It flames up, we both say, “Shit,” in unison, and he quickly extinguishes the flame.

We’re perched on crates of artillery and mortar shells. A flame is likely not a good idea.

“Let’s move to the other end,” Jin says, as if being forty feet from a massive explosion might save our hides.

We crab until we come upon a wall and can move no farther. It’s a wall of basket-woven cases filling the forward half of the freight car. “You got a torch?” he asks, and I know he means a battery-operated light. I dig in a thigh pocket and come up with my pencil light, and this time when we illuminate the obstruction, again both say “Shit,” only this time it’s with some exuberance.

The baskets are filled with liter bottles of *Soju*, the Korean national booze. What bourbon is to the states, vodka is to Russia, *Soju* is to Korea, both north and south.

“Suppose there’s any nutrition in *Soju*?” Jin asks.

“Who gives a flying fuck?” I reply. “There’s damn sure alcohol.”

In seconds, Jin has his Ka-bar in hand, a basket split, and then a bottle, and shortly I hear the pop of a cork and a gurgle. Then he gasps, “Christ’o’mighty.” And coughs. I feel the bottle pushed up against me and gather and upend it.

And, I, too, cough. This is no swill for a sissy.

“Rat poison,” Jin says. Then he adds, “but better than no rat poison.”

“Let’s take it a little easy,” I suggest. “Probably wouldn’t do to be unloaded with the cargo.”

“Yeah. Speaking of that, maybe we should take turns at the hatch. I got to believe this train is headed for Nampo and the port on the Taedong River.”

“And?” I ask.

"And we better disembark this ride before we get there. There's not only a Navy base on the Taedong River but a port that handles only smaller vessels, as a vehicle bridge, the longest in NK, crosses the river near the mouth, and large ones won't clear."

"So?"

"So, a Navy base supply depot is before the port, and I imagine this train will stop there first. I don't know about you, but I'm not thrilled about unloading in the middle of an NK base…of any kind."

"How's your grenade supply?" I ask.

"Three frag, two phosphorous."

"Why don't we leave a little surprise for the boys on the base?"

"You don't suppose this load of ammo might light up the whole place. The fact is, if my memory serves, the base at Nampo is a major fueling depot, and there's several multi-thousand gallon tanks located so they're easily supplied by rail. We might hit a real home run with all these artillery and mortar rounds going off in every direction."

"You think?"

"I think…pity, however…."

"Sir?"

"All this *Soju*, blown to hell."

"Maybe ought to repatriate a couple more slugs before we send it to *Soju* heaven."

"Agreed," he says, and I feel the bottle again shove up against me, after he again coughs as if he's swallowed a slug of gasoline.

"So, how do we rig this baby up?" I ask.

"Nothing to it: a grenade located such as to where sliding the door aside will pull the pin."

"And where the vibration won't release the pin prior to us departing."

"Roger that. Take the lookout. I'll take the rigging."

"How long to Nampo?"

"An hour maybe…but I want us off here at least a couple of miles before target. Agreed, team leader?"

"Agreed. You rig. I'll watch."

Chapter Twenty-Eight

CAPTAIN SOON SHOVES the door to Pieter's apartment open as soon as the latch is released, knocking the occupant aside. Sumi stands back with arms crossed, as if she expected the rude and very physical intrusion.

He is followed by four officers, all with sidearms, two with automatic weapons. Soon says nothing but crosses the room to the windows overlooking the river and picks up the binoculars perched on the rail.

"For what?" he says in his native language, and Sumi interprets.

Pieter cuts his eyes to her and asks, "He doesn't know what binoculars are for?" His tone is a little sarcastic, and she does not relay the comment to Captain Soon.

She says something and then turns to Pieter. "I have told him you're a bird-watcher."

Pieter shrugs.

Soon, with a scowl, points to the kitchen, walks in, and waves Pieter and Sumi to take a seat, which he does as well.

"Tea?" Sumi asks, as if Soon is making a social call.

He looks a little confused for a moment. Then he nods, and she rises, goes to heat the teapot, and returns to the table.

The other four officers begin to rummage through every drawer, cabinet, and closet. Sumi doesn't even flinch as they flip the queen-size mattress over and leave drawers completely pulled out and on the floor, after being dumped and the bottoms searched for taped items.

Pieter, on the other hand, rises and yells, "What's the meaning—"

"Shut up," Sumi snaps at him, and he glances back to see Captain Soon with his hand on his sidearm. "Put on your nice face, now," she snaps. Then she walks over and places a hand on Pieter's shoulder and pushes him back down in the seat. "They will merely report to your embassy that you died of a heart attack, not a bullet to the heart. They will deliver your ashes in a small cardboard box."

Pieter stares at her a moment. "Uh, sorry," Pieter says, turns with a sheepish and subservient look to Captain Soon, and repeats in his limited Korean, "Sorry, sir."

After at least a hundred questions, asked by Soon and interpreted by Sumi, the captain rises from his chair and the cup of tea Sumi has fixed him, and instructs Pieter, via Sumi, to rise, turn, and put both hands on the table.

He pats Pieter down as if he is a drunk stopped on the highway; seemingly satisfied, he yells to his men, who line up near the door.

"When do you return to work?" Sumi repeats in English what Soon asks.

"Tomorrow, I hope," Pieter relays via Sumi.

Soon merely nods, and without a goodbye, leads his men out, taking both Pieter's and Sumi's laptops with them.

"Are we good here?" Pieter asks Sumi, who exhales a long breath of relief, as the door closes.

"I pray so."

"Our computers?" Pieter asks her.

"When they are through with them."

"My school work…."

"When they are finished, if it suits them, they will be returned. Do you feel like eating supper?" she asks, as if nothing has happened.

"I guess," he says, still shaken.

***

BO AND BUTCH STAY as close to the bottom as possible, encouraged by the fact the traffic above is up ten-fold. The prows of fast-moving vessels — patrol boats, they presume — are cutting the water overhead with increasing frequency.

Due to the extended time of the op, they have expended a good part of the oxygen supply of the SDV's canisters, and, when no more than a click and a half downriver, Butch realizes the alarm is going off on his Dräger, his re-breather. Even Drägers have limitations, and his is near its limit or malfunctioning. A person utilizes only five percent of the oxygen in the breaths inhaled, and the function of a Dräger is to process the bad gas out of exhale. But even that process has limitations.

Butch pats Bo on the shoulder and shows him that his re-breather canister's function indicator is in the red. Bo motions with his thumb up that he is going to surface and heads for the shoreline, hoping for another pier or wharf, or at least heavy growth of brush or cattails to help hide them.

But the up-angle of the bottom, as they near the bank, will not allow them to stay deep enough, so their upper bodies are still submerged.

And it is bright daylight as both their heads appear above water.

They have three unused rockets for the AirTronic, but firing it this close to the city is like ringing the dinner bell for a band of jackals. They might take out the immediate threat, but they'll be signaling their location to half of North Korea's one point two million-man army.

Two couples in an outboard-driven pleasure boat are putting along, not forty yards from them, when they turn to look behind. And one of the men is pointing at them. Then he stands up from the tiller on the outboard and points again, saying something to the others, who turn, shade their eyes from the morning sun, and stare.

Bo raises a little higher out of the water and waves at the man, who hesitates but waves back. Then, seemingly not liking what he sees, he returns to his bench seat, and the outboard shoots forward as he gives it the gas.

"What the hell—" Bo manages, as Butch steps out of the craft, his M4 slung.

"Going ashore to raise a little hell," the old man says. "You haul ass." He reaches in the SDV and retrieves the AirTronic and a satchel with the three remaining rockets, a few M4 magazines.

"Get your ass back—" Bo yells, but Butch is already slugging through the water.

He turns back. "I got my jollies. Get 'er down before one of those patrol boats shows and riddles your ass with them cheap Chinese bullets. You're a good pard."

"I can't leave you," Bo says.

"Fine, stay here and be a dead hero, you dumb fuck. My goose is cooked if'n I stay or go, and if I stay, you got a chance. And I don't have one either way. Now, get on that water horse and beat a trail."

As he speaks, they both hear the beating of a diesel engine but can't see it for the undergrowth…probably a patrol boat waved down by the couples in the outboard.

"Go, Bo. And don't forget my daughter. She gets my cut."

"What the fuck," Bo says, but he already has the SDV in reverse and is flooding its tanks. He is no more than five feet underwater and turning into the current when he sees a four-foot-deep prow cut the water no more than fifty feet upstream. And it is idling, heading for the spot he'd just left.

The current catches him as he accelerates, and maybe fifty yards downstream, the water lights up behind him, followed by a shock wave that nearly unseats him. His head swims for a moment as he regains control of the SDV, getting her back on course.

It seems Butch has put the rocket launcher to good use.

As soon as he recovers course, he hits the throttle even harder and hunkers down to reduce the resistance of his body.

Bo can't help but admire the old man, and he hopes he'll live long enough to personally deliver the old man's share to his daughter and to tell the Sink the *Pueblo* organization what a hell of a job the old man has done.

If he lives long enough, which is damn unlikely.

Chapter Twenty-Nine

LUCKILY THERE IS VERY little traffic on Avenue Emile Duraylaan, only after-supper and after-theatergoers, and the night creatures who roam the world's big cities.

Paddington and the Ambassador occupy the rear seat of the black Mercedes limo; the driver and another, both agents, occupy the front. They are followed by a four-door black Mercedes 550 coup carrying four very capable CIA agents. The limo is armored with fairly substantial bulletproof glass; the 550 is stock, but powerful.

They are no more than three blocks away from the restaurant, Le Truffe Noir, heading into the heart of the city, toward the U.S. Embassy, when the driver turns and, through the sliding glass separating driver from passenger compartment, yells, "A pair of vehicles that were parked at the restaurant are closing fast."

Paddington pulls a small two-way radio from the pocket of his robe. "Bravo, are you onto the closing vehicles?"

The Bravo car comes back. "We're about to execute a blocking maneuver."

Paddington, seeing a potential international incident in the making, says, "We're going to avoid city center." Then he yells to the driver, "Break left around the gardens and back outside the city."

Both pursuing cars are Audi four doors, one blue, one brown. The brown one is in the lead.

As they near, one following the other, the Mercedes 550 waits until the last possible instant and then swings violently from the slow lane into the fast of the four-lane street, causing the Audi to slam on its brakes hard enough to smoke the tires.

The blue Audi barely misses the brown one and shifts to the slow lane, only to have the Mercedes swing into his path, but blue doesn't slow and rams the larger car. The Mercedes leaps ahead from the collision and quickly swings left. His rear driver's-side quarter panel slams into the front left fender of the brown Audi, forcing it up onto a planted center medium.

When he does, the blue Audi manages to get alongside the Mercedes; a barrel appears out of the rear window of the Audi and spits flame.

"Gunfire!" Paddington, who's been watching the rear, shouts.

The four agents in the Mercedes disappear from sight, but the car swings hard right, sideswiping the Audi and driving it into the line of parked cars. It spins out behind the escaping Mercedes, and it stalls, sliding across both lanes, blocking oncoming traffic. Three of the four heads in the Mercedes reappear. Both front and back, they are smashing out what remains of the windows, as there is no opening them otherwise. And firing through glass does not make for accuracy.

At almost the same instant, a Korean appears out of the open sunroof of the brown Audi, which has recovered from the planted center median, and, simultaneously, an American CIA agent pops up from the sunroof in the limo, now a half-dozen car lengths ahead.

Both have assault rifles in hand. The American, Paddington, has a Heckler and Koch HK237 in hefty .300 cal. But before they can shoulder the weapons, the recovered 550 swings hard into the Audi, this time knocking it into the center median only to be stopped in a shattering and steaming impact with a tree at least a foot in diameter.

Both offending vehicles seem out of the fight, and Paddington again yells at the driver. "Back to the original route. Straight to the embassy."

Then his radio crackles. "We've blown a rear tire, and the other one is rubbing badly. Williamson has a bad crease on his thigh, and I'm hit in the right shoulder. We'll be out of the fight shortly."

"Roger that. Hold on." Paddington grabs a map. "Better if you can make the embassy."

"Car won't make it, and we need a doc ASAP."

"Okay, I'm calling for support. There's an emergency hospital…Hospital Etterbeek at Rue Jean Paquot 63. Only five blocks. Head there, and another team will meet up with you. If you're capable of travel…a fully equipped bus with EMT will meet you for transportation to Chièvres."

"The Air Force base?"

"Yes, full hospital."

"We'll do our best."

"Just get to Etterbeek, and get there as whole as you are now," Paddington says and disconnects. Then he calls his control officer at the embassy and gets the standby team and ambulance on the way.

Now, if he can just make it to the embassy without shooting up any more of the town.

***

WITH HIS EYES ON his GPS, Jin finally glances up and says, "This baby should start slowing down when we're a mile away from the base…somewhere in the next quarter-mile, we need to beat feet as soon as she's slow enough to bail."

I pull the SATphone, hit "1," and connect to the TOC.

Pax answers, "Ain't you about ready to x-ville?"

"We got a surprise coming for y'all. Watch if you've got eyes on. July 4th coming up soon."

"Don't tell me. Looks like it's gonna be bird time as Juliet can't operate in daylight?"

"We might catch another Mark Twain, but if not…." I hope he understands I mean a boat on the river.

"Advise. The options can is nearing empty."

"No shit, Sherlock. You should see it from my side of the fence."

"Standing by."

And with that I disconnect, just as we pitch forward a little, indicating the engineer has let off the throttle. We probably never exceeded thirty-five MPH, so unless we're on a steep downhill, we'll slow quickly.

We've got to exit the right side of the car as the left door is rigged to pull the pin on a phosphorous grenade.

And, with luck, start a conflagration in the center of a tank farm full of fuel.

I wish we'd been able to booby trap both doors, but we couldn't figure out how to jump from the left side and rig the door.

We crack the left door just enough to see what we're facing and are surprised to see a cliff not four feet from the side of the train car. No jumping that way, at least not yet.

After a quarter-mile or so, the cliffside falls away, in fact, too far away, as the bank is now so steep that, if we jumped, we'd likely roll fifty feet or more down a rocky slope.

Murphy's fucking law.

Then we're crossing a streambed, and it's a fifty-foot drop, a suicide jump, to the small creek. Then things seem to level off, and the train has slowed to fifteen MPH or less. And there's deep undergrowth and grass alongside the track.

"You ready?" I ask Jin.

"Hit it," he says, and I say a quick prayer under my breath, jump, hit, roll, and thankfully, there are no rocks in the deep grass. As I set up, I see Jin fly from the door, and he disappears into some underbrush.

I scramble his way and am not happy to find him out cold. His head is at a bit of an odd angle up against the four-inch-thick trunk of a heavy stalk of brush.

Damn, damn, damn.

I can see the NK base in the distance, no more than one-half-mile from where I'm hoping he'll recover quickly, and the river beyond. On our side of the tracks, there's base housing, some two story, some only one. On the far side, as Jin had determined, are a few huge tanks, each more than a hundred feet in diameter, and then some warehouses.

Loading docks line both sides of the tracks, and I can only hope they'll unload our car from the far side, the rigged side.

And hope that Jin comes to and we're far away before all hell breaks loose — as it will, if our plan works.

But Jin's not moving. He's breathing and has moved his legs a little…which I hope means his neck is not broken.

A couple of hundred yards away is a farmhouse and small barn, and between us and it is an orchard…plums maybe. I see no one around, which could mean they've gone to town, which could be the good news. The bad would be that, if they have a vehicle, it's likely gone with them.

But, no matter. I can't wait more than a few minutes to get some transportation.

Although, come to think of it, if the tank farm goes up in flames, the place will be so crazy, that might be a good time for Ji Su to make an approach with her chopper.

With a glance at my GPS, I figure we're only ten clicks upriver from the Yellow Sea. But that will mean waiting until dark.

I slip my canteen from its holster and wet Jin's face.

But get nothing in response.

Chapter Thirty

IF THERE'S ONE THING constant about a battlefield, it's that nothing is ever constant. It's improvise, improvise, improvise. I hope Bo and Butch are having better luck than Jin and I…and Gun has had. I've been remiss not checking on them…but I've been a little busy. I actually caught a few minutes of shuteye on the train, as Jin and I traded off sleeping and standing watch. Sleep is a critical part of being able to stay alert later, when you're awake.

Now, to figure out how to get Jin out of here.

Deciding I must give the farmhouse and barn a look to see if I can commandeer a ride, I cover Jin with some brush so he won't be easily seen from the train track, and I leave an arrow drawn in the dirt and an arrangement of twigs pointing the way I've gone — which any good Eagle Scout would look for — and set out.

Even with my American rucksack and battle rattle belt, I'm still in a Korean Army uniform, although it's getting a little ragged, and I'm still carrying my M4, which most North Koreans have never seen in the hands of a soldier. And I sure as hell don't speak the language. Now with Gun dead and Jin out of commission, if I'm challenged — which I surely will be if I'm seen, as my skin color will give me away — I'll likely have to fight. My uniform is dirty as hell, so as soon as I cross into the orchard, I find a muddy spot and apply some liberally to my too-white face and the back of my hands. I have no interest in killing some poor dumb peon of a farmer, but way less interest in being hung for a spy…so, if I'm challenged, I may have no choice than to make sure the farmer buys the farm.

I laugh at myself. I know that *yeoboseyo* is the greeting "Hello" in Korean, but I know that I can't say it nearly well enough to pass for a native. Maybe they'll think I'm a friendly Russian, but, even if so, I know every North Korean has been schooled to turn in anything and anybody suspicious…even if it's something done by your own mother — or your own mother herself. They wouldn't think twice about turning in a passing stranger. Dear Leader spends lots of time and effort indoctrinating every child to believe the state and he are more important than family, friends, or God. And God is a non-entity in North Korea, or so he tries to convince the people.

As I near the house, something moves on a wide front porch, and I realize that, in the deep shade, an old grandmother is in a rocking chair with a shawl over her knees. I'm close enough that she sees me, so I merely nod, wave, and walk on to the barn and out of her line of sight. She appears to be shelling peas, as there's a bowl in her lap and one on the porch beside her.

She raises a gnarly old hand and waves…no smile, but at least a wave. And, to my relief, she goes back to her chore. I smile and wave in return.

There has been a vehicle in the barn as there are tire tracks leading out. I slide the door aside carefully. It's dark inside, and I need my eyes to adjust, as someone could be working there. But I see nothing…then something that makes me smile again…a motorcycle parked between a scraper and a harrow. An old red Honda 90, just like one I owned thirty years ago that took me all over the Wyoming hills.

It'll be all the little bike can do to haul Jin and myself, and Jin will have to be conscious, as it's not like I can throw him in the back of a truck.

I check the fuel level, as there's a fifty-gallon drum nearby with a hand pump, but, luckily, she's full to the brim.

Not wanting to alert grandma — not that I think she could hear, anyway — I push the Honda out, pause at the barn door, and look for life. Seeing no one, I roll the little bike to the orchard, being careful to stay out of sight of the front porch, and push it on through until I'm a full hundred yards from the buildings. Only then do I switch her on and kick the starter. There is a motorcycle god. She fires right up. I kill her and go on pushing until I'm close to where I left Jin, as close as I can easily push the bike. Then I go downhill through the brush on foot.

I'm hoping against hope that I'll hear a huge explosion coming from the base in short order, but, right now, I'm disappointed. I'm thrilled to see Jin sitting upright, holding his head in his hands. And he has the presence of mind to have his weapon in hand.

"Thought you ditched me," he says.

"Nah. I need you on the back of the motorcycle I just hooked. If they shoot at me, I want your fat ass to block the bullets."

He smiles and then winces, as it obviously hurts to even grin. Then he asks, "No, shit? You got a motorcycle?" Then he remembers our adopted mission. "Any boom from down the base way?"

"Not even a pop. But if they're unloading, they've got to get to it. A half-dozen cars ahead of our favorite one."

He tries to stand but flops back down, holding his head with both hands. "Concussion, maybe," he mutters.

"Well, I can bury you right here, or you can catch a ride with me. Your choice."

"Do we want to try to ride out in the daylight?" he asks.

"Whoever owns the Honda might come home, and we'd have to stitch a farmer if he followed the easy trail the bike left coming through the muddy orchard. Or he might just call the police to track us down. Now that we've got the ride, I don't think we've got any friggin' choice."

"I'm dizzy as hell, so lend me a shoulder, and lead the way." I help him to his feet this time, pick up his M4 and re-sling it, and we work our way slowly through the underbrush to the Honda.

"You call that a motorcycle?" he says. "It sucks."

"Yeah, but gear adrift is a gift. I'll wait here if you want to go steal us a Harley."

"I'd probably have to break into Dear Leader's garage to find a Harley…and if I did that, I'd go ahead and steal us a Ferrari or a Lamborghini."

"I love the thought, but not likely. As it is, embrace the 'suck.' This is our last easy day. I'm gonna check in."

Digging the SATphone out of my thigh pocket, I hit the "1" and the dial button.

"The lady is standby for another run," Pax answers, without bothering with a

"Hello."

"You got a location on us?"

"Sure. You're an anemic red dot on the screen, unless someone has hooked your GPS."

"No time to chat. There's a road, not much more than a two — " I don't get the sentence finished when a small explosion echoes up the hillside from the direction of the base.

I hold my breath for a few seconds, and, sure as hell, a much larger one follows…large enough that we can feel the shock at our half-mile distance.

"It's a fine fucking day," Jin says, and I laugh. "Good shot, Jinny."

"What the hell was that?" Pax asks.

Before I can answer, we are rocked by four or five secondary explosions.

"It's friggin' Fourth of motherfriggin' July," I say. "Our ride was filled with artillery and mortar ammo, and we rigged it so the longshoremen would get a surprise. And the base warehouse is flanked by fuel tanks. We're as good as a flight of Stealth bombers. We gotta haul ass."

"Call back in twenty if you get clear of all the action. Juliet can't come in till dark, if at all...trouble with CIA shitheads. But Ji Su and the tweety is ready and willing."

I shrug, even if Pax can't see me. I guess "tweety" will work for "bird."

Feeling the need to make this quick, I talk machinegun fast. "We're hauling ass toward the briny blue, but we just put out an all-points-bulletin on ourselves. Half this shithole of a country will likely be here as quick as they can get here. We'll be the center of the bee hive, so it's sure as hell x-ville."

"Then hit the trail," Pax says, and I can hear the worry in his tone. "Take the road just west of your now, direction from Lost Wages to L.A. There's a small range of fuzzy bumps between you and the Yellow Sea. In four clicks, turn toward Frisco, away from the crick, for a half-click. There's a Dodger's size…looks like on Google Earth. Look skyward. Pop canary if you have to, if it's sunshine time, when you see a wasp snooping around."

I know he's trying to confuse anyone lucky enough to have broken the encryption on our radios, but it all makes sense to me. Looks like we're gonna get a ride, if we can get to the clearing as big as Dodger Stadium. A mostly yellow bird, as sleek as a wasp. Ji Su.

This leg of the journey will start with a kick-start, so I do so, and Jin straddles the rack on the back and holds onto me like a bitch on a Harley.

"Fuck, I'm dizzy," he complains but hangs.

We kick mud out behind, and we're doing some cross-country scrambling until we find the road.

Grandma watches us go by but barely looks up; then she returns to her peapods.

I glance to the southeast after we clear the farm buildings and am a little astounded by the hundred-foot flames and billowing black smoke reaching to the heavens.

Heaven sent, I'd say. And pure hell for anyone anywhere near.

Of course, speaking of heaven, when I look up, I scan all directions, I spot a half-dozen fighter jets and a pair of heavily armed choppers converging on the base.

We've attracted lots of interest.

Time to get the rubber on the road.

Chapter Thirty-One

BO HAS DECIDED TO HOLE up and has grounded the SDV underwater, near the remnants of a pier…a series of pilings sticking up four feet above the surface. He's perched behind one, ducking below the surface with his re-breather each time a surface craft passes. The river is more than two hundred yards wide, but it's covered with fast-moving patrol boats and other craft, and all of them seem to be searching for the invader.

Overhead, a helicopter passes every few minutes. It's obvious there is an intense search underway.

Butch thought he was doing Bo a favor by leading his pursuers away, but the fact is he is verifying the fact there were interlopers on or in the river. And probably they — whoever *they* are — are responsible for the destruction of the *Pueblo.*

Bo slips underwater again as he hears the beat of a diesel engine, waits for it to pass, and then slowly rises so his eyes and nose are above the surface but hidden behind a piling. He feels the vibration of his SATphone and digs it out.

"Speak to me," he answers.

"Status?" Pax asks.

"Down one. Pard decided he'd play decoy."

"Fuck! His status?"

"Unknown. Heard lots of lead flying in the direction he left, one rocket flying, and a patrol boat went up. The ol' boy deserves a Medal of Honor. You know better than me."

"We saw you'd parted ways. His marker was still for a half-hour. It moved a little at a high rate of speed but then went dead."

"As is he, I fear," Bo said.

"So, now you got room for a passenger?" Pax asks.

"Are you fucking nuts?" Bo replies.

"Asset needs an extraction."

"You're fucking with me!" Bo says, incredulously.

"Nope. A half-mil bonus, you get him out. Just got a call from the company. Can you get back under the over-the-water, number three against the push from you, for a dark-thirty pickup?"

"You know, I'm way past x-ville. My Dräger is about history. If I make three or four clicks against push, I'll never have juice to make my extraction."

"We'll recon a place for a snatch, a place you can reach."

"Who is this fucker?" Bo asks.

"Spotter who gave us the go-ahead, at great risk to himself. Goose likely cooked if doesn't fly. A farmyard goose, way out of his element."

"Same shade as D.C. house?"

"Yep."

Bo wanted to ask why the fuck a white guy was in the center of Pyongyang. But now he knew it was a white guy, probably an American, who was needing extraction. *What the fuck?* he thought. *In for a penny, in for a pound.*

"I'll hang. Stupid, stupid, stupid, but I'll hang. Text me the name of the over-p so I don't make an error that I can't afford." He presumed the meet was the Choyngu Bridge, back upstream, but wanted verification.

"Ten four. Probably better not to move."

"Yeah, yeah. I get it. How will I recognize?"

"This ain't L.A. Won't be any homeless hanging under the over-p."

"Ten-four," Bo says and disconnects. Now all he's got to do is wait another six hours and then make his way upstream, to find some asset…asshole…he's never met, and then retrace his path in the current with half of Pyongyang trying to hoist his head on a pike.

So, ten or twelve hours more. Then again, fifty grand an hour ain't bad. If he lives to collect.

***

PIETER DE VRIES AND Sumi are surprised when Duri shows up at their door.

"I have come to see how Mr. Pieter is feeling?" Duri lies. "I was told he was ill."

Sumi waves him in and offers tea, and he takes a seat in their small living room while she disappears into the kitchen.

"We must talk," Duri says, nervously watching to make sure Sumi is out of sight.

"I'm feeling much better," Pieter says in a loud voice. Then he whispers, "Go to the roof and wait after you leave."

Duri nods and smiles at Sumi, who reappears with a tray, three cups of tea, and a stack of sweet and nutty *gosomi* crackers.

He tries one and smiles. He asks both of them, "You make?"

"No, no," Sumi says.

"I teach," Duri says.

"That would be nice," Pieter replies.

They chat for a while, until the tea is drained, and then Duri excuses himself.

He's gone only a short time when Pieter stands and stretches. "I think I'm feeling so good after that wonderful tea that I'll get some exercise."

"You should wait — "

"No, I want to sweat this poison out of my system."

"Then I'll come — "

"I'm going to run, and you know you hate it. What's for supper?"

"I have a small portion of ground pork and will mix with *kimchi*."

"Fine. Let's eat early. I'll cut my run short."

"Be careful," she says and seems genuinely concerned.

He heads out for the stairway but goes up rather than down. Duri is waiting for him.

"You will be extracted tonight. It is believed you will be arrested…as will Sumi. But she is not your concern."

"Tonight?" Pieter asks, a little shocked as he thought he'd done so well with Captain Soon.

"Be under the Choyngu Bridge, on this side of the river, at midnight. Dress warmly. A boat will pick you up."

"I think I'm doing fine and don't need to go. I need to complete my assignment…which is two years."

"You won't do so fine in a re-education camp."

"Why do they think I need — "

"They have ears in some places we can only imagine. You must go. You know who I am, and you will tell if arrested."

Pieter is offended. "I would not."

Duri laughs, sardonically, and shrugs. "Jesus Christ himself would tell what they want to know, as even what he went through would be nothing compared to what they will do to get you to confess…and tell all you know. You must leave.

For my sake, if not your own. If you do not, I have orders to make sure you never talk. I like you, Mr. Pieter, and that would make me very sad."

Pieter gasps, looks astounded, and then sighs deeply, but concedes with a nod.

"Midnight?" he asks.

Duri confirms with a nod. Then he adds, "A man, alone, and you will know he's there for you. In the unlikely event he does not show, do not return to the apartment. Attempt to make your own way either south or north." Duri hands him a thumb-drive-size device. "This will help them track you, if they need to attempt another extraction. But let us pray this night will be successful."

As he returns to the apartment, Pieter worries that Captain Soon will return before it's time for him to leave.

Chapter Thirty-Two

THE ROAD WE'RE FOLLOWING was paved at one time, but much of it has been washed away, and the little Honda 90 is bouncing from side to side on deep ruts and potholes. Jin moans audibly on occasion. We're moving along a side hill, with spotted evergreens above — but mostly stumps, as I presume the populace has cut most of it for firewood. It's cold and snowy during NK winters, and with power out in the suburban areas…the whole country other than the capital…staying warm has to be a challenge.

Below us the hillside falls away, mostly barren, toward the river a mile or so away.

Private vehicles outside of the capital city are a rarity, other than a few motorcycles, horse or donkey carts, and bicycles.

So I'm a little surprised to see an old Toyota coming our way. If there was a turnoff before we're going to meet, I'd take it, but it's a six-foot bank uphill that we couldn't traverse and one at least that distance on the downhill side; taking it would likely result in a crash, and, besides that, it would look very suspicious.

So, it's charge forward.

I speed up a little to pass them as quickly as possible, but to my surprise, they slow to a halt. As I near, the driver's window is going down.

Two couples, the men in officers' uniforms. The driver is opening the door as I gun it around him, giving him a slight acknowledgement of a wave as I do. But I'm looking uphill, away from him, so he might miss the Caucasian face.

He yells something after me, but, of course, I ignore him and push the little Honda up to what seems its forty-five MPH top speed.

The road curves to the right, crosses a culvert over a ravine, and then curves back to the left. I glance back and see that the driver is making what will have to be about a four-point turn, as the road is narrow. But he's maneuvering to come after us.

There's no chance to outrun him, so as the road makes another turn and he's out of sight for a moment, I ditch the bike to the side, let Jin fall with the bike, and yell at him, "Trouble. Stay down if you can't fight."

He's gamely trying to unsling his M4 as the Toyota rounds the curve behind us, less than forty yards and slams on its brakes. Just as he reaches a sliding stop, I put a three-shot burst through the driver's-side windshield.

He's already jerked left and applied the gas, but I'm sure he's a dead man, as the Toyota drops a wheel off the edge and stops. The opposite rear passenger-side wheel is off the ground as the car teeters.

The rear door behind the driver opens, but I'm at a disadvantage and can't see as the other uniformed soldier tries to unload.

Luckily the slope is so steep he tumbles; he's firing his sidearm, but wildly. My second burst stitches him from belly to throat, and he does a backward somersault. He fires one more round but into the ground. Then it's still. I note by the braid and brass that I've killed a colonel...that'll likely piss someone off.

I move quickly to the passenger side and see both women with hands up, as if I'm a highway robber, and both are wailing.

Opening the driver's door, I have to put my weight on it to get the little car back level.

To my surprise, Jin has managed to shoulder his weapon and is close behind me. He snaps something in Korean, and both the ladies scramble out of the car, cross the street, and go down on their haunches. He yells something else, and both of them turn to face the slope and cover their eyes.

"You think you can get her back on the road?" he asks.

The driver — a major, I think — is dead, with a hole in his forehead. His head is hanging back over the seat, his cover gone, the back of his head mush. He's a fat fuck, as only military types are in NK.

"Can you put your weight on this so I can kick porky out of the driver's seat?" I ask. Jin re-slings his weapon and puts all his weight on the front passenger door.

I slip into the passenger seat, reach across, open the driver's-side door, get a foot up, and kick porky out. He hits the ground below and rolls away, but the car comes back to level.

"Keep your weight on it," I yell to Jin. I slip into the driver's seat and turn the engine over. It must have stalled, as it takes a few turns but fires up. I get her in reverse and back up enough, dragging Jin along, so that we're back on the road.

Jin climbs in the passenger seat and lays his head back on the seat. "Fucking dizzy." Then he looks up. "What about the women?"

"It's at least three, maybe four clicks back to anywhere that might have a phone, and I doubt if any of these farmhouses have even that."

I climb out of the Toyota, jog over to the Honda, tear the wiring off the sparkplug, jam it in my pocket, and jog back.

"They're on foot now."

Jin shrugs. "I hate the thought of killing some dumb broad, but I'll put one between their eyes."

I shake my head. "No way. We'll be long gone before they can sic a posse on us."

"Then let's exfiltrate."

"Big word for 'haul ass,'" I say, and do.

We drive only a click until we're in a fairly thick cover of trees above the road, and I figure it's time to head uphill and see if we can find a clearing the size of a football field.

An easy LZ for a bird. But it's at least four hours to dark, and she won't come in — can't come in — in the light.

***

PAX STANDS FROM HIS laptop and turns to Su Li, who is leaning against the bulkhead, watching the monitors. "I'm going in with you."

"Not many Koreans have black, curly hair and lily-white faces."

Pax rubs his chin and gives her a smile. "This four days' growth of beard will help. Besides, I don't plan to be face to face with them."

"You don't get airsick, I suppose? This trip may call for some aerobatics."

"Never have."

"Then you've never flown with me."

Pax laughs and gives her a look, up and down, that isn't exactly in the military manual. His voice lowers. "Maybe not flying, but I bet I can keep up with you any other way you'd like to try."

"If we live through it, I might just challenge you."

"Then let's make damn sure we live through it."

"I've gotta preflight the bird. Wouldn't hurt to have a couple of boxes of M4 magazines to spare, since you're another barrel."

"How's your bird armed?"

"Belly-mounted M134 GAU-17 Vulcan Gatling, hidden in what looks like an air scoop, custom-built 2.75 inch 3-pod rocket launcher, one on each side, also disguised in scoops, so six total. She's no Cobra or Apache, but then, again, she looks harmless, and surprise can be as good as another two-dozen rockets. And nothing but a MIG can outrun me."

Pax turns to Connie Nordstrom, whom he's judged as the most competent of the whiz kids. "Connie, I appreciate how you've handled things. I'm leaving you in command here as our number three. Can you handle?"

"You bet, so long as Von Reif stays out of my hair."

"I'll make sure Scroder handles that for you." Then he turns back to Su Li. "We lift off at sundown thirty, so it's near dead dark?"

"She's mounted with TIR, thermal imaging radar, so if we can get over them, even if they're hiding deep in the weeds, and I've got a sixty-foot radius, I'll get in and them out."

Then Pax picks up the ship's intercom and dials the gym, where he is sure Guido Garino and four of his SEALs are working out. As he suspected, Garino answers. "Garino."

"Commander, I'm going in-country at dark thirty. Just in case, is your team ready to follow up, if need be?"

"My orders were to get involved only if the women need extricating…and they're safe. Sorry, but those are my rules of engagement. We're heading out with the next supply boat."

"Too bad there's not a team of Recon Marines around."

"Why? You need some latrines squared away?"

"No time for it, Commander. We'll do the heavy work. You squids go back to whipping your pencil dicks and kissing the cake-eater's butts."

Pax cradles the receiver before Garino can reply and then turns to Ji Su. "Looks like it's just you and I."

"Shit happens. I gotta recheck the bird," and she spins on a heel and heads for the landing pad.

"I'll be locked and loaded, and, hopefully, Reardon and Jin will be standing by."

"Make sure. I'm not up for a sightseeing trip," she says and slams the hatch.

Chapter Thirty-Three

THERE IS NO TRAIL LEADING away from the road, and, even if there were, driving off road will leave easily followed tracks for anyone pursuing. So, it's ditch the Toyota and head into the woods on foot.

Below the road, now no more than one hundred yards from the ruts, is the river. And there's a steep thirty-foot-high bank down to the water's edge.

I help Jin out of the little car and up a twenty-foot bank into the first of the copse of trees…a mix of deciduous and evergreens, and get him settled against a tree trunk. As we've utilized the Toyota for only a little over a click I almost wish we'd stayed with the Honda, as we could have found a way into the forest with the bike…but looking back is not productive.

Returning to the car, I find a spot where I can dump off the road toward the river and purposefully spin the wheels and whip it back and forth, leaving ruts deep in the steep, soft earth I want those dogging us to follow away from the woods.

When I'm only forty feet from the bank to the water, I have the door open and slow to about ten MPH; I hit the gas pedal and then dive and roll. Gathering myself up, I get to my feet, run to the high side of the bank, and see that the Toyota has made the river, which I'd hoped.

For a moment, I'm wondering if the brackish water is too shallow to swallow the car. Then I realize the old, but still tight, Toyota is afloat. She turns her nose downstream, and it's a hundred or more yards before she takes on water and noses down to the bottom — then another twenty-five before she deep-sixes.

My hope is that our pursuers — and there will be plenty of those — will think we dumped it off the road and drowned with the Toyota. But I fear that's a hard sell.

Hustling back up the slope, I cross the road, happy there're no vehicles in sight. Then, as I climb toward the trees and Jin, I hear the fearsome *Wop! Wop! Wop!* of a chopper, and it's growing in volume. I don't bother to search the horizon but bust my butt to get under cover.

I scramble under the same pine boughs hiding Jin and find a spot to survey my six. Sure enough, as I settle in, a military chopper roars past, only a couple of hundred feet above the road. She's bristling with machine guns and rockets, and looking for a target.

Us, I'm sure.

She passes, without slowing or turning our way, but still it's not good news. It likely means the explosion and continuing fires — the distant horizon is now occluded by black smoke — are considered sabotage, or the women I foolishly and softheartedly let live have somehow already communicated the carjacking and killings.

Jin is a long way from recovered, still dizzy and unsure, and likely will be for weeks until his suspected concussion is healed. If we live that long. But I get him on his feet and sling both the M4s and head uphill to where I pray we'll find a football-field-size clearance — more than large enough to land a bird.

We passed some signs along the road — Korean characters, which, of course, I couldn't read. My suspicion is that the signs say something like, "You cut trees and we'll cut off your nuts," but have no way of knowing. Where the signs began, the cutting of the trees ended, and I suspect where we are is some kind of park or protected area. I hope so. Too bad they didn't have a sign with a circle with a tree in it and a slash through it, like a "No Smoking" sign. Then even this jarhead would understand.

It really doesn't matter a hoot, as my Ka-bar won't go far in cutting down a tree, and I'm sure as hell not going to chop up enough firewood to start enough of a flame to warm our hands…as a curl of smoke would give away our location.

Jin's hurting but doesn't complain as I lead him, stumbling, uphill, deeper into the forest. We aren't moving fast, but at least we're moving, until I hear a nearby shot and pull Jin to the ground with me.

But there're no follow-up shots, and it sounded like a very small caliber. I'd presumed it was a shot at two ragged-looking guys in Korean uniforms but carrying American arms and battle rattle, one of whom is way too pale to be Korean, but now I'm reconsidering.

I get Jin again situated deep in the boughs of an evergreen; then I begin my recon. I'm wondering if what I heard was a poacher. Having done a little poaching myself when young and needing to fill our freezer, I know the basics. And the basics are only one shot, never a second that would serve to pinpoint your location. And consequently, I'm having a hell of a time trying to figure out where the shot originated from.

But I move stealthily up through the trees, in a hunting mode — five steps, and then stop and look, for at least a count of one hundred. Check each visual lane through the trees; if there's nothing, move on. I do this five times before I find my game. And this game is a young man, skinning a small animal — a rabbit or possum or something. He's facing me, no more than forty yards away. His small rifle is leaning up against a boulder, and he's concentrating on his work.

I'm considering slipping away unseen when he glances up and panics. He goes for the rifle but gives me his back. Carrying rifle and critter half-skinned and dragging its pelt, he makes like he's in the hundred-yard dash and hotfoots it quickly into the trees.

I can't help but smile. I presume he thought me a ranger or soldier. He, too, is an interloper in this forest. But as far as I'm concerned, young men like him are the hope of this country. Willing to risk his freedom and imprisonment — or, worse his life — for the betterment of his family, is the basis of all revolutions against the world's despots. And I wish him, and those like him, the very best.

Following my own tracks back to Jin, I fish him out of the pine, and we continue uphill, negotiating a rather steep embankment. At the top, I stop to take a blow and realize I can see a portion of the road a little over a click below.

The good news is that we should be nearing the clearing. The bad news is that a half-track and a deuce are parked on the road, and at least two-dozen soldiers are dumping out and following the Toyota tracks down to the riverside.

Now I'm wishing I was a better escapee and had used one of the abundant pine boughs to brush away our tracks as we climbed up and away from the road. Damn, damn, damn. But there's no time like the present and better late than never, to risk a couple of clichés.

So we duck off the steep slope — if we can see them, they can see us — and this time, I take on double duty. Jin is using my shoulder, and I'm trying to obliterate our footsteps with a bough…until I realize I'm doing neither well.

"Fuck it," I say to Jin. "Let's just haul ass. If we can stay invisible for another three hours, we should tie up with the bird, and in four we'll be sucking a Corona on the mother ship."

Holding his head with a hand, Jin managed, "I'm wishing I had a quart of that *Soju* to tide me over."

"Hang on, pard. God willin' and the creek don't rise, we're x-ville soon."

"Your lips to God's ears," Jin mumbled, pushed away from me, and started upchucking what little he had in his gut.

Chapter Thirty-Four

PIETER DE VRIES HAS butterflies in his stomach. He has no idea what is about to take place — only that, if he believes Duri, he has to move. Move in the dark of night, when few North Koreans are on the streets and those who are will likely be stopped, questioned, and searched.

Even so, he feels there are a few things he must take with him, so he packs a small backpack with some toiletries, a couple of cans of sardines, a rain slicker and a sweater, and a pair of the most waterproof trousers he owns. He's planning to go out in his jogging clothes, as he'll at least have an excuse to be on the riverfront walkway — in his case, the jogging pathway — at that time of night. It is a shallow excuse, but at least an excuse.

Sumi is at the kitchen table reading, while he quietly packs in the bedroom, out of her sight.

He is stuffing in his warmest pair of wool socks and is surprised to look up to see her studying what he's doing.

"You are leaving?" she asks.

"No, no," he stutters, "just storing a few things in this backpack.

She walks over and reaches for it, but he clings to it, pressing it against his chest.

"Why are you hiding what you're doing?" she challenges. Then her voice softens. "I know that you and Duri have been talking about much more than cooking. I knew it was something strange when he showed up at our door, and when you two whispered as I made tea — "

"We didn't — "

"And I know you better than you may think."

He shrugs. "And I know you and care very much about you. I know you've watched my every move and searched my things every time I've been away."

She smiles. "Then you should know I was instructed by my employers at MPS to report anything suspicious to them."

"And that's why we live together?" Pieter asks.

"Yes, that's why we live together…at first…but not now. We live together now because I have fallen in love with you."

Pieter is silent for a long moment, studying her, wondering if she is being truthful. He had long ago admitted to himself that he cared far too much for her and cautioned himself against it…time and time again. But he did care for her…even if suspicions tempered his fervor. Still, he didn't reply.

"You know," she said, "I have no family left?"

"I know that's what you've told me."

Pieter could swear there's a tear forming in her dark eyes. "You are now my family. Nothing holds me here…nothing."

His voice softened. "I care very much about you, Sumi. I'm happy to leave my job and this…this terrible country. But leaving you may be the hardest thing I've ever done. Even harder than burying my first wife."

"Then take me with you," she said, and looked so very, very hopeful. *No one,* he thought, *can fake that yearning look.*

He took only a second to decide. "Then pack your backpack, as I have."

"You are not aware, but I have a small handgun…part of my job. They will not search me, as I have identification. I think I should take it."

"Take it," Pieter said, "if and only if you're willing to use it." But the butterflies in his stomach kicked it up a notch. "Let's get some sleep, if possible. We have an appointment at midnight, and I doubt if we'll get any sleep for a while."

She walked over, softly put her arms around his neck, and pulled him close.

***

BO WAS CHILLED TO THE bone from staying submerged up to his neck in the river. The wetsuit he was wearing was the best, but even it, after a prolonged time, let the cold go bone deep. He wondered how long he could stand it before he became hypothermic.

He would be useless if that happened, and he could die if his core temperature fell to that level.

The sun was nearing the western horizon, and he had nearly four hours before he started upstream to his meet. But he decided he must warm up first. He always carried a tiny magnesium bar and striker in his rucksack that he could use to start a fire. If he had fuel of some kind.

Up above him, on the shore, above the ruins of the dock, were the remains of a metal building. It would hide a fire, and he could recover some body heat.

If he could get there without being seen from watercraft.

There was a twenty-five-foot-wide clearing, up a ten-foot-high bank, from the edge of the water to the building. That's all, and that seemed so much at the moment, as his teeth were chattering, his knees watery, and his confidence waning. He wanted to wait until after sundown but decided that would be too late.

So, moving like an alligator through the water, he moved to the river's edge, listened for a long moment for the beat of diesel engines, and, hearing none, scrambled on all fours, dragging his rucksack with some survival gear, including some energy bars, and his M4 up to a wide sliding door, and was quickly into the building.

He sat and shook for a few seconds. Then he began collecting anything that would burn. A table, smashed so it folded in the middle, provided some chips, and four legs and some soiled and torn pamphlets, showing pictures of farm equipment, would flame easily.

With chattering teeth, he moved to the far end of the hundred-foot-deep building and came to a large, iron, welded boiler, luckily with one end laying nearby like a huge bowl. It was perfect, and he climbed inside and used his Ka-bar to shave some magnesium from the bar, formed some kindling around the shavings, and, with the first strike of the steel, it flared. With its super hot flame, he had a fire. As soon as he got the four two-inch-thick legs going, he stripped the wetsuit off.

The boiler was the perfect shelter and directed the heat at him. As he warmed, he couldn't help but remember the Robert Service poem, "The Cremation of Sam McGee."

There are strange things done in the midnight sun
By the men who moil for gold;
The Arctic trails have their secret tales
That would make your blood run cold;
The Northern Lights have seen queer sights,
But the queerest they ever did see

Was that night on the marge of Lake Lebarge
I cremated Sam McGee.

For the first time in hours Bo smiled, amused at the recollection. He'd learned that poem in the eighth grade and received an "A" for reciting it in class. However, he sincerely hoped he met an entirely different end than did old Sam.

Then he stiffened…voices!

Chapter Thirty-Five

IT'S GETTING DARK — a little too early for the sun to have set — and then I realize it's the smoke from the fuel dump blocking the setting sun. I'm wondering if we've messed our own nest, as, if Ji Su can't see the deck, she can't land. And if she can't land, we're dicked. Half the NK Army is looking for whoever sabotaged their Navy base and fuel dump.

All we can do is hope the smoke stays high enough that she can sneak under, or clears enough that she can see the meadow. But if anything, it seems to be getting thicker.

It's close to time to give the TOC a call, as I can see a clearing up ahead. As we near, I see it's a football-field-size meadow…the football-field-size meadow we've been directed to, I hope. But presuming our GPS locators are still active, it doesn't matter. For it's ten times bigger than what Ji Su needs to put down. And the meadow's covered in deep green grass, late for green, but the meadow is likely sub-irrigated. The grass is so thick I'm hoping we won't leave tracks, and charge forward, leading Jin out into the open meadow, stomping to make sure I leave a trail.

"What the hell are you doing, Big Foot?"

"Making tracks easily followed, that's what."

"I thought the object was tough to follow?"

"Hell, a blind man could follow what we've been leaving. So, let's use it to our advantage."

"How so?"

"Just try and keep up. I don't think we have much lead on the tangos."

"We're circling back."

"Yep, if you can't outrun them, we'll let them slip past. I saw a cave in that pile of rocks and ledge we had to skirt around. Looks like home to me, and least until we get a ride. So, step lively now."

We work our way in a forty-yard diameter half-circle and luckily come out of the meadow heading south on a dry streambed, with lots of rocks, and we're careful to keep hard surfaces underfoot. After a hundred yards going back south, we leave the bed and head east. My dead reckoning is right on as we come out atop the ledge and rock pile. We slither over and drop fifteen feet, and I find the deep, dark opening I saw. It's only two feet high at the mouth, nicely hidden by brush, and we slither in. The good Lord is on our side, as it's more than twenty feet deep and opens to more than five feet of clearance.

Now, if only the NK dipshits don't have dogs.

I dig the SATphone out, hit the "1" key, and send. Pax answers before the first ring is complete. "Chee," he says.

"We're playing football, only about that length Dixie from there. But we'll soon have company…two dozen if my estimation is right." I know he knows "Dixie" is "south."

"We're thirty minutes out. Keep your heads down."

"We?" I ask.

"I told you, you ain't having all the fun."

"Roger that." Then I'm forced to whisper. "Got to go," and I disconnect, as I hear voices. And they're way closer than they would be if they were following our track forty paces away.

***

BO QUICKLY EXTINGUISHES the fire, as the voices he's heard raise in volume. He slips out of the boiler and pulls his wetsuit back on. In moments, he sees two raggedy young men at the far end of the building.

He remains unseen, hiding behind some tractor-size equipment that's rusted and disassembled.

The two are not soldiers — in fact, they seem to be wayfarers. Hopefully, the NK version of hobos. Even better, military deserters. Like him, they are chilled and begin to build a fire, and one of them begins plucking a pigeon-sized bird. Looks like it's supper time.

They're busily talking about stealing some vegetables from a nearby farm, as Bo slips up behind them and speaks in his good Korean.

"Hello." They both nearly jump out of their skins. Seeing the M4 he's carrying, both fall to their knees and start begging forgiveness.

They are surprised when he starts to laugh, and both their faces go blank. Then, when he reaches in his rucksack and hands them each an energy bar, he gets a tentative smile.

"You have stolen a bird," he says, and their smile fades again; he laughs. They nod and smile. Bo says, "I am no longer with the Army. You do not tell about me, and I will not tell about you." Both nod enthusiastically.

"We caught this grouse wild. We would not steal — "

"Even the vegetables you were discussing stealing?"

"We are very hungry," he says, looking sheepish, and adds, "and you will share our bird." This time, the nods are less enthusiastic, but still nods.

As they eat a few bites of roast bird and energy bars, they ask about the strange suit he's wearing. He explains, "I am, like you, hiding out, and this black suit is hard to see in the dark."

He doesn't think they are buying his BS, but they don't challenge him, nor do they ask about the re-breather on his back. He figures they must think he's an alien from outer space and are afraid to antagonize him.

He moves back and retrieves the waterproof rucksack he's left by the boiler and returns. They're fascinated as he pulls out his GPS and checks the time and his distance to the bridge and his dark-thirty contact, but they have no idea what he's up to.

He has three hours to kill. But the company, if strange, is fine. And, not threatening.

***

FROM THE DEPTH OF our cave, I can see a squad of NK soldiers who don't seem overly interested in the hunt. Six of them are nearby, standing in a circle, smoking, and, I would guess, either telling dirty jokes or speculating on what they'll do to us if caught. I prefer to presume the former. They are laughing and elbowing each other.

I'm praying they don't see the odd imprint of our boots where we might have missed a hard surface while hunting for the cleft under the ledge we now occupy.

Hoping they leave, as I may soon want to catch a ride home from a location clearly in their line of sight, I'm disappointed when they not only don't leave, but four of the six take a seat on nearby boulders. I wish I could translate what they're saying; Jin could do so easily, but he reclines in the deep darkness of the cave, trying to recover from the crack on the noggin, and I don't want to drag him forward.

One of the talkative ones, who must be a sergeant or some higher rank, walks nearer and bends with hands on knees, studying something on the ground. I can only surmise it's our footprints. I'm strung as tightly as a fiddle.

I bring the M4 to shoulder and track him as he moves back to his charges. His voice raises, and he sounds excited.

Switching the M4 to full auto, I drop to a prone position and wonder how many of the six I can take out before the narrow cleft of the cave entrance buzzes with AK47 stingers.

Chapter Thirty-Six

PAX SUCKS IT UP AS JI SU flies so close to the deck that spray flies from the bird's downdraft, and she's moving at two hundred fifty knots, if the airspeed indicator is correct. She takes a course directly east to the shore of South Korea. Then she gains a hundred feet altitude and turns back northwest, staying below the altitude of a shoreline cliff and the hills beyond.

She's concentrating on her flying, so Pax remains silent. Then she turns to him. "We're in the DMZ…and," she hesitates a few seconds, "now in North Korea. I'm going to circle the dam at the mouth of the Potong, as if we're some brass inspecting the progress. Even though it's dark, they are working twenty-four-seven. Then we'll take a course upriver as if we're heading to the capital. Short of it, we'll swing north to pick up Mike and Jin."

"Roger that," Pax says, and lets her return to concentrating. After they're fifteen clicks into North Korea, she climbs to a thousand feet and cuts her speed back to a hundred sixty knots so she's not so obvious to radar…and flying at two fifty or faster would identify her as not being an NK bird. Too damn fast.

In minutes they drop to two hundred feet, slow to eighty knots, and see the dam below, well lighted, and a beehive of activity. Only one other bird is airborne, and it's a twin-rotor Russian crane, carrying a load of construction material.

Some of the workers look up and wave as they circle. She makes three full circles from one end of the long dam to the other, and then regains altitude to head up the Potong toward the capital. In ten minutes, she has dropped again to less than two hundred feet.

Pax taps her on the shoulder and points to oncoming lights at about their same altitude. She nods. "I've had him on the radar since we left the dam."

She climbs again to four hundred feet, and a military chopper, bristling with cannon and rockets, passes below. She drops again and turns due north.

Pax is watching the other chopper and sees he's turning as well, and pats her again. "He's coming back."

She nods but continues to watch her surface radar and ahead, and she's right. The other chopper is retracing its path along the river.

"You think they're hunting Bo and Butch?" I ask.

"Bo, maybe. Sounds like Butch has played the sacrificial lamb."

"I hope not, but it sounds that way. What's our ETA?"

"About twelve minutes. Try to raise Mike."

Pax picks up the SATphone and pokes in a "2," and it's four rings before Reardon picks up, and he's whispering.

"Chee here. Keep it short."

"Twelve minutes."

"Kill time."

"Roger that. How many mikes?"

"Fifteen extra, unless I call."

"Ten-four."

Pax turns to Ji Su. “He wants us to kill fifteen mikes. And he was whispering.”

“Then we kill fifteen, but I’m going to put her down so we conserve fuel.”

“Risky,” Pax says.

“Help me hunt a clearing. There’s hardly enough wires or high-lines in the whole damn country to worry me much.”

“The hilltops look to be pretty barren.”

She turns to starboard, slows almost to a hover, drops, and switches on her landing lights, but only for a literal second.

She speaks without taking her eyes off the chosen LZ. “We’re good a hundred feet ahead.”

“Your lips to God’s ears,” Pax says as she drifts the bird forward, flares, and gently drops — throwing up a cloud of rotor wash dust — until the skids settle on the hilltop, and she cuts power.

Pax inhales, and realizes he’s been holding his breath. “Nicely done,” he says.

“Piece of cake,” she says. “I saw nothing of civilization, but keep a sharp eye, as there could be a house a hundred yards away. No power in this crummy country. We don’t want a bunch of farmers thinking we’re in trouble, and charging in to help.”

“Sharp eye, yes ma’am,” Pax says, and does, with his M4 cradled in his lap.

I HEAR SOMEONE IN the distance yell and watch as the six soldiers snap to attention. An officer stomps up, now barely visible to me in the growing darkness. He berates them and slaps one across the cheek…the one who appeared to be a sergeant or at least the highest ranked of all of the slackers. He takes the slap and talks like the proverbial Dutch uncle. Then the officer points, yells at his troop, and they scatter into a line twenty or so feet apart. One of them is only six feet from the cave opening. I hold my breath; then Jin, in the rear of the cave, coughs.

I realize I'm gripping the M4 so tightly my forearms are beginning to ache.

The nearby soldier turns, but the officer yells again, and the line moves out, crossing the meadow. The officer stands, hands on hips, and watches.

Just as I think we've got a break and he, too, is leaving, the officer pulls a cigarette from a pack in his shirt pocket, lights up, and takes a seat on a boulder. Glancing at my GPS, I see it's been nine minutes. We don't have time for him to get ambitious. So I slip back to where Jin is prone on the cave floor, among small animal bones and other debris, and whisper to him.

"The squad has moved off, but the damned officer has decided to take ten and poison his lungs. I may have to make sure he stays silent."

"Do what you gotta do."

Jin rolls to his belly, slings his M4, and moves along behind me as I slip up to the edge of the opening. He takes a prone position, ready to back me up. The officer is quartering away from me, at no more than thirty yards. It's getting so dark about all I can see of him is the glow of his cig. My back is to the sundown, and I'm hopeful there's no hint of light behind me. I'm not sky-lined, thanks to the ridge that's at least fifteen feet high.

Unhooking my battle rattle, so it doesn't, I leave it and take only my Ka-bar and sidearm, and move out of the opening, where I'm shielded by some thick brush. I'm able to use it until about only ten yards from the glowing cig, and thirty feet is a long way to walk in the dark and not break a twig underfoot.

I wish I was in my stocking feet but am not, so I do the Indian walk, putting toes down lightly first, trying to feel for anything that might make noise.

When only ten feet, Ka-bar at the ready, I'm surprised as he stands and stretches. Then his radio crackles, and he takes it off his belt and to an ear.

It might arouse a little suspicion if I cut his throat in midsentence, but am given some advantage as he's yelling into it, obviously berating his troop.

He has both hands on the unit, trying to fit it back on his belt, as I close the last three paces.

In trying to replace the radio, he's turned a little my way and catches a sound or my movement in his peripheral vison. He swings the radio, backhanded at me, and I don't have an opening to go for his throat, so I drive the blade under his arm, all the way to the hilt.

He manages a loud grunt, and I shove him away and off the blade; he collapses to one knee. The next thrust takes him under the jaw, and now the only sound is a gurgle as he goes to his back, his hands on the gaping, blood-gushing hole in his throat.

Knowing he's going nowhere, I run back to the cave, strap my belt back on, grab up the SATphone, and raise Pax. "As good a time as ever," I say. "Troop should be at or near the north end of the LZ. Land at the south end if you can."

"Roger. Give us five mikes, and be ready. Stand at the south end, ten paces apart in an east-west line so we can spot and confirm you on TIR. Our LZ should be just north of you."

"TIR?" I ask, searching my memory for the acronym.

"Thermal imaging. Move it."

Chapter Thirty-Seven

PAX GIVES JI SU the signal of a circling finger; she cranks on the turbojet, and, in less than a minute, they're in the air.

"TIR," he says, and she switches the unit on. They cross a little more than two clicks of country and come in over the north end of the meadow. They see the heat images of over two-dozen men below, spread out over a two-hundred-yard line.

They receive no ground fire as the troop below don't know they are not friendly.

Ji Su makes a half-circle and one pass over the south end of the meadow, and Pax points to a pair of heat images, men, twenty yards apart, in an east-west configuration.

"Put it down — north of them should be clear," he says, but she's already lining up, and in two minutes she's settling with her skids in the deep grass.

Pax moves to the rear, opens the slider, spots Mike, and is surprised when he doesn't run for the chopper but rather runs to Jin, and together, they close on the chopper.

He helps them both aboard, slams the slider, and Ji Su doesn't wait; the chopper leaps into the air.

Jin, who's flat on his back on the chopper deck, hands his GPS to Mike. "No man left behind."

Mike leans forward and hands the GPS unit to Pax, who says, "That was too frigging easy-smeasy."

"We're not home yet, Pax-man. We got another passenger at that waypoint."

"Who?' Ji Su asks.

"Gun."

"I thought Gun was dead!" she says as she takes a bearing back to Black Gold and the thirty clicks to get the hell out of North Korea.

"Gun is dead. But we don't leave our dead if there's any way…."

"So, we know he's at this spot."

Pax leans back and eyes me. "You sure?"

"I'm not even sure the frigging world is round. But we gotta try."

"And Butch?" Ji Su asks.

"We have no idea his twenty, but we know where we left Gun, so let's get him home."

Ji Su says nothing, but the bird swings back to the northwest, and she's at two hundred knots in a few heartbeats.

"An LZ," she asks no one in particular.

"Exactly that spot," I reply. "A railroad track. No wires that I remember — "

"That you remember?" she asks, obviously concerned.

"From a hundred feet," I suggest, "hit your landing lights, and we'll look for poles."

"Comforting," she says and adds, "usually a pole line along a railroad" but keeps the ship heading for the waypoint.

I suggest, "This is North Korea, and I'm sure they don't worry about right-of-ways. Anywhere Dear Leader or his pricks want a line to go, it goes."

And we're nearing the waypoint in eight minutes, and she flares and loses altitude.

"All eyes," she yells; I look to the rear, and she and Pax look forward and to their respective sides. She hits her landing lights.

"All clear," I yell.

"Clear," Pax follows.

She settles on the tracks, her skids far longer than the width of the rails, and I pop the sliding door and hit the ground between them, with Pax close behind. Out, down the rocky escarpment that's the rail bed, and under the bridge.

I'm a little surprised to find Gun, still under the brush — cold and about the color of an aging side of beef — but there. Pax and I wrestle him out and down to the little creek, twenty feet upstream, and we haul him up out of the streambed, hoisting him into the back of the bird — and then we're flooded with light.

"Patrol boat, on the river," I yell to Ji Su.

"Mount up," she replies, but, as we do, tracers light the night and are only a few feet above our rotor. I have no idea if they're shooting at us or just putting a warning shot over our bow. I'm sure they're unsure about this strange helicopter, a model never seen in North Korea.

With my feet still on a skid and Pax hanging onto my arm, Ji Su lifts off. She's already facing the river, but the patrol boat is quartering down stream from us, and I expect her to swerve right and away from the threat. To my surprise, as Pax hauls me aboard, she turns directly at the patrol boat, and it's our turn to light the night.

The six-barrel 20mm Vulcan shakes the chopper as it spits six thousand rounds a minute, and she applies the weapon for only a few seconds. Some NK crewmembers have about five seconds to rue the fact they started a fight with an innocent-looking helicopter with no weapons apparent. The forty-foot boat with the bow-mounted machinegun looks as if it's parting at the seams. Then it explodes as one of the Vulcan's tracer rounds hits what's obviously a gasoline tank.

The acceleration of the X3 pins me back as she flies overhead the blazing boat and into a cloud of flying debris. There's a hell of a whack, and I think we've taken a cannon round as the chopper jerks right forty-five degrees, shudders, and heels over to the starboard side. Our rotors can't be more than ten feet from the water, and if they hit water, they'll become a hundred flying scimitars, and we'll become a submarine in short order. I can see Ji Su fighting the controls. Bending over, I grab one of Jin's legs, as he's not strapped in, and as the bird ducks even closer, I'm sure we're going into the river.

But the lady on the cyclic has no give-up in her, and the craft levels and begins gaining altitude.

"That was fun," Pax says.

You don't see the whites of Pax-Man's eyes often, but this one got his attention. He guffaws as we clear the trees on the far side of the river and turn downstream. Thirty clicks and we're out of NK, presuming a MIG doesn't put a rocket up our butt before we're in South Korean air space…and maybe even after.

We're all dead silent as Ji Su puts the pedal to the metal, not bothering to gain a lot of altitude, but soon moving at nearly three hundred knots in a direct line to *Black Gold.*

If you've never had an aircraft buzz by you at Mach one or above, you have yet to be thrilled. Not only one, but one on each side.

Now I know we're about to be toast.

"Whoopee," Ji Su shouts, and I'm wondering if she's lost it. Then she turns and yells to us in the back, "F-16s, friendlies."

"Are we in friendly territory?" I ask.

"A half-click," she says, and then, almost as quickly, "home free. Now if we can just land this dude…."

"Pardon me," I can't help but say.

"Whatever we hit took the starboard skid."

Chapter Thirty-Eight

JI SU IMMEDIATELY GETS on the radio to *Black Gold.* "We've got a mayday here. Need your EMT standing by with a stretcher for one wounded. Need a body bag. Need you to survey damage to our ride."

"Roger that," the *Black Gold* radio operator comes right back. "ETA?" he asks.

"Before you can get topside," Ji Su says. I look out the windscreen and see the lights of the ship ahead.

Pax turns back to me. "There's a hundred feet of half-inch behind your seat. If worse comes to worse, we can lower Jin and Gun's body."

"And you and I?" I ask. As we normally do when we're in bad trouble, we laugh. As does Pax.

"We can take a swim," Pax says, "if sweet Su will get us down to the ten-meter-dive high."

"And me?" she asks, but she's smiling, too.

"Auto pilot. You jump and take a swim with us. Miss X3 heads out to sea. Then the MIGs can have her."

"I think I'd just as soon put her on the landing pad. I just had my hair done before this op."

"Oh, what the hell, then we'll ride in with you."

I slap Pax on the shoulder. "Five to one on a ten spot we live."

"Right, and how are you gonna pay up if we don't?"

"Technicality."

Ji Su slows the X3 to a hover over the landing pad as a half-dozen, including Commander Scroder, gather below. She remains in place for most of a minute when the radio crackles, and it's Scroder on a hand-held.

"We're setting a fifty-gallon drum on its side. If you come in so it's aligned with where your skid was located, it should catch what's left of the struts and keep you damn near level."

Ji Su shakes her head. "You know what will happen if we dip thirty-seven degrees to either side."

"Shit hits fan," Scroder says.

"Yes, sir," Ji Su answers. "Suggest you clear the pad."

"Give us five," Scroder comes back.

Ji Su pulls the craft back to keep the downwash off those working below, and, in moments, the radio lights up again. "Sorry we won't be here to help you dismount, ma'am," Scroder says.

"No problem, Commander. I can handle it."

"Break a leg," Scroder says, joking, but you could hear the worry in his voice. "The pad's yours," he says, and from fifty yards north of the ship, we can see them clearing off the pad.

Ji Su slips it in like she was parking a Volkswagen in an empty three-car garage, but when she's only five or six feet off the deck, the radio crackles. "Pull up, pull up. The damn drum moved. Give us another five."

She moves the X3 forward, makes a complete circle of the ship, and lines up for another approach. This time, she drags the trailing edge of the left skid across the deck until the drum is just ahead, lifts the craft no more than a foot, and drops it onto the drum. It collapses, folding in the middle about three inches and taking about three years off all our lives, but it holds.

She immediately winds it down.

None of us say a word as the rotor slows. Jin, still flat on his back on the deck, speaks up. “Any chance one of you honyocks might get me a beer and a shot of morphine?”

We all laugh, as the crew pours out up onto the pad.

Then I get serious again. “What’s up with Bo and Butch?”

***

BO IS SURE THE TWO NK hobos will say nothing. They, too, can look forward to many years in a re-education camp or to a firing squad should they be caught, so he leaves them with two more energy bars, gives them a short bow, and excuses himself just before nine PM. As soon as he gets far enough away from the ramshackle metal building, he pulls the SATphone from the thigh pocket in his wetsuit, hits the “1,” and dials.

He’s surprised when a female voice answers. “TOC. Talk.”

“Where’s Chong?”

“Catching a few, just back with Chee and Jin, in case you might interfere with his sleep later.”

“He’s been in-country.”

“He’s ready to go again, soon as we ring him.”

“And Gun?”

“We’ll read you in when you’re back in the hutch.”

Gun is Bo’s good friend, and his stomach turns over with her hesitancy. But he has a mission to complete, so he doesn’t press it.

“Okay. I’m back on track and soon underway. Schedule still a go?”

"I know your twenty. I'm following you. We have a tracker on your target; he's moving to rendezvous and will inform if not on schedule."

"Please get Chong back in play, if you would."

Connie Nordstrom was only slightly offended by Bo wanting Pax back in play, but she is used to it, as it seems to be endemic in the CIA, but more and more women are proving themselves to be as good as or better at spycraft than the men. So, she quickly agrees. "Ten-four. Stay safe."

"Roger that."

With his re-breather still functioning, Bo sinks to the SDV and checks the onboard air, figuring there's still at least an hour for each of them. Butch left his Dräger on board when he boogied, but Bo knows it's no longer viable. He checks the batteries on the SDV and figures them good to get upriver to the pickup spot, but he has no idea how long after that they'll have power. They'll be coming back with the current, but propulsion will be needed to keep them out of trouble.

He maneuvers the SDV out into the stream, turns her upriver, laughs at himself for risking his hide for someone he's never laid eyes on, and sets a speed against the six MPH current that will get him to the Choyngu Bridge in two and a half hours.

Chapter Thirty-Nine

SUMI AND PIETER FIND they cannot sleep. So, they make love as those who think it may be the last time might; then they lie in each other's arms for a while.

"You know," Pieter says, "just in case MPS decides to pick me up tonight, let's leave now."

"I was thinking the same thing," Sumi says. "They like to come in the very early morning," and she is dressed in five minutes.

As they open the door to leave, Pieter turns back and eyes the apartment. "You know, I loved much of my time here, because it was spent with you. And now I love it even more, knowing you want to risk leaving with me.'

"We will have a lot more time together…if we succeed. Please, let's go."

Both them are wearing jogging suits so they'll have some excuse for being out this time of night. The backpacks will be suspicious, but they've packed them with a plastic container of *kimchi*, cheese, and crackers and a small bottle of *Soju* on top of their warm clothes. The scheme is to tell any inquisitors that they plan to have a romantic midnight snack overlooking the river.

If there is a busy roadway in Pyongyang, it's the one crossing the Choyngu Bridge, but at this time of night, a vehicle every quarter-hour will be heavy traffic.

They've jogged only the first kilometer of three on the riverfront walkway when a police car with two officers shines a spotlight on them.

Pieter saw them coming, has turned, and is comically jogging backward alongside Sumi. As the car slows, he tells her, "Laugh. Laugh loud." And both of them do.

"Move to the car," a voice rings out on a bullhorn.

Smiling and laughing, they jog across a grass divider and over to the car.

"It is past curfew," a small policeman accuses as he climbs from the passenger side. The taller driver, with furrowed brow, exits also and draws his sidearm, but stays on his side, leaning across the hood, his semi-auto casually in hand.

"Yes," Sumi replies, digs in the pocket of her jogging suit, and pulls out a small leather folder, her MPS identification, and hands it to the officer.

The cop studies it in the car's headlights and waves her over. He holds the ID up, and his vision goes from it to her and back again. Finally, seeming satisfied, he asks her, "Who is your direct superior?"

"Colonel Hoon Eun-Jung," she says, without hesitation.

"And who is this foreigner?" he nods to Pieter.

"Professor Pieter De Vries, University of Science and Technology, here, teaching nuclear science, at the special invitation of Dear Leader."

He nods, looks only slightly impressed, and then says, "Be careful. You know there has been a terrible accident up the river?"

"We heard something," she says.

"If you see anything unusual, report it immediately."

"Of course."

He starts to return to the car. Then he turns back, and his tone is suspicious. "You jog with backpacks?"

"We plan a late snack, with the moon over the river. And this time of year, it's wise to have warm clothes at hand, don't you think?" She reaches out and takes Pieter's hand and smiles lovingly at him.

It's obvious the officer is offended by her affection for a Westerner, but he says nothing — only curls a lip and retakes his seat, as does the driver.

"Wait," Pieter says in English, and Sumi repeats the request in Korean. He has her bend a little, and digs her pint of *Soju* from her pack. He steps over and hands it to the cop, who smiles.

Then facetiously, with a small smile, he says, "I must confiscate this. It is too late to be drinking on the road…even jogging." He's twisting off the cap as he speaks.

Pieter laughs. The officer smiles tightly, and they spin the wheels leaving. He turns back to Sumi. "Let's walk a while. We will be more than an hour early, and it will look suspicious if we hang around waiting."

"Fine," she says, "but let's hope he doesn't call Colonel Hoon. They will be back if they do…and not to pick up another bottle of *Soju*."

"Then maybe it would be wise to jog and find a place near the bridge to hide."

"Go. I will keep up."

***

I CANNOT SLEEP, EVEN though I need to catch up. I'm totally exhausted — not so much from the physical exertion as from the many rushes of adrenalin.

But the job's not over until we get the team home. I'm saddened to hear that we're missing another man. I really liked and respected old Butch, a rasty old bastard who put his head down and tail up and would charge the fires of hell to complete his mission. And did, as the satellite has taken many great pictures of a missing *Pueblo* from the Potong riverfront. And, although we yet have no way of knowing, his success has taken the heart out of Kim Jong-un's nuclear program and maybe a good chunk out of Iran's.

The first reports from Pyongyang are of a terrible accident involving a recreational facility…but then we knew the North Koreans would never hear the truth from Dear Leader. The fact is, even in NK, word of mouth is the best purveyor of news, and the whole country will know their prize, their example of American imperialism, is no longer available for gloating.

I can't sleep. Pax has filled me in on Bo's new mission, and I won't be left out of it when it's time to recover him and this asset the Company wants extricated. I wander up to the landing pad, where a team of welders is working on the X3.

And *Black Gold* likely has some of the world's best welders on board.

Not only are they on the skid, but thcy've constructed a gantry, and the bird is in the air, hoisted off the deck with canvas slings holding her four feet off the pad while the welders work away.

I'm pleased to see a six-inch-wide by ten-foot-long heavy chunk of aluminum channel being refitted to where the skid ripped away. The fact we're not feeding the catfish at the bottom of the Taedong River testifies to Ji Su's ability at the cyclic. The fact is I hate choppers, but would climb in one with her at the controls anytime I'm called to defend God and country.

Ji Su, standing with arms folded, is watching the work, so I sidle up next to her. "Great job with the bird and the Vulcan, lady."

"Thanks." I get an appreciative glance. "A great bird. And those pricks…. No hill for a stepper."

"And, as I understand, you've stepped around Iraq and Afghanistan?"

"If I told you, I'd have to kill you," she says, and laughs.

"A general question."

"And a general answer. Yes. Apaches, mostly."

I give her a coy grin. "Watch out for Pax. He's got his beady little eyes on you, and he's worse than any Afghan warlord when it comes to getting what he wants."

She laughs again. "I think he's got big, beautiful eyes. I thought you two were buddies."

"Way more than buddies, and now you and I are buddies, if you'll allow. You get a gold star for coming into the belly of the beast to fetch us. And I'd walk on hot coals for Pax and would love to see you two tie up, if you want the truth."

"I'm being nicely compensated for my work. Pax may be a bonus. The military, and jobs like this, are the one place a girl gets equal pay with the hairy-legged boys."

I nod and agree. "We all are being well paid. We're rounding third toward home. I hope you'll come to Vegas and let us treat you to a fat steak, if we get out of this in one piece."

"Already have a date for that very thing."

I laugh. "Took Pax Man ten minutes from meeting you to seal that deal?"

"He asked in about three minutes, but I didn't accept until this morning. But you can come along…at least for the dinner part."

"I'll even buy. In fact, right now, I'll buy you a cup of coffee if you're tired of watching this operation."

"You're on."

It's still super dark as we've only got a fingernail moon, and after we've had our coffee and a piece of berry pie, she's eager and anxious about the bird, so we return to the pad to find them finished.

"I'm gonna test fly her and see how she performs with two slightly different skids. Wanna go for a ride?"

"I'm saving it for later." I laugh. I really do hate helicopters. Unlike fixed wing, you throw one bolt in a bird, and it's very likely shit city.

So I go to the TOC, to return to my work.

When I walk in, Constance Nordstrom is concentrating on the big monitor, and I can see that Bo's orange dot is making its way up the Potong. Another maroon-colored dot is only a click from the Choyngu Bridge, coming from the other direction.

"That your asset?" I ask Connie.

"It is. Unfortunately, he has no SATphone, and this ID unit is not a GPS, as you're carrying, but only an inch or so long. It doesn't seem as strong, as reliable, and fades in and out."

The time is displayed on the monitor, and I see it's only forty-five minutes until the meet is scheduled.

My voice goes cold. "The asset is not moving."

Chapter Forty

THEY ALL STARE AT THE maroon dot on the monitor for a full minute. Then Connie speaks up. “He hasn’t moved for an hour. We presume he’s found a hidey hole and is killing time. There’s so much activity on the water and in the air, since the *Pueblo* went up…or down, I should say…that I’m sure it’s a risky business being anywhere in Pyongyang other than tucked in your beddy-bye.”

“Have we zeroed in on a rendezvous spot yet?”

“We’re worried about his air and his battery. Once he gets the asset aboard, then he’ll be travelling with the current. We’ll have better data then, when we get a readout on both….”

“But we have some thoughts on a location.”

“Several. Since you were recovered, that’s about all we’ve been doing — trying to figure a half-dozen different LZs.”

“Good, let’s make it end. I want to get back to Vegas and the night lights.”

She glances up and talks while she’s studying the screen on her laptop. “Hey, I like night lights.”

“You look like a girl who would. We can make it a foursome. Pax and Ji Su have a dinner date, and you’d look good on my arm.”

She laughs, still without looking up. "And you'd look good on mine. Stay whole, and we'll talk some more."

It's time to refill my magazines and my belt. Even though I'm going in on the bird, one never knows when it might be cross-country time again.

And we tangled with a patrol boat on the Taedong. If any of the crew lived, the NK military is likely zeroed in on a wild new chopper that is painted like those repairing the dam across the Potong.

It's time for a confab, as we're only an hour away from dust up. We've been assigned a cabin with a couple of bunks, so I head down, as I know Pax is there, who can sleep through a hurricane, and roust him out. We head up to the TOC and put heads together with our beautiful bird driver and equally luscious CIA agent, Constance Nordstrom. She'll be running the TOC while Pax and I are riding shotgun with Ji Su.

We're perched around a table, three of us with coffee and Su with a cup of tea.

"I think there's a good chance the NK dipshits are onto the X3, as someone may have lived through Su's very good shooting."

"Agreed," both Pax and Ji Su say at the same time.

"So, my thought is we avoid the dam, stay away from the river and the plethora of patrol boats, until we head to Bo's preferred LZ."

Su thinks for a moment, and both of us await her input. Then she says, "There are constant patrols along the DMZ. Radar will think nothing of another bird moving along that line, so let's go in-country a half mile inside the line and then cut north to the LZ when it's the quickest line to pick up our people. I'll get down on the deck and maybe," she laughs, "they'll think one of their own crashed and send a rescue party."

Pax shrugs. "As good as any, so long as you don't do something to screw up our dinner date."

"If I screw up…if we screw up," she corrects herself, "then we'll be dining perched on a cloud. I'd rather do Vegas."

I get us back on track. "Okay, the Vulcan is back to one hundred percent?"

Su nods. "As soon as they finish the skid, we check everything out, and she's good to go."

I turn to Pax. "You've resupplied?"

"Hell, I didn't fire a shot, so I'm as good to go as I was the last time we lifted off."

"Then let's get aboard and ready to lift off, the instant we hear from Bo."

And we do.

***

BO HAS TRIED TO STAY on the surface as much as possible, dropping down only when he saw traffic on the surface or a chopper coming his way.

When he was a half-click from the bridge, he dropped six feet below surface and moved slowly until he was sure he was under the overpass.

Easing to the surface a hundred feet short of his target, he was glad he'd underestimated the distance. He scanned the bridge and was only slightly surprised to see a uniformed guard marching, long arm on shoulder, like he was pacing in front of Buckingham Palace. Luckily, he did not glance over. Even if he did, he'd likely think Bo's head was something floating on the surface, as it was far too dark to make out details at that distance. However, over the three-hundred-foot span of the bridge, a light was spaced every fifty feet or so.

Bo's meet was supposed to be under the southbound lane on the north side of the river. He placed the SDV just below the surface, up against the upstream side of a square pillar so the current held him in place, and just deep enough that he could keep eyes and nose above the water. He'd been told the extraction was to take place at 0030. Glancing at his GPS, he saw the time, 1157, so he had thirty-three minutes to wait, presuming the asset wasn't early.

He was getting chilled to the bone again. If he could anchor the SDV in place on the surface, he'd wait, tucked up under the overpass, but he couldn't, so it was tough it out.

***

SUMI AND PIETER HAD jogged past a wide drainage ditch and five-foot-circumference culvert from a park across the four lanes that the cops had been on and ducked down into the pipe to wait.

"I'd like to be there early so we can check it out," Pieter said, after glancing at his watch and seeing they had only forty-five minutes.

"We can jog on past and check it out."

"Let's go," Pieter said, and they ducked out of the pipe and struggled back up to the walkway.

As they reached the top, Sumi noticed a patrol boat on the river. "How will we ever escape on the river with boats and helicopters running up and down it?"

"There will be an American picking us up. He does not want to die, just as we don't. Trust in the Lord, Sumi."

"There is no God in North Korea," she said, and they jogged on.

"Then trust me, and the Americans."

They came to the bridge and walked the last hundred feet with Pieter as far to the riverside as he could get, visually searching under the broad span.

"Nothing there yet," he said. "Let's go on past and take another look from the other side."

"Look," she said, and motioned to the center of the bridge, where a guard was marching, in unison with another across the four-lane width. "How will we get under with them watching?"

"It's a very wide bridge. When they're on the far side, we can slip off the path and under."

"Let's jog," Sumi said, and they picked up the pace again.

They continued a couple of hundred yards past the bridge and then stopped; Pieter checked his watch again. "Midnight," he said. "Let's watch and time it so the guards are going the other way and are at least to the center."

Sumi threw her arms around his neck. "Are we really doing this?"

"No backing out now. The MPS will be waiting or showing up soon if we go home. With luck, we'll be in Seoul sipping the best *Soju*, for supper tomorrow."

They stood and watched until the guards reached the center of the bridge on their going-away march.

"Now or never," Pieter said, and they started jogging back.

They were only twenty yards from the bridge when a police car slid to a stop along the curb in their path, and the policeman they'd given the *Soju* to, climbed out, his semi-auto side-arm in hand.

Chapter Forty-One

THE COP HOLDS HIS HAND OUT, palm facing them, and orders them to freeze. Which they do, in their tracks.

"What?" Sumi asks, looking very innocent, but her right hand finds its way to the small of her back and wraps around the butt of her firearm.

"Up," the cop says, motioning to them to put their hands up.

Pieter, knowing Sumi has the firearm, decides to distract the cop, as his partner also exits the vehicle, slamming the door. Pieter steps to the riverside and off the edge of the walk; he pretends to stumble and goes to his knees.

"Hands up," the policeman shouts and hurries forward to Pieter.

While the cop concentrates on getting Pieter on his feet, Sumi jams her firearm into the man's ribs and pulls the trigger.

As he is sinking to his knees, she turns her attention to the other cop, who is rounding the trunk of the patrol car. He presumes his partner has fired as both the cop and the jogger are on the ground. It is a fatal mistake, as Sumi takes a bead on the second cop. Three bursts from another weapon, a full auto, rattle the night, and the cop spins and sprays blood across the trunk. He goes to the ground in a heap.

Pieter scrambles to his feet and steps in front of Sumi, afraid that the shooter, who he presumes was his contact, might shoot her as well.

He holds out both hands, palms out, and yells, in English, "She's with me. Guards on the bridge," he says, and points.

Both guards, four lanes apart across the bridge, are running their way. The man, dressed in a black wetsuit with some device on his back, rises to a standing position between the lanes.

With Pieter's warning he spins, and as the guards near, he picks the nearest one and fires a burst of three; then he swings to the other and, with less than a second in between bursts, drops him as well, knocking that one off the bridge. He spirals fifty feet to the river and disappears underwater.

"Come on," Bo yells at Pieter, and both he and Sumi run and follow the man down to the water's edge.

"Tell her goodbye," the man says.

"She's coming with us."

The big man in the wetsuit gives him a hard look. "No, she's not. It's a two-man vehicle."

"Then I'm not going."

"We don't have time to argue — "

"There is no argument. She doesn't go, I don't go."

"We will be underwater. There is only one breathing device."

"We'll trade off."

"Fuck," the man says and waves them down to the waterside.

He directs Pieter to the second seat and says to Sumi, "There's room in his lap." Then he removes his re-breather and hands it to Pieter. "You breathe through this re-breather. If you begin feeling faint, it's no longer functioning correctly. Pat me on the shoulder, hard, and I'll surface."

"Got it," Pieter says, as the man turns to Sumi. "The hose and mouthpiece on your left is your air supply. Turn the red switch where it connects to the sidewall after you have the mouthpiece in place." Then he reaches into a thigh pocket on his wetsuit, pulls out a device with a thick antenna, dials, and speaks only two words before hitting the disconnect. "Assets aboard."

As he finishes his instruction, a siren blares in their ears, and they see the reflection of a rotating red light.

"It's go time. I'm Bo. Let's go."

They settle into the SDV, and Bo quickly backs it into the current, turns it downstream, and, as they move out from under the bridge, their heads disappear under water.

Now all they have to do is stay alive with half of North Korea hunting them, down a few clicks of the Potong, and figure out where to catch a ride on a hot-looking bird.

Nothing to it.

***

CONSTANCE STARES AT THE phone and then turns to the other two, who are working on their laptops "Did he say assets? Assets? There's only supposed to be one. If there's more than one, how the hell are they going to get downriver?"

The other two, Terrance Walters and Archie Turnston, both shrug. "Couldn't hear," Terrance says, and they turn back to their screens.

She picks up her handheld and double clicks its button.

Almost immediately, Reardon comes back. "Reardon."

"Bo called. Simple message. 'Assets aboard.'"

"'Assets'?" Reardon asks.

"I'm sure that's what he said."

"Didn't you say you were worried about battery and air?"

"I did."

"Battery probably won't make much difference, but if they're sharing air, that'll cut them down by a third. Ten or twelve knots with the current. Looks like no more than thirty minutes to pickup. We're dust up!"

"Break a leg," Constance says. "Don't forget — you owe me a fat steak in Vegas."

"Ten-four," Reardon says and is gone.

Chapter Forty-Two

"CRANK IT UP," I SAY, with a rotating finger, and Su has us in the air in less than a minute.

"You got a location?" Su asks.

"Not yet, but we might be going closer in than we thought. There's some indication there are more than two on board the SDV, which means air will get rare quickly. You can't stay underwater without oxygen."

"So, the DMZ route still holds?" she asks.

"Safest way in, right."

"My thought still."

"Stay the course unless we hear different."

Pax, who's in the back, taps me on the shoulder. "I'm gonna take a snooze."

I nod, and as usual am astounded that he can sleep anywhere, anytime.

Ji Su keeps us at a comfortable five hundred feet with the DMZ a quarter-mile to our right. After twenty clicks overland, she dumps it like a rock.

"What the fuck?" Pax yells from the back.

After she levels out about fifty feet over the deck, and I get my stomach out of my throat, I answer, "Thought you were snoozing."

"Thought it was a permanent snooze there for a minute."

I laugh. "Su wanted to get a closer look at the locals. We're on leg two."

"Not the last leg, I hope," he says, and neither of us laughs.

***

BO HAS GONE AS FAR as the busted-up pier where he'd waited earlier, expecting a tap on his shoulder at any time, and decided he'd better give his passengers a break. He was surprised he hadn't drowned them, as the re-breather takes a little instruction that he'd had no time to offer. He took the SDV up to heads-above-surface, saw that his dead reckoning was a quarter-click off, and stayed at that depth to move to the shelter of the pilings. When behind one, he killed the motor and turned. "Y'all still with us?"

The woman was a little blue in the face and shivering, and the man didn't look much better.

"Who are we?" Bo asks.

"I'm Pieter, and this is Sumi."

"Are we…going…much…more?" the woman asks.

"I don't think we can," Bo says. "Another click or so?"

"'Click'?" she asks.

"Kilometer," Bo answers.

"Then?" she asks.

"We catch a ride."

"With a heater, I hope," Pieter says.

"I'm proud of you two. Not an easy day."

"Let's get it over with," Pieter says, "before we freeze to death."

Bo digs his SATphone out again and raises the TOC. "In seven minutes, I'm going to surface. How's chances for catching a lift?"

Constance comes right back. "Will relay. If a problem, will advise."

They situate their breathing apparatus, and Bo floods the SDV again. In minutes, they are ten feet under the surface and moving at more than ten knots southwest.

***

JI SU TAKES THE COMM message from Constance and pokes in a target on her avionics.

"Seven minutes to pickup,' she says. "Locked and loaded, gentlemen."

"Roger that," I say and turn back to make sure Pax is with us. He has his M4 in hand and gives me a nod.

Su does some quick calculating, climbs to two hundred feet, and kicks her airspeed up to exactly one hundred eighty-seven knots. In a few minutes, she comes off the speed and slows.

And ahead of us we see the Potong, identified by the few running lights on boats moving up and down her.

Su is back on the radio with Constance, who's trying to bring the icons on her screen to merge together, giving Ji Su constant corrections.

"Less than a half-click," Su says. "Let's get a visual ASAP."

She's dropping down to fifty feet when Pax, who has eyes out the port side, says urgently, "We've got company. Another bird, a half-click and closing fast."

"And there's Bo and two passengers," I say, seeing the repeated flash of a mag light.

“I’m going to do a fly-by and see what the bird is,” Su says and turns into the path of the oncoming chopper.

We pass with them on the port side so quickly it would be hard to identify the other ship were it not for the machine guns and rockets.

“You strapped in?” Su yells to Pax over her shoulder.

“Secure,” he answers. She shoves it to the wall, and we’re pinned in the seat as she climbs. I wonder if she’s ditching Bo and the asset when she hits two thousand feet altitude. Then I know better when she rolls hard and goes completely inverted, doing what in a fixed wing would be a split S, and we must be exceeding three hundred knots by the time she levels out at a couple of hundred feet altitude and I see the bogie is a half-click dead ahead of us. He must be doing a hundred fifty knots, but we’re closing on him as if he’s standing still.

From three hundred yards out, she hits the trigger on the Vulcan, and the bird rattles and shakes. We pass over the top of him, clearing him no more than ten yards, before he even knows he’s dead. Behind us, which we can’t see, an explosion lights the night.

“I’m not setting down,” she says as she comes around to head back to Bo. “A rope ladder behind the rear bench. Recessed rings in the deck. Hook it up and deploy when I begin to hover.”

In no more than three minutes, she’s over the SDV, and Pax has the ladder out. It has hard plastic rungs so it’s easily climbed.

Pax and I position ourselves flanking the ladder and are both a little surprised when the first face we see is a very good-looking Korean woman, nicely showing off her body in a wet, clinging jogging suit. The next up is a middle-aged man, also in jogging attire. Then Bo, smiling as if he was the cat who just ate the canary. As soon as his butt hits the deck, he yells at us, "Close that damn freezer door," and we shut the slider.

And none too soon, as Ji Su rolls a hard port turn and an RPG or some kind of rocket roars by, so close it lights the cabin and would likely have singed our eyebrows had we still had the slider open.

"Hang on," Su says, and this time, the turn is to the starboard. "Let's solve this crap," she says, and as soon as she levels out, I return to my forward seat and see there's a large patrol boat a couple of hundred yards dead ahead. A second after seeing the problem, and we've closed a hundred yards, our own rockets streak away from the cowlings on either side of the ship, and she's taking no chances as we close to no more than sixty yards, and she fires two more before she peels it to the port as green tracers fill the air all around us — as well as flying rubble from the exploding patrol boat. But this time, we clear it.

I figure we clear the collapsing superstructure of the boat by no more than a few feet.

Su drops the chopper back near the surface of the river and as she gains speed, rises to no more than fifty feet over the water.

"Poke something in that hole," she yells at me, and I see why my face is suddenly washed in freezing cold. A hole, at least a 50mm, is in the now spider-webbed windscreen, luckily splitting the difference between us.

I turn quickly to see that no one in the rear is hit, and see Pax picking plastic shards out of his face.

"Bad?" I ask.

"I'm pretty enough. A few more chicken-shit little scars won't keep the women away."

I just shake my head. The boy never ceases to amaze me. The other three are huddled together, trying to get warm.

"A little more heat in the back," I suggest to Su, who adjusts a dial.

In eighteen minutes, I see the lights of *Black Gold* ahead.

"Son of a bitch," I say, loud enough for all to hear.

"What?" Pax asks, a little apprehensively.

"I think we're going to make it."

Epilogue

I ALMOST WANT TO GO back and see if I can scale the ramparts of the Dear Leader's — Dick Licker's — palace and see if I can make a capon out of the chicken-shit. They have displayed Butch's body in a parade, with no mention of the *Pueblo*, to demonstrate what happens to American spies who try to infiltrate the motherland. The State Department has disavowed any involvement in the incident.

And, of course, the NK press reported that the *Pueblo* was subject to a terrible accident. Unfortunately, a propane explosion at an inopportune time while preparing lunch for some visiting dignitaries from the northern regions. No mention of losing several of their leading nuclear engineers, or a number of visiting Iranians of the same stature. We only hope the Iranians take umbrage and bomb the hell out of NK, but they know deep in their black hearts who killed their people and sunk the ship.

However, our own press has reported the truth — of the explosion, not the cause — and, as we'd hoped, a dozen prominent Koreans and a half-dozen Iranian engineers and scientists are among the missing.

That would please Butch, but not so much as the fact the *Pueblo* is sucking scum off the bottom of the Potong. I'm confident he's perched on the edge of a silver-lined cloud with his old man, laughing and chortling about the successful mission and the culmination of decades of wishing and planning.

We're back in Vegas, after a week of debriefings in Okinawa, and then a week of chores: visiting with Butch's sister, and handing her a check, taxes forgiven, for a cool million, and then to Gun's mother and father in Santa Ana, delivering the same. After more than a dozen missions with his SEAL team, Gun bought it during an unofficial foray into a pissant country with exemplary service for which he'll never get credit, nor of which his parents will learn of his contribution to his country. If things change in North Korea, I'll return and tell them their son's story. But I'm forbidden, and I abide by my agreements.

I know the million-dollar check I hand them, along with the assurance that it's not necessary to report it on their income tax and an accompanying letter from the IRS affirming same, won't assuage their grief. But they have some assurance their son did something of great value for his country.

The oldest steakhouse in Vegas is The Golden Steer, and Pax and I have been there so often more than one waiter and bartender know us by name.

And we're pleased to introduce the joint to the two ladies who've flown in to spend a few days with a couple of beat-up Marines.

A couple of Jack rocks, a fat T-bone and a baked, and I'm in the middle of dessert, looking at CIA agent Constance Nordstrom and hoping she's my after-dinner treat, while Pax and Ji Su eye each other like the other one is dessert, when my phone vibrates in my pocket.

I'm tempted not to dig it out, but I know my newly fattened bank account won't last nearly as long as I'd like.

"Reardon," I answer.

"Word is you take jobs no one else will touch," the rather sexy but worried-sounding voice on the other end says.

"This is my last easy day, I guess," I reply, and Pax stops eyeballing the beauty and turns his attention to my conversation.

A Look at West of the War by L.J. Martin

Young Bradon McTavish watches the bluecoats brutally hang his father and destroy everything he's known, and he escapes their wrath into the gunsmoke and blood of war. Captured and paroled, only if he'll head west of the war, he rides the river into the wilds of the new territory of Montana where savages and grizzlies await. He discovers new friends and old enemies...and a woman formerly forbidden to him. Action adventure at its best from the author of Nemesis, Mr. Pettigrew, the Montana Series, and many more acclaimed westerns and historicals.

About the Author

L. J. Martin is the author of over three dozen works of both fiction and non-fiction from Bantam, Avon, Pinnacle and his own Wolfpack Publishing. He lives in, and loves, Montana with his wife, NYT bestselling romantic suspense author Kat Martin. He's been a horse wrangler, cook as both avocation and vocation, volunteer firefighter, real estate broker, general contractor, appraiser, disaster evaluator for FEMA, and traveled a good part of the world, some in his own ketch. A hunter, fisherman, photographer, cook, father and grandfather, he's been car and plane wrecked, visited a number of jusgados and a road camp, and survived cancer twice. He carries a bail-enforcement, bounty hunter, shield. He knows about what he writes about, and tries to write about what he knows.

Other Works by L. J. Martin

West of the War. Young Bradon McTavish watches the bluecoats brutally hang his father and destroy everything he's known, and he escapes their wrath into the gunsmoke and blood of war. Captured and paroled, only if he'll head west of the war, he rides the river into the wilds of the new territory of Montana where savages and grizzlies await. He discovers new friends and old enemies...and a woman formerly forbidden to him.

Windfall. From the boardroom to the bedroom, David Drake has fought his way…nearly…to the top. From the jungles of Vietnam, to the vineyards of Napa, to the grit and grime of the California oil fields, he's clawed his way up. The only thing missing is the woman he's loved most of his life. Now, he's going to risk it all to win it all, or end up on the very bottom where he started. This business adventure-thriller will leave you breathless.

Bloodlines. When an ancient document is found deep under the streets of Manhattan, no one can anticipate the wild results. A businessman is forced to search deep into his past and reach back to those who once were wronged, and redeem for them what is right and just. There's a woman he's yearned for, and must have, but all is against them…and someone want him dead.

Overflow. No. 1 on Amazon's crime list! Got a problem? Need it fixed? Call Mike Reardon, the repairman, just don't ask him how he'll get it done. Trained as a Recon Marine to search and destroy, he brings those skills to the tough streets of America's cities. If you like your stories spiced with fists, guns, and beautiful women, this is the fast paced novel for you.

The Repairman. No. 1 on Amazon's crime list! Got a problem? Need it fixed? Call Mike Reardon, the repairman, just don't ask him how he'll get it done. Trained as a Recon Marine to search and destroy, he brings those skills to the tough streets of America's cities. If you like your stories spiced with fists, guns, and beautiful women, this is the fast paced novel for you.

The Bakken No. 1 on Amazon's crime list! The stand alone sequel to The Repairman. Mike Reardon gets a call from his old CO in Iraq, who's now a VP at an oil well service company in North America's hottest boomtown, and dope and prostitution is running wild and costing the company millions, and the cops are overwhelmed. If you have a problem, and want it fixed, call the repairman…just don't ask him what he's gonna do.

G5, Gee Whiz When a fifty million dollar G5 is stolen and flown out of the country, who you gonna call? If you have a problem, and want it fixed, call the repairman…just don't ask him what he's gonna do.

Who's On Top Mike Reardon thinks his new gig, finding an errant daughter of a NY billionaire will be a laydown...how wrong can one guy be? She's tied up with an eco-terrorist group, who proves to be much more than that. And this time, the group he's up against may be bad guys, or kids with their heart in the right place. Who gets lead and who gets a kick in the backside. And if things go wrong, the whole country may be at risk! Another kick-ass Repairman Mike Reardon thriller from acclaimed author L. J. Martin.

Target Shy & Sexy What's easier for a search and destroy guy than a simple bodyguard gig, particularly when the body being guarded is on of America's premiere country singers and the body is knockdown beautiful...until she's abducted while he's on his way to report for his new assignment. Who'd have guessed that the hunt for his employer would lead him into a nest of hard ass Albanians and he'd find himself between them and some bent nose boys from Vegas! Another in the highly acclaimed The Repairman Series...Mike Reardon is at it again.

Judge, Jury, Desert Fury. Back in the fray, only this time it's as a private contractor. Mike

Reardon and his buddies are hired to free a couple of American's held captive by a Taliban mullah, and, as usual, it's duck, dodge and kick ass when everyone in the country wants a piece of you. Don't miss this high action adventure by renowned author L. J. Martin. No. 6 in The Repairman series, each book stands alone.

No Good Deed. Going after some ruthless kidnappers, who want NATO,s secrets, is one thing...going into Russia is

another altogether. But when one of Reardon's crew is being held, he says to hell with it, no matter if he's risking starting World War 3! Why not add the CIA and the State Department to your list of enemies when your most important job is staying alive hour by hour, minute by minute.

Overflow. Mike Reardon, the Repairman, hates to mess his own nest—to work anywhere near where he lives. If you can call a mini-storage and a camper living. But when terrorists bomb Vegas, and a casino owner's granddaughter is killed…the money is too good and the prey is among his most hated. Then again nothing is ever quite like it seems. Now all he has to do is stay alive, tough when friends become enemies and enemies far worse, and when you're on top the FBI and LVPD's list.

Quiet Ops. "…knows crime and how to write about it…you won't put this one down." Elmore Leonard

L. J. Martin with America's No. 1 bounty hunter, Bob Burton, brings action-adventure in double doses. From Malibu to West Palm Beach, Brad Benedick hooks 'em up and haul 'em in…in chains.

Crimson Hit. Dev Shannon loves his job, travels, makes good money, meets interesting

people…then hauls them in cuffs and chains to justice. Only this time it's personal.

Bullet Blues. Shannon normally doesn't work in his hometown, but this time it's a friend who's gone missing, and he's got to help…if he can stay alive long enough. Tracking down a stolen yacht, which takes him all the way to Jamaica, he finds himself deep in the dirty underbelly of the drug trade.

The Clint Ryan Series:

El Lazo. John Clinton Ryan, young, fresh to the sea from Mystic, Connecticut, is shipwrecked on the California coast…and blamed for the catastrophe. Hunted by the hide, horn and tallow captains, he escapes into the world of the vaquero, and soon gains the name El Lazo, for his skill with the lasso. A classic western tale of action and adventure, and the start of the John Clinton Ryan, the Clint Ryan series.

Against the 7th Flag. Clint Ryan, now skilled with horse and reata, finds himself caught up in the war of California revolution, Manifest Destiny is on the march, and he's in the middle of the fray, with friends on one side and countrymen on the other…it's fight or be killed, but for whom?

The Devil's Bounty. On a trip to buy horses for his new ranch in the wilds of swampy Central California, Clint finds himself compelled to help a rich Californio don who's beautiful daughter has been kidnapped and hauled to the barracoons of the Barbary Coast. Thrown in among the Chinese tongs, Australian Sidney Ducks, and the dredges of the gold rush failures, he soon finds an ally in a slave, now a newly freedman, and it's gunsmoke and flashing blades to fight his way to free the senorita.

The Benicia Belle. Clint signs on as master-at-arms on a paddle wheeler plying the Sacramento from San Francisco to the gold fields. He's soon blackmailed by the boats owner and drawn to a woman as dangerous and beautiful as the sea he left behind. Framed for a crime he didn't commit, he has only one chance to exact a measure of justice and…revenge.

Shadow of the Grizzly. "Martin has produced a landlocked, Old West version of Peter Benchley's *Jaws*," Publisher's Weekly. When the Stokes brothers, the worst kind of meat hunters, stumble on Clint's horse ranch, they are looking to take what he has. A wounded griz is only trying to stay alive, but he's a horrible danger to man and beast. And it's Clint, and his crew, including a young boy, who face hell together.

Condor Canyon. On his way to Los Angeles, a pueblo of only one thousand, Clint is ambushed by a posse after the abductor of a young woman. Soon he finds himself trading his Colt and his skill for the horses he seeks…now if he can only stay alive to claim them.

The Montana Series – The Clan:

Stranahan. "A good solid fish-slinging gunslinging read," William W. Johnstone. Sam Stranahan's an honest man who finds himself on the wrong side of the law, and the law has their own version of right and wrong. He's on his way to find his brother, and walks into an explosive case of murder. He has to make sure justice is done…with or without the law.

McCreed's Law. Gone…a shipment of gold and a handful of passengers from the Transcontinental Railroad. Found…a man who knows the owlhoots and the Indians who are holding the passengers for ransom. When you want to catch outlaws, hire an outlaw…and get the hell out of the way.

Wolf Mountain. The McQuades are running cattle, while running from the tribes who are fresh from killing Custer, and they know no fear. They have a rare opportunity, to get a herd to Mile's and his troops at the mouth of the Tongue…or to die trying. And a beautiful woman and her father, of questionable background, who wander into camp look like a blessing, but trouble is close on their trail...as if the McQuades don't have trouble enough.

O'Rourke's Revenge. Surviving the notorious Yuma Prison should be enough trouble for any man...but Ryan O'Rourke is not just any man. He wants blood, the blood of those who framed him for a crime he didn't commit. He plans to extract revenge, if it costs him all he has left, which is less than nothing...except his very life.

McKeag's Mountain. Old Bertoldus Prager has long wanted McKeag's Mountain, the Lucky Seven Ranch his father had built, and seven hired guns tried to take it the hard way, leaving Dan McKeag for dead…but he's a McKeag, and clings to life. They should have made sure…for now it will cost them all, or he'll die trying, and Prager's in his sights as well.

The Nemesis Series:

Nemesis. The fools killed his family…then made him a lawman! There are times when it pays not to be known, for if they had, they'd have killed him on the spot. He hadn't seen his sister since before the war, and never met her husband and two young daughters…but when he heard they'd been murdered, it was time to come down out of the high country and scatter the country with blood and guts.

Mr. Pettigrew. Beau Boone, starving, half a left leg, at the end of his rope, falls off the train in the hell-on-wheels town of Nemesis. But Mr. Pettigrew intervenes. Beau owes him, but does he owe him his very life? Can a one-legged man sit shotgun in one of the toughest saloons on the Transcontinental. He can, if he doesn't have anything to lose.

The Ned Cody Series:

Buckshot. Young Ned Cody takes the job as City Marshal…after all, he's from a long line of lawmen. But they didn't face a corrupt sheriff and his half-dozen hard deputies, a half-Mexican half-Indian killer, and a town who thinks he could never do the job.

Mojave Showdown. Ned Cody goes far out of his jurisdiction when one of his deputies is hauled into the hell's fire of the Mojave Desert by a tattooed Indian who could track a deer fly and live on his leavings. He's the toughest of the tough, and the Mojave has produced the worst. It's ride into the jaws of hell, and don't worry about coming back.

Made in United States
Troutdale, OR
02/19/2024

17797792R00166